T
H
E

L
E
M
O
N

J
E
L
L
-
O

S
Y
N
D
R
O
M
E

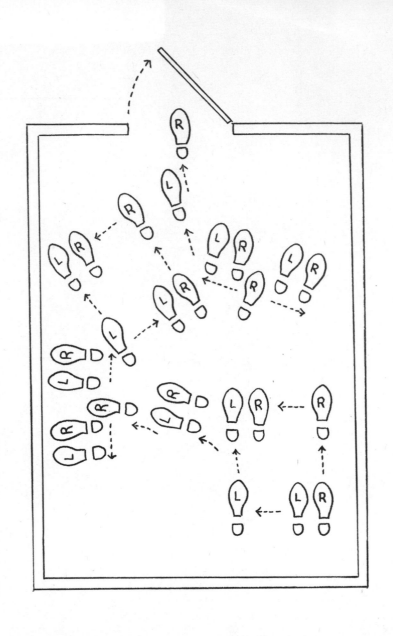

THE
LEMON JELL-O
SYNDROME

Man Martin

UNBRIDLED BOOKS

This is a work of fiction. The names, characters, places and incidents are either the product of the author's imagination or are used fictitiously, and any resemblance to actual persons living or dead, business establishments, events, or locales is entirely coincidental.

UNBRIDLED BOOKS

Copyright © 2017 by Man Martin

Library of Congress Cataloging-in-Publication Data

Names: Martin, Man, 1959- author.
Title: The Lemon Jell-O Syndrome / by Man Martin.
Description: Lakewood, CO : Unbridled Books, [2017]
Identifiers: LCCN 2016035732 (print) | LCCN 2016044811 (ebook)
| ISBN
9781609531416 | ISBN 9781609531423 ()
Subjects: LCSH: Life change events--Fiction. | Self-perception--Fiction.
|
Psychological fiction. | Medical fiction.
Classification: LCC PS3613.A7833 L46 2017 (print) | LCC PS3613.
A7833 (ebook)
| DDC 813/.6--dc23
LC record available at https://lccn.loc.gov/2016035732

1 3 5 7 9 10 8 6 4 2

Book Design by SH ∘ CV

First Printing

For my agent Sorche

for her tireless efforts and faith in me

In the universe, there are things that are known,
and things that are unknown,
and in between, there are doors.

WILLIAM BLAKE

CHAPTER ONE

A, a

From the Semitic *aleph* (⟨), "ox." The Greeks renamed it *alpha*, twisting the neck to point the horns downward. In the lowercase, the ox head can still be seen in profile, a single horn curving like a cricket's antenna: a.

alpha and omega: The first and last letters of the Greek alphabet (A and Ω). Metaphorically, God, i.e., the "first and last," from Revelation 1:8, "I am Alpha and Omega, the beginning and the ending, saith the Lord."

alphabet: The characters of a written language arranged in an established order. From *alpha* and *beta*, the first two letters of the Greek alphabet.

atone: To reconcile or make restitution. A compound of *at* and *one*, that is, to be "at one with," or in harmony.

The night before being struck by the Lemon Jell-O Syndrome, his private nickname for his terrible, incapacitating illness, Bone King taught Wednesday-night Composition 1101 at Fulsome College with an unease with which it has rarely been taught. When reminding his students that the object of a preposition could never be a subject, he spoke as if it came as a personal tragedy. Suspecting your wife of infidelity, and only suspecting—*if my wife is cheating*—is a subordinate clause that wrings the heart like a mop until there is a declarative sentence to complete it.

The clock by the door told him motion by motion when Mary would be coming home from Grace Church and changing to go out to Jelly Jam: now letting herself in the kitchen door—now making the orbit from kitchen to bedroom to bathroom, changing from work clothes, getting ready to leave—putting perfume behind her ears?

Born in the Tennessee back hills, Bone was an unlikely candidate to become a scholar. He could quote Seneca in Latin, but he was haunted by the dread that he'd never really overcome his pronunciation of "pin" for "pen" nor lose that weighty one-word imperative, "gih-yawn-owwa-hye-ah!," he'd once used against hound dogs in the kitchen or chickens on the front porch. Through monkish solitude and dedicated study, he'd climbed the greasy trunk of academe and published his master's thesis, *Misplaced Modifiers*, which had won first place for Books on Grammar and Usage in the Southeast. His further ascent seemed a foregone conclusion, but the struggle had cost him. Wherever he went, a silent inner voice went also, a running commentary on usage and etymology. Mary had once loved his dreaminess but now complained he didn't pay enough attention. The truth was he paid too much, only never to the right things. Sometimes he wondered if this weren't a sign of mild lunacy, but then he'd spot in "luna-cy" the ghostly lexical thumbprint of the moon, and with that he'd be off in another world.

By the time he got home, the sun had set, and it was dark. She was at the club.

"Chicken and rice on the counter," Mary's note said. He turned on the TV and listened from the kitchen as his dinner rotated, humming in the lighted window of the microwave. He sat in the recliner, plate in his lap, bathed in the vapor from his chicken and rice and the blue-white glow of Wednesday-night reruns: a medical comedy with a hardworking, no-nonsense doctor, a wisecracking nurse, and a quirky patient with a strange diagnosis. After his solitary meal, Bone went to bed.

Mary.

Had another man touched that smooth white skin? Her naked back, where it tapered to her waist. A masculine hand, black hairs bristling around a heavy old-fashioned wristwatch, resting itself along the curve, two fingers lightly curled along the cleft …

Bone noted, observed, and tagged the minutes passing on the glowing alarm clock as he lay alternating between sweats and shivers. At last the front door opened. Boards creaked down the hall and into the bathroom. Flush. The shower ran. A toothbrush scrubbed. A drawer opened and closed. Mary—soap smell and scrubbed skin—eased into the covers beside him. Bone pretended to have just awoken.

"So, how was tonight?" No response. "How was Jelly Jam?"

"It was great." She readjusted herself on her pillow.

"So who else was there?"

"Hmm?" Like a drowser surfacing reluctantly from a dream.

"Who else was there? At Jelly Bean?" He hoped the whimsical substitution of "bean" for "jam" would evoke a smile. "So who was there?"

"Oh, you know—Laurel, Cindy Davis, Ruth—the usual."

"That's nice." He lay rigidly in bed. "Did you run into anyone else?"

"What?" She turned toward him. "Why are you asking all this? You're cross-examining me."

Something hot settled in the back of Bone's throat. "No, I'm not," he said, forcing a smile to the darkness. "I'm just talking is all." Bringing up the next question was like pushing a stalled car over the crest of a hill. "Was Cash there?"

"Oh, Christ, Bone."

Stupid, stupid, stupid. Why had he asked that? Bone's throat was dry and scorching hot. He was trembling. He ought to roll toward her, tuck his head into her neck and lay his thigh over hers, his hand on her ribs, smell her hair, whisper, *Work has become a run-on sentence for me, with neither period nor semicolon. I am past tense, restless and incomplete in this world, a dependent clause, and you are the comma at which I rest. Conjugate with me and teach me the sweet syntax of your body.*

"Was he there? If he wasn't there, just tell me."

"No, he wasn't there." She sighed; in the crooked trapezoid of yellow moonlight falling over their bodies, he could feel as well as hear her lungs expand and expel.

When my love swears that she is made of truth,

I do believe her, though I know she lies.

How wise Shakespeare was; he knew it all.

Bone pretended to sleep and pretended not to know she was pretending also.

THE NEXT MORNING was Friday, and in theory Bone had all day to work on his manuscript, *Words*. We who take grammar so lightly may well give a thought to men like Bone working in dark library basements safeguarding the subjunctive mood while the rest of us are out living our lives.

After vacillating whether to mention his nemesis, E. Knolton, in the introduction, Bone settled on a haughty and dismissive "some": "*Some* might say the concept of correct grammar is outmoded." In the Grammar Wars, waged with the tenacity only professional academics can muster, Bone defended Standard American English against the E. Knolton faction, anarchists claiming no such thing as "correct usage" existed, only "different dialects," each with its own "worthy grammar."

How Knolton would have jeered to know the pains it'd cost Bone to pluck "might could" out of his speech, the sweat spilled mastering "it is I." And—highest price of all—the rejection by his own kind, pursued along the quarry tracks by jeering boys and pelted with gravel for *talking like a Yankee.*

Finally, Bone rose from his desk and went to the window. One of Cash's Mexicans cut grass in slow zigzags; another applied clippers to a boxwood. Mary and Cash talked in the side yard. The fragrance of the gardenias was at its height, and Bone imagined the heady smell sweetening the air around them.

A yellow butterfly lifted from the red salvia and darted between them. Mary had brought Cash a glass of iced tea— how corny! Does anyone really bring tea to the yardman? Cash's sleeves were rolled up, the better to show off his biceps, Bone supposed. Cash made some yardman witticism, and Mary laughed and touched his forearm near the heavy, old-fashioned watch he always wore. Cash looked toward Bone's window and stepped rightward out of sight behind the sash. Mary followed. Bone gazed at the vacancy, then went into the bathroom.

LAST MARCH, CHARLOTTE, their aging landlady, informed them of their new arrival in the subdivision. "Cash Hudson?" Mary repeated when she heard the name. It transpired she'd dated Cash in high school. Chilly fear rose in Bone's chest.

The fear took concrete shape on a day Bone had spent yanking a lawn-mower cord until sweat dotted the Briggs & Stratton. Each time Bone was on the verge of pounding the damn machine flat with a sledgehammer, the motor condescended to puff an oily "phut," provoking a fresh frenzy of useless yanking.

All the while, Cash talked with Mary, who stood *beaming* in a sleeveless cotton top, the silk concavity in the small of her back peeking out above her jeans. Two years into their marriage, her discontent punctuated their lives with increasing frequency: Bone's work on *Words* took all his time and attention; there wasn't enough money; they never did anything; there was damn medieval poetry on the shower wall; she was bored and feeling trapped.

Cash Hudson, you could tell—and if you couldn't, Cash himself would tell you—wasn't destined for the humble subdivision of Ashford Park forever. Instead of renting, he owned his two-bedroom ranch, and when he'd saved enough, he'd buy another and rent that one. His sole topics of conversation, as far as Bone, crouched wheezing and dripping by the lawn mower, could tell, were the money he made last year, what he was making this year, and what he'd make next year. This information Mary found *riveting*.

Cash's business, ironically enough, was landscape maintenance: a big green truck with a steel-mesh gate that lowered like a navy landing craft, deploying mowers and blowers over Ashford Park and beyond. For the time being, he made do with day workers, but business was growing so fast, soon he'd need to take on someone full time.

If you're such a damn expert, Bone thought, pausing between his labors, why don't you damn well offer to help? I'd sure like to see how you do it.

Then, to Bone's horror, Cash *did* offer.

"Let me see what I can do with that thing," Cash said, dropping his voice into the baritone of someone wise and helpful taking charge, and with a pull, he brought the mower shuddering and puttering to life. "Let's adjust the choke," Cash said, and pushed a lever until the mower sounded a little less tubercular.

Even the best of lawn mowers, Cash explained, would not put up indefinitely with owners who never bought a new spark plug or a yearly oil change, and without these attentions would eventually freeze up altogether—to which Mary replied, "Oh, we didn't know that."

We didn't know that. Thank you, Mary, for making me look like a fool in front of our neighbor.

"You know what," Cash said—I know what, Bone thought, do *you* know what?—"why don't I take care of your yard for you?" And before Bone could protest that they didn't have money for lawn service, Cash said, "I'll make it half-price."

"Oh, I couldn't let you," Mary said, *meaning, she could let, and definitely would let him, but she wanted to be forced.*

"I insist," Cash said smilingly, *meaning, he would force her.*

"Isn't that sweet?" Mary asked. "He's going to do our yard half-price."

ON THE OTHER side of the shower curtain from where Bone stood at the toilet, unable to pee, the tile still bore the faint traces of Chaucer's "Prologue," which he had written in Sharpie while studying *The Canterbury Tales.* Behind that was a window, from which vantage someone, if he chose, could watch unobserved as Mary and Cash resumed their conversation, although doing so would require stepping into the tub to spy on them like an emasculated cuckold.

The tub, Bone realized, offered ample space to stand, which shouldn't have surprised him since he showered there every day, but illogically he'd expected to feel the enameled side curving up against his toes. Soap's mild smell clung to the window. Cash and Mary stood near the privet bushes by the back fence. Nothing untoward was afoot, at least for now. Cash plucked a handful of wild violets from amongst the liriope, a yardman's habit.

What a ridiculous situation. Or was "preposterous" the better word? **Ridiculous:** worthy of ridicule. But **Preposterous:** a nonsensical combination of *pre* (before) and *post* (after). Yes, "preposterous" was nearer the mark: there was something definitely before-after, topsy-turvy, bass-ackward about all of this. Bone pictured how the scene would look from the perspective of a hypothetical witness: a man, *fully dressed*, mind you, in a bathtub looking longingly, like the foolish fathead he was, out the window at his wife. From above, their heads would form a proverbial lover's triangle, acute, in this case, Bone at the vertex, thirty feet from the base of Cash and Mary, standing in the speckled shade of the privet. From Bone's perspective, Mary and Cash stood framed in the proscenium under the lace curtain, a sunlit stage broken into nine tiles by windowpanes. Had Cash and Mary glanced at the bathroom window, they'd have noticed first Bone's red hair, then his blue eyes staring curiously, and then it would have been their turn to be curious. Unless they really were lovers, in which case they'd merely be indignant.

Screw it, Bone thought, I'm getting out of here.

Which is when he discovered he couldn't.

Bone told his legs to move, but they didn't.

Move! But that's not how you do it, is it? You don't tell your leg to move; you just move it. *How* do you move it? It'll come naturally if you don't think about it. *Don't think about it?* What else *can* you think about?

Windowpanes need cleaning—mildew on the sash—spider walking on the sill—eight legs and not a problem with one of them—la-tee-da-tee-da-dum-dumtee-dum-dum-dum—damn it, *move!* This can't be happening. Spider almost to the other side, goddamn spider!

Bone was sure he could move now.

Ha-ha-ha, it would be just a silly false alarm, and wouldn't he feel like a chump? It was a temporary thing, like when your jaw locks, and you have to pop it into place. Unnerving at the time, but perfectly harmless. Just wait a little, and then move your leg without thinking.

In just a moment now he'd do it. He was absolutely positive when he attempted to move his legs, that's just what would happen.

...

Goddamn, goddamn, goddamn.

...

He thought of lifting his legs with his arms, but when he tried reaching down, he found he couldn't.

Damngoddamngoddamngoddamngoddamn. Jesusjesusjesus, oh, Jesusjesusjesus.

Cash and Mary had disappeared. The bathroom window now held only the backyard, broken into nine panes: the crooked little dogwood traversing the lower left pane, continuing in the upper corner of the middle pane, its crown of leaves extending over the three panes above the sash, a triangle of yellowing May sky. An anxious squirrel scooted partway down an oak and studied the ground below in a head-down position. Bone still could not move.

Someone rattled the bathroom doorknob and found it locked.

Now Bone spoke. "Help!" The words resounding on the white tiles alarmed him, and he hollered, "Help! For God's sake! Help! I'm stuck!"

The door rattled again. "Bone?"

Mary.

Hot tears rose in his throat, and outside the window, the scene shimmered like a reflection in rippling water. He realized with ironic detachment that at least his tear ducts still operated. "I don't know. I've forgotten how to move."

"What?"

"I can't move. I'm stuck. I need help."

"I'll get Cash."

"For God's sake, don't bring him into it."

But Mary was gone already, and in a few minutes it sounded as if a small, heavily booted army were mustering in the hallway.

"Bone, are you still in there?" A foolish question, but Bone replied in the affirmative. The lock clicked—someone picked it, evidently. Bone heard rather than saw Mary, Cash, and the Mexicans tumble in—his view of his own rescue confined to the little window, its frame, the yellow-painted wall, and the white tile below. No one commented on his being in the bathtub fully dressed, but they couldn't understand why he didn't simply step out. They seemed to believe that he'd merely been awaiting an audience before doing just that, and kept inviting him to turn around and extricate himself. Only after reiterated explanations did they accept that his inability to do so was precisely the problem.

Finally, Bone, who'd had more time to consider this calamity than anyone, said, "Just work my legs. Like a marionette." Cash's hands grasped Bone's calf, bending the knee's hinge. It took several experimental manipulations—accompanied by much onlooker advice—to get the hang of walking with someone else's legs. As Cash lifted and planted Bone's feet in turn, marching him in place like a life-sized toy soldier, several sets of hands assisted in turning Bone by the shoulders. Worried faces of Mary and several curious Mexicans, and the top of Cash's head—he was still kneeling to work Bone's legs—rotated into view. A cautious clomp of one foot across the porcelain wall, and then, carefully, precariously—ready, steady!—he swayed back dangerously like an unmoored scarecrow before they could seize his shirt to stop him from toppling—they brought his second foot alongside the first.

Once he stood on the bath mat, the spell was broken, and, lo, he could walk.

CHAPTER TWO

B, b

From the Semitic *beth* (◁), "house," e.g., *Bethlehem*, "house of bread." The Greeks upended the letter, renaming it *beta* and, in the upper case, adding a balcony on the second floor.

Babel: The legendary site of a tower threatening to reach "unto heaven itself" until God "confounded the tongues" of man, creating the world's profusion of languages. Tempting as it is to believe, **babble** does not descend from this but from **baby** and the Germanic suffix **-le**, which connotes small, repetitive actions, as in **wobble, twinkle,** and **gobble. Babel** is derived from **Babylon,** an ancient city whose cuneiform script was cousin of the Semitic alphabet, whence all Western European alphabets are derived.

backformation: Removing what appears to be a suffix or prefix from an existing word to form a new one. Thus, **buttle** is derived from **butler, burgle** from **burglar,** and more recently **conversate** from **conversation.**

barbarian: A native of a land where they aren't as civilized as we are. From *barbarikos,* a derisive onomatopoeia for foreign languages, which to the Greeks sounded like baby talk or bleating sheep: hence, *baa-baa-rian.*

Cliché inventory compiled by Bone King during visit to the Northside Hospital Emergency Room

CLICHÉ ITEM	YES	NO
Interminable and meaningless forms to complete[1]	X	
Time passing with gelatinous slowness while waiting to be seen by physician	X	
Young man with head wrapped in bloody gauze		X
Suspiciously juvenile-looking physician	X	
Mysterious and alarming tests performed	X	
Phrase "overnight for observation" used	X	
Humiliating hospital gown that fails to cover backside	X	
Room with motorized hospital bed capable of achieving any angle, slope, incline, or combination thereof conceivable to Euclidean geometry, but which on no account can be made comfortable	X	
Flavorless hospital food served on plastic tray	X	
Visit from priest	X	
Referral to specialist with exotic-sounding name[2]	X	

Notes
1. *To wit: "In case of emergency contact." What do they mean, "in case of emergency"? This is the emergency room. And the person to contact is who came with me. (Pointed this out to Mary, who was not amused.)*
2. *Dr. Limongello, whom everyone calls "Wonderful Dr. Lemon Jell-O."*

ALTHOUGH BONE WAS capable of navigating on his own steam once he was free of the tub, helpful hands herded him to the living room. Cash and the Mexicans stood stupefied, stiffly shifting from foot to foot, while Mary stroked Bone's cheek with her fingertips and smoothed his hair, as if this terrible episode were somehow attributable to grooming. "Sweetheart," she said, "what happened?"

Bone couldn't say what had happened because he knew only that he couldn't move, and that's what he told her. Her kiss left a tingling spot on his forehead, like a priest's blessing. Her dark eyes looked into each of his eyes in turn, as if trying two doors to find the unlocked one, while down her blouse he could see the silken hemispheres of her breasts. "We're taking you to the emergency room," she said, the first order of business as far as she was concerned. But Bone demurred; it was only a onetime occurrence, surely.

"I bet you're right, buddy," Cash said with a man-to-man sort of compassion. "Probably just a onetime thing. But don't you think you need to go to the emergency room anyway? Just in case." A Hispanic murmur of consent rose from the Mexicans, and Bone thought what a good friend Cash would make. Bonhomie's sudden sunshine filled the room. So Mary drove Bone to the hospital, her face filled with the solemn joy of taking sensible measures in a crisis, Bone suppressing the unspeakable urge to smile.

At a traffic light Mary asked, "What were you doing in the bathtub?"

"Oh, just looking at those lines of Chaucer," Bone said as nonchalantly as he could, gazing with unusual attention at a sign offering to buy ugly houses.

"But I thought you were done studying Chaucer," Mary pointed out.

"There was just something I wanted to check on," Bone explained. In the subsequent silence, Bone felt uncomfortably certain she knew he was lying.

In the emergency room, Bone invited Mary to join him in a game of Cliché Hunt while filling out forms, but she only said, "You can't make everything into one of your little games, Bone." So he retreated into his ruminations, leaving Mary to hers.

He was calm throughout his examination by his Clearasil-scented physician: the futile formalities of reflex testing, blood sampling, X-raying, and peering into his skull holes. He was unruffled at being made to walk from one end of the room to the other, stand on one foot, then the other, squeeze with his left hand and then the right. Bone was a patient patient with all of it. It was incredible that the bizarre episode of immobility—already so remote it seemed to belong to another lifetime—would recur; nevertheless, it was charming to be the object of Mary's concern.

The inconclusive tests having reached their inconclusions, Boy Doctor confessed himself stumped and referred Bone to an expert in neurological circles, Dr. Limongello, "a double-doc."

"What?"

"A double-doc," the physician repeated, clearly enjoying Bone's puzzlement. "He's an MD in neurology and psychiatry. He's unorthodox, eccentric even. He's sort of famous for unusual methods, his bedside manner. But he's wonderful."

The hospital staff set up an appointment for Monday. Meanwhile Bone was to stay overnight for observation. The room they assigned came equipped with:

- *A bed evidently designed for use in outer space*
- *A wall-mounted TV*
- *A screen where Bone's heartbeat rose and fell in a fragile white line, steep mesas dropping into craggy valleys, like someone turning the knob on an Etch-a-Sketch.*

A nurse came to check on him—"Oh, he's wonderful," she exclaimed when she heard Lemon Jell-O was going to look at Bone. He lay pretending to write notes on his pad, staring at Mary from the corner of one eye as she sat in an armchair by the bed watching the local news.

Car wreck. Crime. Politician. Weather, with a forty percent chance of other weather later on. Then something upbeat to close—a girl gets her dying wish: a photo op with a pop star.

Mary's shoes lay on the floor, one upright, one on its side. The curve of her smooth calves tucked beneath her made a tilde (~), and two brunette strands fell across her forehead, escaping her bun after a day's confinement at work, her studious frown and black-framed glasses accenting her beauty:

a "plain girl" sitcom character destined to transform into a knockout by removing her glasses and shaking her hair free of its restraint. He did not deserve her, and he knew it.

Father Pepys arrived at suppertime and chatted as Bone lay ill at ease, ruins of chipped beef and two pale peas wading in liquefied red Jell-O in his plastic tray. Since starting work as the church secretary, Mary had become a churchgoer, and Bone attended as often as he could stand it. What got to him was not the homogenized nonsense of Christianity but the unchewable chunks of Father Pepys's own contribution. Once Mary came home from service and wrote "atonement" on a piece of paper. "Look what Father Pepys showed us," she said, adding dashes to make the word "at-one-ment." "It means at-*one*-ment. Jesus died so we could be at *one* with God. At-*one*-ment." This particular piece of Pepysian poppycock had practically put Bone into apoplexy. Bone's fury at this was in no way assuaged when to his astonishment he later discovered that the priest's goofy etymology was actually correct.

After the priest left, Mary looked around the room. "Not many places for me to sleep," she remarked.

"Oh, you don't have to stay here," Bone said. "Go home." But what he was really thinking was, stay here.

"Don't be a dope," she said. "Of course, I'm staying."

"I appreciate it," he said. "But I don't think they'll allow it anyway. Why don't you go home and get a good night's sleep? You can pick me up in the morning." He heard the words, but they seemed to be coming from someone else's mouth. What was he saying? *Stay here, stay here.*

"Are you sure?" she asked. She seemed disappointed.

"Absolutely, I'll be fine. Go home." Why was he saying this? What was wrong with him that he didn't just say thank you, I love you, I'm grateful for you? But he didn't. She asked if he wanted the light off, and pressed the switch. Her silhouette leaned forward to kiss him, a moment of gardenia. And she was gone.

Even with lights out, a hospital room gets only as dark as an arctic midnight in June. Bone lay disconsolate in what darkness there was. She would have stayed if he'd asked; why hadn't he? Somewhere along the way, he'd stopped telling her how he loved and needed her and entered the realpolitik of marriage, where above all else, you must never risk shifting the all-important balance of power. Bone rolled onto his side. On the screen, the beat of his heart drew and erased, drew and erased, over and over.

WHEN BONE FIRST met his future wife, he was coming off a near miss of a relationship with Miranda Richter, the medievalist in the office next to his. After a promising start, they'd solidified immovably in the friend zone, the familiar story of Bone's romantic life. Mary Snyder had been a student in his Composition 1101 class, second row, one seat from the middle. Bone immediately made up his mind to dislike her. Dislike or madness: ignoring her would not do.

Ignore the gormless, slack-jawed freshman, with hair that looked as if he'd combed it in a wind tunnel; the chubby, bubbly, gum-chewing co-ed, always squealing first, loudest, and longest at Bone's jokes; the stone-faced business majors resenting this detour from their lifework of relentless acquisition and conspicuous consumption; the savant wannabe smoking clove cigarettes on breaks, appending an interrogative "no" to every statement like some sort of damn European: "The typical syntax in Old English was still subject, verb, object—*no?*"

Ignore everyone else, but not her. The almond eyes beckoning, *Gaze into me, fall into my depths,* the chestnut hair, lustrous and despicable, that you ached to curl around your fingers, and the adorable, detestable, heart-shaped face—who goes around with a face like that?—and the sweater undulating over the swell and dip from clavicle to hip.

If she'd been beautiful, and beautiful only, he'd have gotten over her, but once, as he slipped in just before the unwritten deadline allowing students to skip when the teacher is a no-show, Mary narrowed her eyes and pointed her finger with a stern "This better be worth it." It wasn't the joke that got him but the way she said it, and by the way she said it, Bone knew she was flirting with him. She was flirting with him. The rest of class, his heart hammered at his sternum as if it were putting up siding.

Each semester he held individual student conferences, a chore he enlivened by transforming it into an improvisatory performance, with himself cast in the role of Professor Witherwood, a composite character based on Hollywood depictions of Ivy League professors. The essence of the Witherwood character was his absurdly elevated diction, which fell just short of an Oxford accent. Student reaction ranged from indifference to stupefaction; they never suspected that Bone had drafted them into an unscripted one-act comedy. But then came Mary. During her conference, Bone called her to task for overusing adverbs: "Select sincere verbs and adjectives that know their business, and no further modifiers are necessary." Her smile at this emboldened him to further flights of eloquence. "Your verbs, my dear, and there's no point trying to conceal the fact, are not all a good verb should be. They lack the requisite vim. As for your adjectives, they're evasive and lack conviction. You can tell their hearts are elsewhere." She laughed outright, and that evening Bone went home, feet scarcely touching the ground.

Mary, he learned, worked as Dean Gordon's secretary. Close to himself in age—early thirties, Bone guessed—she became Bone's ally, nodding at cultural allusions no one else shared, laughing at sly aspersions that sailed safely over everyone else's head, getting, in short, him. By the time he realized he'd broken his resolution to dislike her, he was already half in love. Finally, after enduring an entire heavenly, hellish semester under the heat lamps of her almond eyes, developing a sore neck from avoiding looking toward her heart-shaped face, and getting migraines holding his breath lest he whiff the heady sweetness from that lustrous dark hair, Bone determined to act.

For some, asking Mary out would have been a natural next step, but not for Bone. Life had taught him many things;

unfortunately, almost all of them were about grammar and etymology. He could have told you that "kiss" is both common noun and transitive verb, as are "date" and "love"; the mechanics of an actual kiss, however, or arranging a date, let alone finding love, were matters as opaque to him as the steel door of a bank- vault. So, knowing no better, during the final exam, he beckoned her into the hall, "Ms. Snyder," and then when they were alone, the very molecules of the air holding their breath as if before a thunderbolt, he said, "So when are you going out with me?"

The six-year-old at the state fair wins the plush panda a head taller than himself; the housewife ignorant of sports catches the home run cracked to the stands; the Baptist pastor, morally opposed to gambling, who bought a ticket only to soften the embarrassment of facing the cashier with his wife's tampons, wins the million-dollar jackpot. In this way, by the mysterious cosmic force known by envious runners-up as beginner's luck, Bone's untutored tactic brought home the metaphorical bacon.

"How about this Saturday?" Mary asked.

On Saturday at sundown, therefore, Bone stood ready to press the doorbell of Mary's townhouse apartment. Twilight gave each skinny tree—precisely one per lot—a poetic, wistful beauty. Someone was grilling a steak. Birds tittered in the eaves. But Bone was aware only of the starched shirt leaning on his shoulders like a cardboard sheet. Even he knew that arriving this early was a faux pas; wouldn't it save embarrassment to wait in the car a few minutes before announcing himself? He turned, stepped toward his car, hesitated—on second thought. Turned. Raised his hand to the doorbell. Stopped. Lowered his hand. Considered. Raised it. Lowered it.

He never knew how long Mary's roommate, Laurel, had been watching before he finally noticed her face in the window. Once he stopped, Laurel called, "Mare-ree! Your date's here!" The door opened, and he slunk across the threshold.

As he waited, making strained replies to Laurel's small talk, Bone's surroundings—the Jacques Brel poster over the unused ten-speed; the dusty potted ficus; the plastic crate-cum-bookshelf housing Salinger, Vonnegut, and *The Fountainhead*—stamped his memory, the way the priest's face, guards' clasping hands, and clanking leg irons imprint the consciousness of a prisoner en route to the electric chair. Bone had an unignorable foresense of failure.

Indeed, the date was not precisely a success.

He took her to dinner and a movie, which, he'd gleaned, is standard operating procedure on dates, but sitting across a table from the woman he'd fantasized about, rather than inspiring him to gallantry and charm, merely stunned him.

She gave him a roll from the bread basket and held it in his fingers as she buttered it for him, an unexpected intimacy that sent electricity crackling up his arm. "It must be exciting being an author," Mary said. Bone said it was not that exciting. "When do you find time to write?" Mornings, Bone told her. "I always wished I could write." Bone said she should try it.

After a few more failed gambits on her part, the silence went unspoiled by human speech until the theater, when Bone's two-quart paper cup of crushed ice and syrupy grape soda, which a sign at the concession counter ludicrously identified as "medium," managed to upend into Mary's lap.

After this episode they left without seeing the rest of the movie.

Back at the apartment, Mary gave Bone her cheek when he went in for the kiss, and his attempt to land on her mouth only resulted in an evasive maneuver resembling an experiment in magnetic repulsion. "So," Bone said. He felt shortchanged and short-tempered. He was no skinflint, but this rendezvous had run him—between tickets, popcorn, and soda, not to mention the lavish dinner he had barely tasted—a great amount of money, money he could ill afford on a college teacher's salary. In contrast to this, a kiss—the memory of which might have warmed the cold baloney sandwiches on which he would subsist next month to economize—would have cost her nothing, and yet she withheld it. He hated himself for having these thoughts, but in no way did that stop him from having them.

"So," he said, "can I ask you out again?"

"Sure," she said, her reply as insincere as his request. "Give me a call."

He did call—why, who can say, unless to confirm his bitter hypothesis—four times: the first time she answered; the next two times it was Laurel; each time Bone was informed Mary had a prior engagement. The fourth time no one answered at all.

Bone heard, through a vine of particularly sour grapes, that Mary, "you know, that pretty secretary who works in the dean's office," was "involved with" Dr. Gordon, the dean, a serial womanizer whose wife would no doubt "just die" if she found out.

In its long existence the word "love" has acquired its share of false etymologies, to wit: in French *l'oeuf*, "egg," is metonymy for zero, the egg's shape suggesting 0, as "goose egg" does in English. The British anglicized *l'oeuf* to "love," and in the way that meaningless coincidences sometimes become meaningful, to this day, in tennis, as in life, love means nothing. Bone warmed himself reflecting on this chilly irony.

The gossip about Mary he added to a preliminary but quickly growing store of data regarding the bad character and otherwise undesirable qualities of Mary and women like her, indeed all women generally, coolly committing himself to the solitary life. As for Gordon, if Bone had not especially liked him before, he loathed him now.

Therefore, when Bone answered his telephone one day and heard Mary's voice on the other end, you could have knocked him over with a hummingbird feather.

"What's up?" she asked. The question flummoxed; what was up? The white clouds, he supposed, the yellow sun that warmed the earth, his soaring heart; these things were up, and yet he could make no reply. "You haven't called in a while," Mary chided, as if above all things else the anticipation of his call were the chief delight of her existence. "I thought you and I were going out again."

He gurgled, "I'm glad you're using the correct case."

"What?"

"You said 'you and I' instead of 'you and me.' I was congratulating you for using the correct pronoun case."

"Oh." A longish pause while Mary waited for Bone to speak. "So, you wanted to go out?"

Mary, it transpired, had already picked a place and date, sparing Bone the chore of planning suitable entertainment. At her townhouse, he spent the obligatory awkward minutes with Laurel until Mary emerged in a scrumptious short black skirt and red blouse which offered the additional advantage, which Bone naively believed she did not suspect, of revealing her breast in profile.

It rained; getting lost only once—a shared mishap that seemed to seal the bond between them—they threaded their way through black, rain-bright streets between streetlamps punctuating the night like an ellipsis to the Vietnamese restaurant Mary had chosen. Bone's hot blood roared in his ears, the fine hairs on his neck tickling his collar as if he were sitting on an electrified fence instead of next to this beauty in mute wonder; what glad change of heart accounted for this good fortune? Had he made a better first impression than he'd thought, and was it only bad timing and bad luck that had kept them apart?

The waiter asked if they wanted iced coffee—an odd suggestion coming before they'd even seen a menu. Meeting their puzzled looks with a puzzled one of his own, the waiter explained that Çhao Gio was renowned for iced coffee, implying it was unusual, if not unheard-of, for customers to be unaware of this. Bone and Mary exchanged looks, and Bone said yes, they would have the iced coffee.

Their wait was relieved by an awkward coincidence when Dr. Gordon and his wife arrived. It was a small restaurant, and the couples sat at adjoining tables. Time dripped in strained camaraderie before the waiter reappeared.

"We ordered the iced coffee," Bone announced.

"Yes," Gordon said. "It's the specialty." Gordon was his insufferable self, reclining with his arm extended over the back of his wife's chair. Mrs. Gordon, who even smiling wore frown lines of a long campaign to stay slim and attractive, asked if Mary enjoyed her position and if it got very hard being under her husband, a strange, fierce fire in her eyes. Gordon asked Bone something about teaching, not concealing his lack of interest in Bone's reply; Gordon was after all a dean, and Bone a mere lecturer.

A surreal and uncomfortable situation, but Mary reached across the tablecloth to hold Bone's hand, and beneath the table, her knee pressed his own. In his joy, he lost his discomfort; a thousand Dr. Gordons could have marched in with a thousand wives, and he would have snapped his fingers at all of them, aware only of that sweet touch against his hand

and knee. Bone said something clever and offhand, a remark that later he could never remember, a modest put-down, at which Gordon's nostrils dilated in mild displeasure and Mrs. Gordon laughed.

Mary squeezed his hand, and the waiter returned with a tray to prepare their coffee.

In an era of Starbucks' ubiquity, iced coffee is as mundane a beverage as any, but the folks at Çhao Gio served it with all the solemn ceremony of High Church mass; the only things lacking were a crucifix and incense ball. Before Bone and Mary, the waiter set down two miniature coffee pots, frosty cocktail shakers, and tall glasses with a finger of beige semiliquid that Bone guessed was partially caramelized condensed milk; the waiter made Mary's first, pouring the hot coffee into the cocktail shaker, giving two judicious rattles, then pouring it, chilled but undiluted, over the condensed milk; the result was a glassful of gray dawn: midnight black near the top, tapering to creamy taupe, and finally the antique white of the condensed milk at the bottom. Mary reached for her spoon, but Gordon said, "Don't stir."

Obediently Mary set the spoon back down and watched as the waiter completed the coffee-making operation for Bone.

Velvet.

Each flavor feathered to the next like the color in the glass. The closest thing Bone knew to compare with it was chocolate milk, except it was nothing at all like chocolate milk. Too soon his glass was empty, but he saw it would be gauche to order a second; besides, a single glass, he discovered, was the perfect amount. If only he hadn't finished so quickly.

"Good, isn't it?" Gordon said, as if iced coffee, the Vietnamese restaurant, and Vietnam itself were things brought into being for his private amusement, but which, for the sake of their edification, he graciously condescended to share.

After the restaurant, parked in front of her townhouse, a streetlight shining in the gleaming puddle at the curb, Mary was unexpectedly willing to learn all there was to know on the subject of Bone King; even if she were pretending, Bone, unwilling to end the evening, was unusually garrulous.

He talked about growing up in Tennessee, the sharp, sweet smell of sawmills, gullies choked with rusted car chassis and black plastic garbage bags. He told her about Red Man–chewing junior high boys who loved the music of fists on skin and terrified pleading. He told her how, when still a child, he'd discovered his love of the written word in the Cook County Library, and how his work on Words would be not only his dissertation but an expression of that love. He said that in spite of certain memories, he dreamed of going back someday, having a few acres and maybe a couple of chickens, and she said he was really something and kissed him.

She told him that night that he was real, that he didn't play games, that she was sick of playing games. Bone sensed that she was comparing him to someone else, but he was too wise or lucky to ask whom.

Was that all there was to it? Did Mary, like Othello's Desdemona, love Bone for the dangers he had passed, and did he love her that she did pity them? No, there was one other triumphant moment.

It was when they'd been seeing each other about three months, and Bone had taken Mary out for her birthday, his mood made more festive by the chill January night that made her huddle against him when they left the car. He'd recently read an article on backformation, removing what seems to be a suffix or prefix to form a new word, deriving **buttle** from **butler**, **burgle** from **burglar**, and, more recently, an African American neologism, **conversate** from **conversation**. Walking arm-in-arm to the restaurant, they played at making backformations of their own: "I might seem feckless, but I've got loads of *feck.*" "Give me a hammer, I need to *ham* some nails." "I am so happy. Tonight I am full of *hap.*"

Seeing the homeless man sitting on the sidewalk outside the restaurant, Bone automatically reached into his back pocket—he'd picked up new habits from Mary. The smallest bill in his wallet was a five, but what the heck; Bone gave it to him without further thought.

"Where are your shoes?" Mary asked.

"Someone stole them."

Inside the restaurant, Bone happily studied the menu. Everything looked so good. Did Mary want to start with an appetizer? Mary stared at the menu as if it were indecipherable. Her chin trembled. "I don't understand," she said. "How could they steal that man's shoes?" A tear went down her face.

A month of anticipation, ruined. It would be useless saying not to worry about the man outside, that there were shelters, that Bone had already given him five dollars. Disappointment, frustration, and annoyance flashed by like overhead lights marking the distance in a long, dark tunnel. Then he saw what he must do.

"Excuse me," he said. He returned a few minutes later, his face about to split from his grin. "I think we should start with that artichoke-cheese thingy," he said.

Tears still in Mary's eyes. "I'm sorry," she said. "I just can't stop thinking about it. That poor man."

"Look down," he told her. He lifted the tablecloth. For a second she stared at his toes wiggling in his black socks without understanding. Then she cried again. Then they laughed. That was the night she said she loved him. That was the night he felt worthy of it.

CHAPTER THREE

C, c

From the Semitic gimel (𐤂), "sling" or "throwing stick." Hence, the three great achievements of the Early Bronze Age, as represented by the first three letters of the alphabet, were domestication of animals, man-made shelter, and warfare.

calque: A word formed by translation from another language. Typically, English adopts words wholesale, as in "déjà vu," "amuck," or "kindergarten," but makes **calques** of particularly picturesque or apropos phrases, as in "losing face" from the Mandarin *diū liǎn*, or "scapegoat," possibly a mistranslation of *azazel*, a demon of Hebrew mythology, for '*ez ozel*, "goat that escapes," i.e., [*e*]*scapegoat*.

Christ: From the Greek *khristos*, "anointed," akin to the Sanskrit *gharsati*, "to grind oil from seeds," from the Proto Indo-European, *ghri*-, "to grind," whence also **grind, grist,** and **grits.**

cliché: I will forgo the comical catalog of **clichés** a lesser lexicographer would mistakenly think witty and original. French printers called a ready-made phrase cast as a single piece of type **cliché**, onomatopoeia for the liquid slap and hiss of a hot letter mold dropping into cold water.

cuckold: A derisive term for a wronged man, from **cuckoo,** a bird famed for laying eggs in other birds' nests, from the Middle English *cukeweld* or *cukewold*, from the Latin *cuculous*, and thence from the Greek *koukos*.

W̲hen Mary picked up Bone from the hospital, she quizzed the staff, getting nothing but good news, which is always strangely dissatisfying.

The Etch-a-Sketch of Bone's heart had risen and fallen all night with perfect regularity, his vital signs as vital as ever, his blood pressure neither too high nor too low, his urine all that good urine should be, if not more. Bone's bill of health was a clean one.

"I think we ought to cancel the appointment with the neurologist," Bone said as they drove home. "I know it was scary, but I think I just freaked out for a while there. I've been under a lot of stress, and I just freaked out."

"What's stressing you?"

Bone might have responded he was worried she had something going with Cash Hudson but said instead, "Just the usual. My editor's losing patience waiting for me to finish *Words*. And of course, my dissertation committee's breathing down my neck."

Mary said nothing for a time. He put his hand on her knee, but she ignored it. "You still need to keep the appointment," she said.

Bone couldn't have said what he expected of his homecoming, but it wasn't what he got. It wasn't as if he thought there'd be a banner reading "Welcome Home." That would have been ridiculous. Still, it felt odd that everything was exactly the same as it had been before. Instead of a ritual to smooth the transition, he and Mary did as always: Bone sat on the couch and read *The Journal of Etymology*, and Mary talked on the phone to her friends. They watched TV without speaking. It felt strange acting as if nothing were strange, but at least there was a bright spot about gliding back into the familiar routine: Saturday night in the King household was the customary night for sex.

At bedtime, Bone sat on top of the covers, stripped to his boxer shorts, a singsong going through his head: tonight, tonight, tonight, going to make love tonight. He'd taken care not to disarrange the covers because he wanted to share sliding into a fresh bed with her—like breaking the crust of crème brûlée—pushing their feet down through cool, tight sheets as their arms and bodies sought each other out.

Mary, in the bathroom, was brushing her teeth with astonishing thoroughness, it seemed to Bone. After a while, feeling foolish and self-conscious, he pulled back the covers and got in. So much for his and Mary's getting into bed at the same time. He lay on his side in a roguish pose, head in hand, elbow sunk in the pillow. Toilet flush. Mary came in the bedroom but immediately left.

"What is it?"

"Forgot to set up the coffee maker."

Bone's wrist was going numb. He rolled on his back, hands folded across his chest. Tonight, tonight, tonight. Then she was in the bedroom. She took off her skimpy flower-print robe and got in bed. Her summer nightgown was little more than a slip. Tonight, tonight, tonight. Bone reached for her but only knuckled an elbow. Now she was trimming her toenails. She propped against the pillow and opened her murder mystery. Bone kissed her bare shoulder.

"It's Saturday night," Bone reminded her hopefully. This

was not turning out quite the magical evening he'd imagined.

"You just got back from the hospital."

"So?" He waggled his eyebrows.

"I don't work that way. I can't just turn it off and on." She stared at him. "Are you going to sulk about this?"

"Aren't you glad to have me home?"

"All right," she said. She bookmarked her place, set her mystery on the nightstand, and turned off the light. Her legs were wonderfully cool and smooth. She held his face in her hands and gave him a businesslike kiss.

They weren't exactly setting the night on fire, but even bad sex is better than no sex at all. He kicked his briefs out from under the covers, then turned to kiss her again. But now the angle was wrong; their mouths didn't seal, and a little drool dripped onto the pillow. Putting a hand on either side of her head, he lowered to her mouth in a push-up. The angle was better, but now there was something under his hand.

"Move," Mary said.

"What?"

"Move. You're on my arm."

Bone got out of bed.

"Where are you going?"

"I have to pee," Bone said. "Back in a second." Down the hall in the bathroom, Bone peed and flushed. As he washed up, Bone looked in the mirror and reflected. When had their sex life turned into this dreary cycle of anticipation and letdown? There'd been a time, and not long ago, when adjectives such as "spontaneous" or "joyous" could fairly be applied to their lovemaking, or at the very least "mutual." Mary enjoyed sex, Bone supposed, but she didn't *believe* in it, its power to heal, to make whole, to justify the shabby round of existence. He wondered how he and Mary had allowed themselves to turn into these people. Could they ever turn back?

Bone cut off the water and walked down the hallway to the bedroom door.

But that was as far as he got.

Go on in. *How* do you go on in? Tell yourself to move. *How* do you tell yourself to move?

His immobility had struck again.

Mary said, "What are you doing?"

"I can't move," Bone said. "Oh, God, it's happening again. I can't move."

Mary got out of bed. "I'll get Cash."

He cursed her, which shocked them both, and instantly felt ashamed and said more mildly, "Please, God, no, why do you have to bring him into it?" He saw her mind was made up, and said, "If you have to bring Cash into it, at least put something on me."

Bone uttered a cry of horror when he saw what Mary had in mind, but she ignored him. A crisis is no time to be fussy about dignity. Getting Bone dressed in this condition, his entire body rigid as any mannequin, ruled out slacks and a polo shirt. He blocked the door almost entirely, leaving little room to operate, and it took several unsuccessful trials before she worked his arms, frozen midswing, into her flower-print robe, finally putting it on him backward like a hospital smock and cinching the belt around his waist.

"I'll be back in a sec," Mary promised as she squeezed past him into the hall.

"Don't leave! It's too small! You didn't get the belt tight!" Bone shouted, but he already heard her naked feet pad down the hall and the kitchen door close. "The knot will never hold," Bone said quietly, and as if it to prove that knots could hear, the belt loosened behind his back and undid itself like a vine forced into a shape it will not willingly hold. The robe fell open, and a breeze from the air-conditioning vent ran up his backside.

Bone wondered how long it would be until she returned. How long had it been already? Time hung suspended the way it does when nothing happens to mark its passing. Had she taken the car? He hadn't heard the engine start, but surely she hadn't run over to Cash's house barefoot. Cash lived a street away. Bone imagined Cash answering a doorbell and finding Bone's wife slightly out of breath, dressed in a slip nightie that barely reached her thigh.

Bone's reverie was interrupted by a strangled gurgle emanating behind him that told him Cash Hudson had arrived on the scene. The neighbor, however, did not comment on Bone's wardrobe but merely knelt and set to work getting Bone through the door, which was somehow worse and more humiliating than anything else he could have done.

Bone contemplated the consequences of his actions. If he'd absolutely *had* to use the bathroom, why hadn't he put on his briefs so at least his gleaming backformation didn't stick out behind like two white loaves? This, however, is the sort of thought that strikes one only after it is too late.

Cash gripped and lifted a calf, causing the robe to shift and slide silkily from Bone's shoulders, down his arms, and onto the floor. Now Bone was completely naked.

I will not cry, Bone resolutely told himself. I refuse to cry.

So naturally, a fat tear rolled from his eye, burning his cheek, and frozen as he was, he could not even lift his arm to wipe it away.

CHAPTER FOUR

D, d

From the Semitic *daleth* (◁), "door."

day: The interval between sunrise and -set. The d- rises straight up before sinking to a squinting -a-, after which –y descends beneath the word's horizon, curving back again toward d-. The Proto Indo-European root for **day,** *déi-no-,* is unmistakably kin to the root for **god,** *déyw-o-,* that is, "shining." From these two derive, therefore, not only **date, dial,** and **diary** but also **deity, theology** (owing to a consonant shift d > th), and **divine.**

door: The sideways lid of a room. The word opens with the ideogram for door itself (see **D**), a downstroke with a knob on one side. We pass the portals of two -o-s before reaching -r, a panel with a latch closing the word on the far side. The Proto Indo-European root, *dʰwer,* leads back before **doors** themselves, to the late Paleolithic, evidently a meaning assigned existentially, its creators not knowing what lay behind it.

If there'd been any doubt about seeing the specialist before, there was none now, though Bone still told himself he was keeping the appointment only to humor Mary. As humiliating and frightening as the episodes were at the time, afterward they seemed merely ludicrous. He couldn't get through doors—who ever heard of a thing like that? His disorder was as impossible to take seriously as death by penguin stampede.

That Sunday was tense and solemn. The obvious topic of discussion, neither of them cared to mention, so the day was spent in speaking little and avoiding eye contact generally; accordingly, Bone had ample time to speculate on his own about the cause of his condition. Perhaps his problem was not physical but—and this is preposterous, of course, but after all, who's to say what is and isn't possible?—*verbal*. And would this really be as far-fetched as it seemed? Many theorists claim consciousness isn't a mere nebulous state of awareness granted in some degree even to earthworms and horseshoe crabs but the ability to *verbalize*. Others argue that our identities, our very selves, are constructed out of words. So Bone took a crack at viewing his predicament in light of the subject he taught: grammar.

So what did he know about his condition? Both episodes had to do with crossing a threshold of some sort—stepping out of a tub, crossing into a room. Moreover, each was associated with Mary—spying on her, though he would never admit that, and getting ready to make love.

To demonstrate how syntax could be at the root of his problems, Bone began by diagramming a very straightforward sentence, "Bone loves his wife." The "sentence tree" style, that lopsided mobile of coat hangers and string, would not do; to really grasp a sentence at its core requires the old-fashioned and unfashionable Reed-Kellogg system.

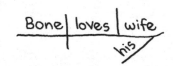

How elegant. Two short vertical lines separate the subject, "Bone," from "wife," the object of the verb "loves," with the tender possessive pronoun "his" touching the sentence stem like a tentative remora so there's no mistaking whose wife it is Bone loves.

He took another simple example. "She loves him no longer."

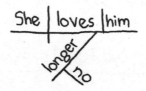

Almost the same sentence, except for that telltale adverbial phrase drooping like a dead branch beneath the verb "loves." The adverb "longer" almost offers hope, except that even in its most positive sense, this necessarily implies a termination, and finally you come to the terrible "no" crouching at the sentence's base.

Interestingly, in diagramming, an interrogative is put in the same subject–verb–complement order as a declarative statement. Thus, a question, such as, "Did you have sex with him?" supplies its own answer when diagrammed:

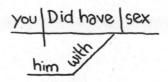

The "him" hanging by its preposition seems evasive, ashamed to be caught in the main sentence stem, an uninvited neighbor slinking across the street at a crabwise angle. None of English's polite, Norman-French-derived vocabulary, however, can express the idea without a preposition: "have sex with," "make love to," "have intercourse with," et cetera. To form a clear, straightforward sentence, Bone had to resort to sturdy if vulgar Anglo-Saxon.

you | Did fuck | him

There. Now "him" was properly the object of the verbphrase "Did fuck," as it should be, and not the wishy-washy object of the preposition.

Having attended to these arbitrary examples, Bone was ready to consider his predicament in a syntactic light: "Bone walks across the threshold."

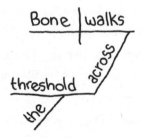

This, perhaps, revealed the source of his perplexity. The all-important verb "walks" has no object, no noun to receive its action. The only proper object of the verb might be the reflexive pronoun, "himself," but if Bone walks himself, he is merely going in circles. "Walks" is intransitive, and yet transition is exactly what the meaning requires. To get where it's going, the sentence has to detour from the stem and cross the narrow footbridge of a preposition only to arrive, where?

Threshold.

The determinate "the" that tells which threshold—the sentence is useless if it only claims that Bone crosses thresholds in general—is a driplet hanging from "threshold" itself. And "threshold"—what does it signify? A vacancy between two places—crossing a threshold necessarily means crossing *into* something, but that something is withheld, a ghostly implicature buried in the deep structure of the sentence.

Who could blame him for his inability to navigate such syntax?

DR. LIMONGELLO'S OFFICE was in one of the medical buildings sprouting around Northside Hospital like mushrooms around a tree stump. When they arrived for Bone's appointment— Mary had taken the day off—a receptionist gave them a clipboard, thick with forms to complete, instructing them to sit in the waiting area. If Wonderful Dr. Lemon Jell-O's wonderfulness were measured by how many people he kept waiting, he was a wonderful doctor indeed.

They waited. Bone perused the periodicals laid out for their delight: sailing magazines (Bone didn't sail) and golf magazines (Bone didn't golf) as morning melted into a puddle of noon and their stomachs began to growl. Mary went to the desk to ask if the doctor would see them soon or if they should go ahead and get some lunch.

"There's a cafeteria downstairs," the receptionist offered.

"If we go down and eat, will we lose our place?" Mary wanted to know. The receptionist didn't answer that one, and so they went back to waiting.

Finally, a nurse bade them follow in the wake of her swishing thighs, out of the waiting room to the final door of a door-lined corridor.

"Wait in here," the nurse instructed.

"I can't," Bone muttered, heat rising in his face.

"What?" the nurse asked, and then repeated, "Wait in here."

"I can't," Bone repeated more loudly than he'd intended. A curious patient down the hallway opened his door a crack but chose not to step out. The hell with it. "I can't get through," Bone said loudly enough for anyone who wanted to get a good earful. "That's why I'm here. Sometimes I can't go through doorways."

So Mary and the nurse walked him through, manipulating his legs, into a room with an examination table, two black-cushioned chrome chairs, cabinets, and a sink.

"Will the doctor see us soon?" Bone asked, still feverish with shame, but this was another question destined to go unanswered. The nurse left, and Bone sat on the examination table, Mary in a chair. Dumbed-down scientific illustrations adorned the walls: colorful branching neurons, glands squeezing out hormones in fat teardrops, arrows indicating potential problems in the temporal lobe and frontal cortex. A poster told a modern-day pharmaceutical fairy tale: in the first panel a smiling man in a white lab coat talks to a damsel slumping sadly under a soot-black cumulus cloud. In the second panel, posture much improved, she ventures a timid smile—not exactly happy but willing to *appear* happy—and the cloud, while still overhead, has diminished, now a manageable dove-gray instead of black. Bone contemplated the implied moral … *and she coped as well as could be expected ever after.*

"Are y'all waiting for me?" A man in a white lab coat, smiling as if it were his first day on the job, stood in the door.

"Dr. Limongello?"

With one hand the doctor took Bone's shoulder, and with the other he gave a vigorous Rotary Club handshake, coming awkwardly close, quizzical, snapping bright eyes scrutinizing Bone as if life's secrets were printed on the inner wall of his skull. "This is the first time I've seen you, right? This is your first appointment?" he said, and when Bone said it was, the doctor said to Mary, "Well, aren't you lovely?" making her blush, and for a moment, Bone thought the doctor was going to kiss her hand, but instead he just shook it and said, "Well, let's take a look-see at the patient."

Limongello bustled around the room as if assuring himself everything was where he'd left it: the sink handles, the glass jar of cotton balls on the counter, even the cartoon woman with her hovering thundercloud received his touch. Bone and Mary had been warned the double-doc was "eccentric," but they hadn't been prepared for this. What accounted for that smile that shone not only from his mouth but from every pore of his forehead? The awareness that patients were his bread and butter? The delight of diagnosis, being able to see through the translucent mystery that others find opaque? An effort to reassure? Happy anticipation of helping a stranger?

Limongello looked in a drawer beside the sink and found an otoscope. "Might as well rule out an inner-ear problem. Say 'ahhh.'" Bone said it, and Limongello chuckled. "Just kidding, you don't have to say 'ahhh' when someone looks in your ear." He looked into Bone's ear with a disappointed "Huh!" Then, "So why don't you tell me what seems to be the trouble?"

As Bone recounted his two episodes of immobility—three counting the one that had occurred just outside the door—the doctor set the otoscope down, looking from Bone to Mary as if gauging whether they found this tale as astonishing as he. "That must have been terrifying. We've got to do something for you folks." Limongello rubbed his jaw and said, "Okay, I want you to walk from the front of the room to the back. Nothing fancy, no heel-to-toe, just walk normally." Bone walked as normally as possible after being told to "walk normally" while Limongello watched, after which he had Bone close his eyes and told him to bring in one hand at a time and touch a finger to his nose, standing first on one foot, then the other. Limongello sat perched forward as far as possible in a chair beside Mary, staring raptly at Bone. "So the first time, you were taking a bath?"

"He wasn't taking a bath; he was just in the bathtub," Mary supplied.

Limongello looked at Mary, then at Bone. "So why were you in the tub?"

"I don't really remember," Bone lied.

Limongello wore a satisfied-dissatisfied look, like a poker player seeing through an opponent's ill-advised bluff. "'Zat so?" The doctor's demeanor said he didn't believe it was so but had decided not to pursue this line of questioning; instead he abruptly slapped his thighs twice, announcing, "I am so hungry I could eat a horse. Well, a *small* one. Ah-ha-ha-ha. I didn't get anything for breakfast but coffee and some damn raisin toast. Have y'all eaten?" They hadn't. "Wait here a sec." He disappeared, leaving them to gape at one another, but came back a few moments later without his lab coat. "I told my assistant to fill in. What say we go to the cafeteria and talk this over?"

"What about your other patients?" Bone asked.

"Ah." Limongello waved dismissively. "They're in good hands. You're now my most important case. Think you can go through?" Limongello invited Bone to go through the door, and this time Bone was able to, a fact that Limongello noted, thoughtfully rubbing his chin. Bone headed toward the waiting room, but Limongello stopped him. "No, no, no. We'll go through the 'Bat Cave.'" He led them through a back entrance at the end of the hall. Bone worried his condition would strike and freeze him at the door, but in the doctor's magic presence, he went through again without trouble.

"Are you sure this is okay?" Bone asked once they were in the elevator.

"Let me tell you something," Limongello said. A hand on Bone's shoulder again, his faint breath on Bone's cheek. "Your case is of real interest to me. It's—not exactly—but very similar to certain other—very mysterious cases that've had me stumped some time now. I think your syndrome holds the key to something major. If we got to you in time."

Leaving the doctor's office felt like taking an unscheduled holiday. Limongello allowed Bone to pay for lunch after warning them off the meatloaf and recommending the fish sandwich, which was what he got himself, along with an orange soda.

They selected a corner table, and Limongello asked about Bone and Mary, learning that Mary was a church secretary and Bone a college professor. He seemed interested in Bone's opinions on grammar and was impressed that Bone had written a book. Soon they became so comfortable that Mary asked, "What kind of name is Limongello? Italian?"

"I'm only Italian on my father's side," Limongello said breezily. "On my mother's side I'm Scotch-Irish." Although he'd said nothing funny, he laughed, and his laugh was so easygoing and natural that Mary laughed, too, and there were good feelings all around.

"So, Doctor," Bone asked, "what's wrong with me? Am I

cracking up?" Trying to match the doctor's breeziness (and failing). "Cuckoo crazy?" He pointed a twirling index finger at his temple, the time-honored representation of broken gear-work inside.

"In a nutshell?" Limongello said. "I think you think too much." Mary gave Bone a sardonic I-could-have-told-you-that look, but Limongello was as unsmiling as a head on Mount Rushmore. He lifted his breaded fish off the bun and, with the delicacy and precision of a surgeon, cut a bite with his spork and chewed thoughtfully before speaking again, looking at Bone with the gaze of an art critic considering a painting by a promising but flawed talent. "I think your problem is neurological. But then, you'd expect me to say that because I'm a neurologist. A priest would say it was spiritual. An accountant would say it was financial. Ha-ha. Each of us only sees what we're prepared to see," Limongello said with sudden seriousness.

"So what do you think is wrong?" Mary asked.

Limongello made a sound between a *tch* of concern and sucking a morsel of whitefish from his teeth. He took a tennis-ball-sized rubber brain from his pants pocket and, halving it like a pecan, pointed out the curve of a pale question mark inside. "We used to think the brain was a bank where you made deposits and withdrawals. Like this neuron is the memory of Aunt Sally, and here's the part that knows the square of the hypotenuse, and down here is why you can't stand rutabagas. But the truth's a lot stranger. It's more like a highway system.

"The brain sends messages to the body, and the body sends messages to the brain, and one part of the brain sends messages to the other parts, and around and around like that. Everything's sending messages: neurons, glands, even blood cells. But there's no place where the messages stop or start, no origin or destination. That's the mystery. What we got at the end of the day is all these messages running around, but what no one's ever been able to find is the self—who's *reading* the messages? Who's *directing it all*? We may never find it. We can find the messages for your emotions easy enough: dopamine and oxytocin to make you feel good, and noradrenaline and calcitonin to make you feel bad—'Good, good, you're happy now,' or 'Uh-oh, uh-oh, you're getting tense,' but we can't locate the *you* that actually reads the messages, the self that feels happy or sad or whatever. Sure, we can go in with a big old scalpel, *skriiik*," with an alarmingly vivid impression of slicing meat, Limongello swiped diagonally across the rubber brain, "and chop out a lobe, and after that you won't hate rutabagas or remember Aunt Sally, but that's not the same thing. We'd never know if we got rid of the memory, that piece of your*self*, or just ripped out the pathway the message goes through. You might blow up the highway the farmer gets to town on, but that's not the same thing as killing the farmer. You understand?"

Limongello didn't wait to see if they understood. "Your problem is so specific, not a general motor deficit, only a problem with doors. Maybe your brain has one tiny road—a one-laner, a dirt road, an alley—for the message about getting through doors. Just that and nothing else. When you come to a door, the message about how to walk through has to travel down that one particular road. For some reason your brain, maybe even your *self*, can't get the message, so you can't go through the door."

"But it wasn't a door," Mary said. "It was a bathtub."

"The first time, yes," Limongello conceded. "When I say doors, I really mean thresholds; I mean transitions. At times the message about doors doesn't go through."

"I don't have a problem with doors," Bone said. "There's one right over there."

Limongello said, "*Logically*, you know what a door is. You can define *door*. You can draw a door. The highways for those messages aren't blocked, just the side road of going *through* doors. I'm not kidding when I say your problem stems from thinking too much." Limongello leaned back and laced his fingers across his chest, tapping his thumbs. He cocked his head, viewing Bone at a forty-five-degree angle. "It's been proven that *thought*, all by itself, alters the brain's function. For example, if you're having a pity party, being a Gloomy Gus, and you clap your hands and say out loud, 'I feel terrific,' your hypothalamus will give you a little boost of dopamine and you'll actually feel a little better. Strangely enough, though, if in the middle of feeling really, really *good* about something, you think to yourself—even briefly—'This is how I feel when I'm happy,' or even 'I'm happy now,' you'll get an immediate *decrease* of dopamine. And if your hormones are signaling embarrassment or fear, and you think 'I'm angry,' you may suddenly discover you're *furious*. The message system is very complicated."

"Is there a medication?" Mary asked.

Limongello's lips twisted briefly in displeasure, and a sigh lifted and dropped his shoulders. "Why's a pill always the first thing people want? Sorry, but I just don't want to risk that. Not yet. We don't know if this is a type of epilepsy, or Parkinson's, or what. Giving the wrong medication could be disastrous. Disastrous. For example, that messenger I told you about, dopamine. When that messenger goes to one part of your brain, it says that things are copacetic. Life's not so bad. But to another part of your brain, that same message, dopamine, is how to do a pirouette. So far, so good. But in *another* part of your brain, that same message tells you to start listening to the voices in your head, how your friends are out to get you, your wife is running around on you, the cable guy is working for the CIA, or your doctor is a loony using you for medical experiments." Limongello waggled his fingers in a witch doctor's *booga-booga-boo* gesture. "The exact same messages mean entirely different things at different times in different parts of the brain."

"Like the alphabet," Bone suggested.

"Yes," Limongello said. "Like the alphabet. Sometimes A's a letter and sometimes a blood type. Might be a grade on a paper or stand for 'adultery.' So we got to be careful before sticking any new messages in the brain. Even a harmless-looking message, if it winds up in the wrong part of the brain—well, *blooey*." Limongello's hands opened and spread, simulating a cloud of smoke and debris. "The brain's an intricate mechanism. There are some tests I want to do." He put away the rubber brain and produced a pad and pen. "I need your address and phone number so I can visit you at home. We can dispense with office visits from now on."

Bone began writing and asked if Limongello couldn't get this information from the receptionist, but the doctor said this way was simpler. Bone asked about insurance, but Limongello said, "Don't worry about it. Like I said, your case really interests me. This may be the key to something major. Say I'm doing it pro bono. It won't cost you a thing. Besides, you already bought me lunch. And the fish sandwich was delicious."

"What do we do if it happens again?" Mary wanted to know. "The doorway thing."

"He might try dancing."

"What?"

"Music messages travel entirely different pathways in the brain. There's been plenty of research to show this. For example, chronic stutterers can communicate clearly when they sing. If this happens again, let's see if we can't throw your ol' brain a curveball. Try dancing through the door instead of walking."

"Dancing."

"Yes, Professor King. Do you dance?" Limongello struck a playful pose of doing the marimba. "Rumba? Charleston? Cha-cha-cha?"

"I can square dance," Bone mumbled numbly.

"Well, there you go," Limongello said, his attempt to lift Bone's mood as effective as a knock-knock joke at a funeral.

"Anyway," Bone said, "I don't expect it will happen again."

"Maybe not," said Limongello. "We'll hope. But next time you get stuck at a door—if there is a next time—see if you can't just do-si-do on through."

"GOOD LORD, WHAT a quack!" Bone said in the musty dusk of the parking deck, shaking his head and fumbling his keys from his pocket. "Can you believe his prescription? Dance?"

Mary stood and considered, elbow resting on the hatchback roof, a cube of daylight pouring between the concrete pylons illuminating half her face and the downy hairs of her forearm like fiber optics. It was one of those times she was so heart-stoppingly beautiful, it made something catch in Bone's throat.

"Well, I don't know," Mary said. "I think he made a lot of sense."

"Really? I think he was a whack job." Overstating it, but Bone would have said anything to keep her standing the way she was.

"Well, we can get a second opinion if you want." An impatient look crossed Mary's face. Bone beeped the unlock button, and she exited the cube of light into the passenger seat. Bone decided not to get a second opinion. After all, the condition was so bizarre, shouldn't the diagnosis and treatment be equally bizarre?

CHAPTER FIVE

E, e

From the flag-shaped Semitic *he* (𝟥), "praise" or "jubila-
tion." (See **hallelujah**. *Haleil,* "praise," and *ya,* "Yahweh.")
If the sequence of the Semitic alphabet reflects the progress of Bronze Age civilization, mankind domesticated
animals (⟨), built shelter (⟨), obtained weapons (𝟣),
and then acquired a door *for* the shelter (⟨) before getting
around to expressing gratitude to a higher power.

English: From *anglisc,* after the Angles, the Germanic
tribe who invaded Britain in the fifth century, from *An-
geln,* a fishhook-shaped peninsula on the Baltic Sea.

euphemism: From the Greek *eu-* "good," a positive or
socially acceptable synonym for a negative or socially
unacceptable concept. No one, for example, asking directions to the restroom is looking for a place to rest, nor is
the salient feature of a bathroom the bath. What a touching faith in language **euphemism** shows, as if reality is
altered by calling it something soap-scented and white.

excruciating: Extreme agony. From the Latin *ex,* "out
of," and *crux,* "cross." Literally, the pain of crucifixion.

The appointment with Dr. Limongello having
hogged the morning and eaten up the bigger
slice of afternoon, only a leftover scrap of time
remained, so Bone went to work early. Miranda Richter,
in the office next to his, looked up to say hello when he
passed, then cocked her head and narrowed her eyes. "Is
something the matter?"

Of course, something was the matter. Any number of things were very much the matter. And also of course, Bone lied. "No, I'm fine."

"You don't sound like yourself." Miranda's girlish face frowned: Shirley Temple playing an oncologist. "Is it, Mary?" A half-beat pause in the banal question, an unexpected comma falling before the nominative "Mary," a silence so brief only the sharpest sharpened razor could have sliced between, but packed with icy implication. Bone stopped short as if someone had jerked an unseen leash tied to his collar.

"No, no." Another lie. "What makes you ask?"

"Oh, nothing. Just came into my head." Her voice resumed its accustomed melody, steering clear of the precipice of consequential topics. "You want some Red Zinger?"

Bone took an armchair catty-corner from her desk His perceptions came in disconnected blots—tea bag plopping in a white mug, steam gurgling from a teapot, Miranda passing a clean spoon—"Well, almost clean," she amended, retrieving it and picking at a speck of annealed organic matter—a fat, tummy-shaped bowl of sugar packets shoved in his direction. "I ought to use honey or something, but I can't help it. I just love the taste of sugar!" Giggling the way she did every time she confessed this weakness.

"What made you ask if it was Mary?" Bone persisted.

"Why?" Absorbed in examining her sugar-packet inventory. "Is anything wrong?"

"No, nothing. I'm just curious why you mentioned her."

"Well, you know people. How people talk." Miranda put the mug in his hand, taking the opportunity to search his eyes. Her long, graceful fingers briefly touched his.

"What people?"

"Oh, people here. You know." She waved, indicating unseen tongues swarming overhead. "The truth is, I've been worried about you two since the start." Her voice dropped, and her hand was on his again. "I don't know if you ever knew this, but the rumor back when you got engaged was that Gordon was *seeing* Mary—" before Bone could interrupt to say he already knew this, Miranda finished with, "—up until the wedding." Bone did not know *that*. "Oh, dear! Oh, my goodness!" With a fat wad of white paper napkins, Miranda daubed the scalding Red Zinger that had spilled onto his crotch, not absorbing it but dispersing it into a broader, fainter, and hopefully less noticeable stain. "I shouldn't have mentioned it. It was years ago. I don't even think it's true."

"*Seeing* her," Bone said—how could Bone ever speak the word "seeing" again without an inward shudder at its new and horrid connotation?—"up to the wedding. Who said?"

Miranda stared, weighing whether to speak. It occurred to Bone, not for the first time, how attractive Miranda was, even with her chipped nails and ridiculous pageboy haircut that looked as if it had dropped on her head from the ceiling. Once, he'd nearly asked her out. But the chance had passed. "It was Dr. Gordon. We were planning your wedding shower, and he said his present was not *seeing* her on the big day so she wouldn't be late for her own wedding."

Blood pounded in Bone's ears. He sat still, concentrating on holding his teeth together so they wouldn't chatter. Heavy silence hung in the air. It was Miranda who spoke. "I don't think anyone took it seriously. He was just being an asshole, trying to be funny. That doesn't mean I like Gordon." Bone did not like him, either. "Watch out for Gordon," Miranda said, raising her mug for a sip. "He was talking to Loundsberry in the copy room, and when I came in, they acted like I'd caught them at something. I don't know what he's planning, but I got the feeling it has to do with the English Department. The look he gave me. Gordon's up to something, and if the excrement juxtaposes the oscillator, Loundsberry won't stick up for us. *Illegitimi non carborundum.*" The last was a joke between them, an ersatz Latin aphorism, "Don't let the bastards grind you down."

"Yes," Bone said, gulping the last of his tea and rising. "I have to get to class."

"Toodle-oo," she said, her customary farewell. A silly phrase, but Miranda Richter was the sort of person who would have disappointed you if she said anything *but* "toodle-oo."

Teaching Survey Literature that evening did nothing to lift Bone's spirits. As a child, imagining being a college professor, Bone had envisioned a somber lecture hall with a blackboard bearing indelible ghosts of bygone notes, tall, wavy-glassed windows, the threshold troughed by generations of students. Instead, he taught in a cinder-block dungeon of buzzing fluorescence and white tile floors. An advertisement-covered bulletin board cajoled the viewer to apply for credit cards and cell-phone plans. A smeary dry-erase board stood vigil over all.

During class Bone heard himself make here an insight, there an observation, his voice flattened and false-sounding, as if broadcast from inside an aquarium. Afterward he wanted nothing more than the familiar ache of home, but before he could flee, Belinda bushwhacked him: eager-to-please, willing-to-learn Belinda, bovine-bosomed Belinda. What madness had once led him to date this loathsome spaniel?

Not really dated. He'd happened to see her at a bar. Later, she'd told him about a band she was "into," and he'd gone along. On another occasion, at a poetry reading, he'd taken her hand at an especially fraught passage. All perfectly innocent.

Well, not entirely innocent. Have we mentioned that Bone was a married man? And that he hadn't happened to run into her; he'd chosen the time and location because he'd heard Belinda talk about it? And that when he'd held her hand, he'd been secretly hoping for much more? Much, much more?

Was that why Bone was jealous of Mary, because in

his heart he'd given Mary cause to be jealous of him? What was it that really galled him: that Mary might be committing adultery or that, unlike Bone, she might be committing it *competently*?

"I finished *Madame Bovary*?" Belinda said. "And it was great? But maybe it was too perfect? Like maybe the great novels are great because of their mistakes, not in spite of them?" An opinion easily gleaned from any book on Flaubert, which, no doubt, is exactly where Belinda had gleaned it, the better to impress Bone with her startling originality. "Are you teaching Advanced Grammar next semester?" So unused was Bone to an actual question from this quarter that she had to repeat it before he said he was. "Because I was talking to Dr. Gordon? And I was telling him how much I liked your class? And that I wanted to take you next semester?" She stared, expressionless as a dry-erase board. "And he said something that kind of made me think you weren't going to be here."

Dr. Gordon again. The fact that Belinda's last statement hadn't come out as a question oddly alarmed Bone and made his heart beat a little faster. "When did you talk to Dr. Gordon?" Bone wiped the dry-erase board. He could talk to her only when he didn't have to look at her.

"I work in his office."

Mary's old job.

"What did he say exactly?"

"I don't remember exactly." She could recite verbatim opinions cribbed from experts, but this she could not re-member.

"Well, I'm definitely teaching fall semester," Bone assured her.

"Well, that's good? Because you're, like, my favorite teacher?"

He shaped his mouth into a checkmark-smile and gave it to her. "I appreciate it." Belinda was back to talking in questions, meaning *crisis averted, back to normal.* Only things weren't back to normal. Miranda had said Gordon was "up to something"; did this something have to do with what Belinda had heard? Then there was the matter of Gordon's *seeing* Mary up until the wedding. What a new and dreadful weight had been forever lashed to that innocent gerund. Once, during their engagement, after keeping Bone waiting an hour and a half at Macy's to register for china, Mary had arrived breathless and uncharacteristically full of apologies: she'd been leaving her townhouse, she explained, when an old friend had bumped into her.

Had she just come from *seeing* Dr. Gordon?

Perhaps it was these thoughts that triggered it, but whatever it was, Bone had another bout of his condition at the door of the English building. Bone thought about moving but could not. So much for the immobility episodes not recurring. Now what? Okay, Wonderful Double-Doc Lemon Jell-O has a plan; let's put 'er into action.

A square-dance caller in Bone's head said, "Take your partner by the hand." Bone reached, and sure enough, he could move as long as it was a dance step. "Bow to your partner, bow to your side." Bone did. "Take your partner and swing her around." With that combination of stomping and skipping, which square-dance enthusiasts will say is the very essence of the form, Bone swung around to find himself face to face with an astonished Dr. Loundsberry. Though he had not yet crossed the threshold, Bone's arms, embracing his invisible partner, fell. His left knee, raised in a high step, also fell, bringing him to rest in a slightly tilted posture that he instantly corrected. Neither he nor Loundsberry found voice for a moment.

A book on positive thinking had once advised Loundsberry that if someone didn't have a smile, you should give him one of yours. He'd fought lifelong to put this dictum into action, stretching his lips in an affable grin but never managing to sustain it more than two seconds before drooping into his natural expression of a fugitive harkening to the distant baying of dogs. Then remembering his resolution, he'd pull his lips back for another go at a two-second smile. On this occasion, however, Loundsberry was too surprised even to give Bone one of his fleeting smiles but just looked taken aback and mildly horrified.

"Professor King," he said at length.

"It's a condition," Bone said. Loundsberry's face registered he'd surmised something along those lines. Thus, the full explanation of Bone's episodic door problem, that the dance Loundsberry had witnessed was not the malady but the treatment thereof, prescribed by a "wonderful" neurologist, poured forth in a rush, a flood of linked and compound clauses, before Bone could plug in a stopper.

Throughout Bone's unburdening, Dr. Loundsberry rose on his toes and lowered to the flats of his feet in a dance of his own, a dance of pensive reflection. "It's really nothing to worry about," Bone assured him.

"Ah," Dr. Loundsberry said, remembering to pull back his lips to show his yellowing teeth. "Ah. Well." The smile lasted two seconds before falling back.

With a shudder of apprehension so powerful it shook his knees, Bone walked to his car.

CHAPTER SIX

F, f

The Ancient Greek alphabet wrenched down the cap of the Semitic *waw* (**Ⴘ**), "peg," to resemble our own **F**, calling the result *digamma*. The Greeks dropped the letter, but not before the Etruscans picked it up and passed it to Latin, where its sound changed from /w/ to /f/. Greek had another version of *waw* as well: *upsilon* (**Y**), ancestor of **U**, **V**, **W**, and **Y**.

factoid: An unlovely neologism from the Latin *fact* and the Greek *-oid*, a bastard compounded by universal misuse as "a minor fact." Logically, the word does not mean "fact" but something that resembles one. An **asteroid** is not a "small star" but merely resembles it, and a **humanoid** resembles a human; it is not a dwarf. Genuine **factoids** include such generally accepted nonsense as domestic violence's rising during Super Bowls (it decreases), Eskimos having two hundred words for snow (Eskimo per se is not a language, but the Aleut and Inuit have about the same number of words for snow as English), and during the equinox its being uniquely possible to balance an egg on end (it is always possible to balance an egg on end; it merely takes repeated attempts). Add to the examples of **factoid** above the mistaken definition of factoid as "a minor fact."

faithful: Full of faith, trustworthy. From the Late Latin *fidere,* "to trust." Hence, **confidence, fiancé, fidelity.** From the Proto Indo-European root *bhidh*, "believe."

false: Untrue. From the Latin *fallere*, "to deceive," whence also **fail, fall, fault.**

The next morning Bone found Limongello on the front stoop. There was a heavy fog, and Bone indistinctly made out a green sedan, fuzzy-looking in the mist, parked in the driveway. Limongello held a large black valise, a cartoonist's version of a doctor's medical kit.

"What a great coffee cup," Limongello said. "'I are a grammar teacher.' Ha-ha. Love it." The cup was a gift from Mary, and Bone had always secretly disliked the weak joke, but Limongello's appreciation made him smile in spite of himself. "I hope I'm not interrupting?"

The neurologist followed Bone to the back room, set his case on the desk, and surveyed the bookcase Bone had been assembling, nodding thoughtfully like Sir Arthur Evans amid the ruins of Knossos. Here a bracket joined another at an appointed angle, there a baseboard ran perpendicular to a side brace, everywhere lay Styrofoam curlicues and plastic bags of silver screws. Bone had been trying to follow the instructions for putting it together, but with only glimmers of comprehension. For openers came the aptly titled "exploded drawing": the bookshelf perfectly arranged but detached and floating apart from itself like an expanding universe, Allen screws caroming off into the margins. The written directions, evidently translated by an idiot clerk from demotic Tagalog, were a veritable masterwork of language poetry, with such delectable rhetorical disjunctions as "Turn screw pieces for tighten. If more untighten wanted, turn other way. Over and over!"

"Any more episodes?" Limongello asked. Bone described the outbreak at the English building, and the doctor clucked his tongue in concern. "I brought some things along to show you," Limongello said. "Let's try and see if we can't isolate this problem of yours."

Limongello sat in Bone's rolling office chair and put the heavy black case in his lap, unsnapping the clips and opening its mouth like a veterinarian peering into the throat of a giant but docile black toad. A series of tests followed, their gravity lightened by the doctor's demeanor. Eyes closed, Bone identified a paperweight, pencil, and feather by touch. Then Bone identified them eyes open. Bone closed his eyes again, and Limongello touched his arm several times, asking how many fingers he felt. One, three, two. He gave Bone a random series of numbers to repeat. Next, Limongello had him sing "Twinkle, Twinkle, Little Star," playfully joining in for a rousing finale, "How I wonder what yoooo are!" He placed a pencil in plain sight, asking Bone to locate and to pick it up. The doctor put the pencil several places, never hiding it or preventing Bone from watching where he put it. After Bone successfully located it the sixth time, Limongello excused himself and went to the bathroom. When the doctor returned, he said, "There's writing on the wall in there." Bone explained it was a Chaucerian passage he'd been studying at one time and wanted to have before him as often as possible. Limongello nodded. "That's right. You're a linguist, I was forgetting."

"Not really a linguist. A grammarian."

"Right. Grammarian. The bathroom was where you had your first episode, wasn't it?" Limongello looked toward the hall door that led to the bathroom as if expecting someone to come through. "Let's go in there. Do you mind?" Bone followed the doctor to the bathroom. Limongello asked him to step into the tub, not a request Bone would ever have anticipated from a medical professional. Limongello stepped in after him, apologizing in case his shoes marked up the enamel. He peered at the faint words like an Egyptologist reading hieroglyphics. "What a great idea. This way you can study even in the bathroom." He read aloud, "'Frenssh she spak ful faire and fetisly.' What's 'fetisly'?" Bone explained that orthography and vocabulary had changed since Middle English. "Ri-i-i-ight," Limongello said. "Everybody treats doctors like we're some sort of shamans, but I think you guys are the real shamans. You scholars." Limongello put a hand on Bone's shoulder and pinched Bone's collar with the other, his eyes quizzical and humorous. "After all, what's grammar but an attempt to find rules? Rules we can live by. What's a definition but an attempt to find meaning?"

Turning to the writing again, Limongello licked his thumb and squeaked it on a letter. "Maybe you shouldn't have used permanent ink. Which way were you facing when it happened?" Bone turned to the window. The fog had lifted, and the sun shone in a bright puddle by the stone steps. "You weren't looking at the writing?" Limongello's brow creased. "But you weren't taking a bath, either?" Bone said he was not. "What were you doing?" Bone said he didn't remember, and Limongello frowned. Bone asked what Limongello was hoping to find out. "Answers," the doctor said with perfect seriousness. "But I don't know which clues are relevant and which ones aren't. It's like being a detective. There's something you're not telling me, Bone." Never having experienced the near-psychic ability of a gifted diagnostician focusing his complete unblinking attention, Bone started. "I wish I had an EEG in here," the doctor mused. "I'd like to get a look at your readings right now. Can you step out of the tub by yourself?"

Bone could and did. Limongello followed, and they returned to the office.

"Apart from your grammar work, Bone, what's on your mind?" Limongello said when they were seated. "What're you concerned about?" Bone did not reply. "I want you to know, anything you tell me will be kept in strictest confidence."

The pressure to tell pounded in Bone's chest. A final, deep, wavering breath, and Bone confided his fears about Mary and Cash, about spying on her from the bathroom window. "My hands are shaking like a leaf," Bone said with a half-laugh when he'd finished. "Do you think that's one of my symptoms?"

Limongello held Bone's hands and studied them. "Under the circumstances," he said, "I'd say it's just a normal reaction."

"The irony is," Bone said, "I'm not a saint, either. I've never done anything, but not for lack of trying." In his comfort with the doctor, he told of his attempted and ill-advised liaison with Belinda of the Bounteous Boobies.

Limongello nodded, neither in judgment nor surprise. "Ah, yes. *Septem Annis Scabiem*," he said. "Seven-Year Itch. It affects women as well as men. We find our perfect soulmate, and then, for some reason, that bores us. We look around for someone new." He raised his hands in a vague gesture. "The human condition is dissatisfaction when everything is satisfactory." Limongello regarded Bone. "But your syndrome, your immobility, is very interesting to me. I think it might help isolate the cause of certain other syndromes, syndromes that were once extremely rare but have become increasingly, alarmingly common. You might even say they threaten to become an epidemic. Now, some of the things I'm going to say may sound bizarre, even incredible, but you have to believe everything I'm telling you is the one hundred percent truth, however weird it seems. I'm going to tell you a story about a patient of mine. We'll call him 'Y.'"

"'Y'?"

"Because if he was 'U' or 'I,' that would just be too confusing. Ha-ha. You stepped into that one, Bone. No, seriously. For obvious reasons, I can't divulge the actual names of my patients. Suffice to say, Y's problem is very real, and by no means untypical. Y was a successful car salesman, a decent person. Wife and family. Deacon at the Baptist Church. Whole nine yards. Got it?" Bone said he got it. "So anyway, one day Y just disappears. Vanishes. They put in a missing-person report, checked the morgue, the hospitals, the works. Nada. No one knows what happened. But then one day, what do you think?" Bone did not know what to think. "Someone recognizes him! He's living in a different town! He has a different name, a new job, he's even got himself a girlfriend. So anyway, they tried reuniting him with his family. Y tried. He moved back with his wife. He slept with her. Helped with the dishes. Called her 'Sugar-Boo.' But it didn't come back; he never remembered his old life. His wife says he was like a whole 'nother person after he returned. It's like he never really came back at all. The fact is, Y no longer exists. His body is still there, nothing wrong with the body, only now there's a whole 'nother person inside it. As far as Y himself is concerned, or the man who used to be Y, there's no such person as Y. To this day, Y has not come back, and the man who used to be Y will swear on a stack of Bibles he doesn't know him."

"Jesus," Bone said.

"'Jesus' is right," Limongello said solemnly. "Neurologists don't like to talk about the *mind* these days, but I'll tell you what I think. I think Y's mind completely *dislodged* from the reticular formation in his brain. I'm not talking about mental illness here. I mean whatever glue or adhesive holds the mind inside the physical brain broke or came loose, and his mind or soul or whatever you call it—his self—dislodged. I know all this sounds incredible, but I'm convinced that's what happened. Wherever Y's *self* is, I suppose it's still somewhere in his skull, if it still exists, it's no longer joined to his physical brain. And Y's not the only one. There are thousands of people just like Y whose selves dislodge, dislodge and float away from inside their own brains. And disappear forever. And there's more of them every day."

"God, is that's what's happening to me?"

"I've been studying Y's case, and it turns out his disappearance maybe wasn't quite as sudden as it looks. If you knew what to look for, there were signs. Symptoms. Of course, Y himself can't tell us what happened before he dislodged, but I've interviewed his wife, and she said some very intriguing things, and very suggestive. For example, one time—this was about a month before he disappeared—Y told his wife he didn't feel like getting out of bed. Not sick or anything, just didn't feel like getting out of bed. So his wife figures, what the hey, calls in sick for him, and Y takes an unscheduled holiday, spending the day in bed, his wife bringing him meals and everything. Next day he goes back to work and never asks to stay in bed again. Only one thing."

"What's that?"

"I've got a hunch," Limongello said. "It's just a hunch, but it's a real strong one, and right now I don't have anything else to go on. We can't know for sure because the only person who could tell us is Y, and Y doesn't exist anymore. But my hunch is Y didn't stay in bed because he didn't feel like getting out but because he *couldn't* get out. Sound familiar?"

"Jesus, oh, Jesus."

"That's why your case is so interesting to me, Bone. That's why this is so important. I believe you may be showing the same early symptoms as Y. If I can isolate those symptoms and find a treatment, I might prevent your self from dislodging from your brain. Even more, I might be able to save any number of Ys down the road. You see why this is so important?"

"Of course."

"I didn't want to alarm you, but I need you to see why I'm devoting so much time to your case and why it's imperative you give me as much cooperation as you can. I know my methods are unorthodox, and I don't act like a regular doctor." Limongello made air quotes around the word "doctor" as if being a neurologist were make-believe. "But I need you to trust that I'll do everything in my power to help you, and I need you to do what I ask even if some of it seems strange." He reached into his case and pulled out a white envelope. "Your eyes only." He shook the envelope twice, and Bone accepted it.

It was an envelope, labeled in green block letters "BONE KING: PERSONAL AND CONFIDENTIAL." It contained a typed survey, and at the bottom of the second page Limongello had written, again in green ink, "Use additional pages if needed." Two attempts at "necessary" had been X'd out before Limongello had settled on "needed." Limongello might be a brilliant neurologist, but a spelling champ he was not.

"Anything, Doctor, whatever you need."

"HE REALLY IS a great guy," Bone told Mary about Limongello when she came home. "He helped me put together the bookcase."

"Not all that great," Mary said skeptically. "What are all these leftover pieces?"

"Nothing," Bone said. "They're just extra. Dr. Limongello says there's always leftover pieces."

Mary was, if anything, even less impressed with the double-doc's diagnosis than with his bookshelf-building ability. "Your self is becoming dislodged? Are you sure that's what he said?" Her brow wrinkled. "I never heard of a diagnosis like that. Is that even a thing? Maybe you should see another specialist."

Mary's criticism, however, only served to make Bone defensive about the double-doc who had dignified his strange condition with a fittingly strange diagnosis.

CHAPTER SEVEN

G, g

Not, as we would expect, from the Semitic *gimel* (⊀), "throwing stick," but from the Greek *zeta* (**I**), resembling uppercase I and pronounced /z/. Latin having no /z/ sound, the Romans pronounced it /s/, a sound already supplied by **S** itself. If we are to believe Plutarch's account, it was a former slave turned grammarian, Spurius Carvilius Ruga, who arbitrarily assigned *zeta* the hard /g/ of **good** and **gold**. (Parenthetically, Spurius means "false" or "illegitimate" in Latin. Plutarch also credits Ruga with being the first Roman ever to divorce.) Ruga lopped the short horizontal stems from *zeta's* western side, making a bracket ([ ), which in time bowed into a semicircle, perhaps under kindred **C**'s gravitational pull. A vestige of *zeta's* original flat base remains as a fishhook in the bottom half of uppercase **G**. In serif fonts, lowercase **G** is a pair of pince-nez orbs joined by a half-loop (g). In sans-serif fonts, it faces left and gapes slack-jawed (**g**).

God: By definition indefinable, the most that can be said is what God is not. For example, God is not a chipped white mug of Red Zinger tea, nor a vagrant standing by Waffle House at the access road to Interstate 285 with "Will work 4 food" lettered on cardboard with a Magic Marker. Unless God actually is those things, in which case we're back where we started. Derived from the Proto Indo-European *gheu*, "to invoke, or call upon." Hence, God is "the one prayed to."

Questionnaire for Bone King
Prepared by Arthur Limongello, MD, MD

Your best friend gets a cash bonus and a big promotion. How would you feel?

1. b. How would you *secretly* feel?

The same friend tells you that his boss threatened to fire him, and also his girlfriend is breaking up with him. How would you feel?

2. b. How would you *secretly* feel?

3. Do you find yourself making "games" out of ordinary tasks or pretending to "play a part" in order to make them endurable?

4. Do you ever have inappropriate emotional reactions? For example, do you ever feel happy when you ought to be sad, or vice versa?

5. Do you ever feel your life is not your own, or isn't "real" somehow? Explain.

6. Do you ever get the feeling other people are "missing something"? Like they're hollow or not really *real*, they're like robots, only made out of meat? It's like their feelings aren't really *real* feelings, not like *your* feelings? Explain.

7. Did you ever wake up from a nightmare where someone you're close to, like your wife, wasn't who they seemed to be, but, along with just about everyone you knew, was in a complicated conspiracy to trick you out of something and maybe even kill you? Explain.

LATELY WHEN BONE called, his editor always seemed to be in a meeting, but today Grisamore picked up. "Bone." Less a greeting than flat identification.

To Bone's question, "How are you?," Grisamore said he was fine, and Bone, unasked, said with a chuckle that he was fine as well. "I was wondering if you got those sample chapters." Grisamore had, and Bone sipped his coffee, awaiting praise or criticism. Neither came. Bone had the sudden conviction that Grisamore was playing Sudoku. Was it his imagination, or could he hear the scritch of graphite on newsprint shaping a 2's half-loop and sidestroke? "What did you think?"

"The truth is, I haven't gotten around to it." *Hadn't gotten around to it?*

"Well, ha-ha-ha, that's okay." (Stop laughing! Bone pressed a mental foot to the floorboard, but it seemed the brake lines had been cut.) "It's not quite the direction we discussed, but I think you'll like it." A pause, verifying the top right corner could be 9 and only 9. "You'll get the finished manuscript soon. Two weeks at most."

"It's not important," Grisamore reassured him.

Bone hung up, swirling his coffee, mulling dark thoughts. Better get to work if he wanted to finish in two weeks. On a yellow legal pad, he blocked out a determined grid: this many pages by noon, a light lunch, annotate 'til three, then proofread until time to go to Fulsome, a little more proofreading before turning in, so his text would be fresh in his head, ready to hit those pages first thing in the morning.

And no goofing off, either.

But thinking *about* work kept him from doing any. His anxieties shuffled through their playlist: Mary, Gordon, Cash, Grisamore. But Grisamore said the book was fine. Even though he hadn't read it—*why hadn't he read it? Had* he said it was fine? Or that he, Grisamore, was fine? Bone couldn't recall.

He brewed a fresh pot of coffee, this time too strong, and drank a mug, fortified with plenty of sugar. Now to focus on the manuscript.

HE SNORTED AWAKE, stiff-necked from lying on the couch. Lunchtime. He imagined an improbable gourmet salad such as bohemian intellectuals concoct from their icebox's random remnants: a handful of leftover blueberries here, a smattering of bleu cheese crumbles there, but all he found of bleu cheese and blueberries was their absence, along with a corresponding lack of field greens and raw asparagus tips that had graced the salad plate of his fantasy. In lieu of these, Bone ate a bag of pita chips.

He continued in a dither until he went to class, and there, thirsting for home and some good solid research, he was cornered by Belinda.

"Professor King? I wanted to talk to you about my paper?" An essay with a sad scarlet C trembled in her hand. Bone put on his avuncular voice, sympathetic but uncompromising. He explained that while her content was acceptable, her errors were legion: "they're," for example, is customarily a contraction of "they are," not the possessive form of "they," as she'd employed it in some places, nor the antonym of "here," as she had elsewhere; that her apostrophe use could only be described as whimsical; and that AYK and BKA were acronyms best reserved for text messages and left out of formal papers altogether.

Her chin quavered, and a shining tear threatened to moisten an eyelash, but she was made of tougher stuff. "I was thinking that maybe there is no such thing as correct grammar?" she ventured, a timid Edmund Hillary touching a tiptoe to the Himalayas.

"What?"

"That maybe what you call correct grammar is only a dialect?" She didn't look from her paper. "That maybe I have my own dialect? And it has a worthwhile grammar, too?"

"Where'd you read this?" But Bone knew exactly where she'd read it. It was a pure pile of E. Knolton, served up brown and steaming, word for word, save for the naive Belindaesque substitution of "worthwhile" for "worthy." Some rash and reckless librarian must have left a heretical journal out in the open. "Listen, Belinda," Bone said. He didn't place a reassuring hand on her shoulder, but his tone suggested he might do so at any moment. "If you're going to succeed in life, if you're going to live up to the wonderful potential inside you, you have to master Standard American English. You understand, don't you?"

Here Belinda inserted a meek "Yes, sir."

"People who speak these other 'dialects' get judged. Others assume they're ignorant and uneducated and don't give them a fair hearing. It isn't fair, but that's the way it is."

Another "Yes, sir," equally meek.

"It's especially important when it comes to writing."

A third "Yes, sir," even meeker.

"I'll tell you what." Now he did put a reassuring hand on her shoulder. "You redo this. Correct every error I marked and proofread carefully, and I'll regrade it, but you have to get it back soon, because it's almost finals. That doesn't give me much time."

A fourth, final "Yes, sir," now with a hopeful note.

"Excellent. We have a plan now." He smiled at her and did up the snaps on his briefcase. Oddly, talking to an annoying undergrad about the richly deserved grade on her mediocre paper and undertaking additional work on her behalf was the happiest he'd been all day.

They found Loundsberry waiting outside class. A soft palm on Bone's shoulder, he asking a delighted Belinda how she liked Fulsome. The department chair had heard of her! She was an up-and-comer! In fine Belinda form, she described her training on the new billing system, complaining and bragging at once—*Look at all the responsibility I have!* She didn't detect the claim-staking hand on Bone's shoulder. He had come not for her but for Bone. When Belinda finished, Loundsberry, not having listened, could say only, "So, well!" No matter; Belinda's studious, gratified-serious face said she took this as an endorsement, or at least as *You've given me a*

lot to think about, young lady, and I'll be discussing this with my colleague here.

Loundsberry and Bone walked to Gordon's office, where the dean half-sat on his desk, dressed as if he'd come from or was on his way to somebody's soccer match. His head bobbed up as they came in, directing a frowning smile now at Bone instead of the manila folder he'd been studying: expecting but not pleased to see him.

"Bone, Chuck, come in." Gordon didn't offer a chair, but after a few seconds Bone sat anyway. The awareness of Loundsberry standing behind him sharpened Bone's anxiety. He was looking up awkwardly at Gordon, but it would look strange for Bone to stand now. Bone took in his surroundings. A framed art-deco *The Fountainhead* poster, a facetious "Who is John Galt?" coffee mug—to Gordon, Ayn Rand represented the pinnacle of intellectual achievement—a photo of Gordon white-water rafting, spray crashing into his grinning face. No Mrs. Gordon photos. "Chuck told me about the other day." Bone made a soft whiffing noise, giving permission to Gordon to continue. "I wish you'd come to us about that, Bone. I wish you'd been up-front from the start." Loundsberry moved from behind Bone to the bookcase. "The first you knew about it, Chuck, was the other night—Monday, right?—you saw him, you know, you said—" Loundsberry nodded, stretching into a smile and falling back into a gape. "That's not the way we do things, Bone. You have to *tell* us things."

"Yes, sir."

"Don't worry about it now," Gordon said, hand out like a traffic cop. "Water under the bridge. The important thing is," finger making a radar sweep from Bone to Loundsberry, "no one knew about your thing until Monday. I want it on the record that Fulsome has never fired anyone because of a medical condition." He leaned in as if to hug Bone or punch him in the chest. "So what I want to know is—" He didn't finish the sentence.

"It's not life-threatening," Bone said.

"What I want to know is—we already have wheelchair ramps and automatic doors, at least one set, for each building." Gordon ticked off accommodations on his fingers, hovering at his ring finger when he realized there were only two. "And I don't know what they're charging you for medication."

"I'm not on medication. The doctor says I don't need it, and I don't need wheelchair ramps and automatic doors. I can walk fine. And I don't have any trouble *opening* doors. It's going *through* them."

The smile portion of Gordon's frowning smile melted into pure frown. "So what exactly do you need?"

"I don't need anything. Sometimes," Bone added, "not very often, when I come to a door, I just can't go through. That's all. Then I just have to square dance."

"That's it?" Guarded, but hopeful, too, like someone foreseeing spring around the corner. Gone was the frown. "Why don't you get us all a soda?" Gordon asked Loundsberry. "Professor King, you want a Diet Coke?" Strange, when calling him on the carpet, Gordon called Bone by his first name, but when the bonhomie was so thick you could scrape it with a putty knife, it was "Professor King." Loundsberry shifted uncomfortably, not keeping pace with the sudden warm front that had moved in, and Gordon gave Bone a sympathetic look: *Loundsberry's not as good at these things as you and I.* "I'd like a Diet Coke. Get us all a Diet Coke.

"So tell me what's up with this door thing of yours," Gordon said when Loundsberry left. Bone told him what was up with this door thing of his, withholding the disturbing diagnosis that his self was dislodging from his reticular formation. "You know what I like about you, Professor King?" Gordon asked, then, as was his modus operandi after posing a question, answered himself. "Some people go, 'Oh, I'm disabled! I'm so helpless! Take care of me!'" Gordon said, imitating the way some people went, people who evidently spoke in high-pitched voices, wiggling their fingers pointlessly in the air. "But not you. No, sir. Why, you don't even have a disability, do you? Here's Loundsberry with the Cokes."

Loundsberry distributed wet cans from the pyramid stack in his hands. "You see, Dr. Loundsberry, I told you he was one of us! Now, here's the other thing." Serious again, manly and matter-of-fact, one fingertip sealing his upper lip, Gordon leaned so far forward, he left the desk, and for a moment, Bone feared he would climb into his lap. Instead, he stood, hand on Bone's shoulder. "Fulsome will never fire you," Gordon's index finger pointed just above Bone's eyebrow, "on account of illness." Gordon waited for Bone to speak, so Bone muttered that this was good news, which it was. But if it was good news, why the pinprick of chilly dread at its core, like the tiny black dot of Yin in the fattest, thickest part of Yang? Gordon straightened. "Look at us, all serious! Who died is what I'd like to know. In fact, while you're here, let's put this in writing." Gordon sat in his black leather chair and tapped his keyboard with the pleased frown of somebody doing something serious and significant. "Something to say your condition isn't a factor in your employment, and what else did we agree to? That we weren't aware of it until Monday's date. Does that sound right? By the way, how's that book of yours coming? Aren't you working on another book?" Bone explained sheepishly that he was way past due getting it to his publisher, and Gordon nodded sympathetically. "Yes, I've been working on a book myself." Two papers whispered from the printer. Gordon signed them and pushed them across the desk, fingertips twisting them around like an ice-skating spider so they were right side up for Bone. Gordon extended the pen to Bone. "You can sign below me." The pen wiggled invitingly.

Bone skimmed the paper. "It's not right," he said.

Gordon's pen halted midwiggle. "What?"

"You wrote my condition doesn't impact my job." Gordon stared, pen frozen. "It should be 'affect.'" Bone coughed. "And 'referenced my condition to Dr. Loundsberry' should be 'disclosed.'" Gordon and Loundsberry exchanged looks, as if Bone had claimed to have been raised by lobsters. "'Impact' and 'reference' are nouns," Bone clarified. After two seconds of clammy silence, Gordon laughed and took back the papers. "I'm sorry," Bone said.

"No, no," Gordon chuckled. "Right is right. We need to fix it. Or should I say 'amend'?" Gordon was tapping keys again. "Now, let's see, it was 'disclose' and 'affect.'"

"I know 'to impact' and 'to reference' are used as verbs in business-speak," Bone said, "but we're educators." Thank goodness Gordon was taking it so well. Two fresh copies came out of the printer. "If you'd used 'to incent,' you'd have hit the trifecta."

"Good old Professor King," Gordon said. "You never change." He passed the papers across the desk to Bone. "By the way, how's Mary?" he asked. "I sure do miss seeing her around here." Good Lord, did Gordon *wink*? And there it was again, that ugly word, "seeing." Bone's chin quivered and he looked down, signing in a writhing scribble, the Coke clamped between his thighs.

As Bone left Gordon's office, his mood lifted as if he'd narrowly escaped from a booby-trapped dungeon, a hair's breadth beneath a massive stone lowering from the ceiling to crush him. He drove home in a bubble of inexplicable elation. How good even the most ordinary life was! Belinda was grateful for his help. Grisamore thought his book was fine. Limongello was looking into his condition. And soon he'd be home with Mary! And as for Dr. Gordon, screw Dr. Gordon! And Cash Hudson. Screw Cash Hudson! Mary was his! He'd won her fair and square, and she'd chosen him. Screw you both, Dr. Gordon and Cash Hudson!

"I'm home!" Bone hallooed as he came in the kitchen door and set his books and briefcase on the counter, but there came no answer, so he said again, louder, over the TV in the next room, "Hello, sweetheart!" His sweetheart replied that his dinner was in the microwave. He punched the button and watched pasta and sauce rotate in the lighted window.

Life was good. Bone was fine. Mary was his. But the exclamation marks had fallen from his joy. Bone drummed "William Tell" on the countertop. The microwave beeped, and he opened the door. "Don't get any of that on the couch," Mary warned as he brought his supper into the living room. She was folding laundry.

Reaching for the remote, Bone asked if she minded if he turned down the TV. She didn't. She said when he put his socks in the hamper to ball them together, and Bone said okay. He kept saying he'd do that, she pointed out, but then forgot. Bone promised to remember. It was just that she always ended up with a sock in his drawer she couldn't find one to go with, and when she did another load, there was a sock missing, and she spent all this time looking for it and didn't realize his other sock was already in the drawer because it had been in the last load. Bone admitted the truth of this and said he'd do better.

While Bone took his dish into the kitchen and rinsed it, Mary said she was thinking of gelatin dessert. What made her think of that? For Betty's cookout Saturday, she was thinking of gelatin dessert. What did Bone think? Bone thought it would be great.

Bone didn't ask Mary about Miranda Richter's employment of the verb phrase "was seeing," as in "Gordon *was seeing* Mary up until the wedding." "Was seeing." The past imperfect tense, the perfect tense for an imperfect past, a tense referring to an action "habitual or continuous" or "left uncompleted." Had Gordon "seen" Mary *habitually, continuously*? Had Mary *completed* "seeing" Dr. Gordon?

The Norton Anthology lay on the counter where he'd left it, Limongello's questionnaire sticking out of it. Bone looked at it for the first time since yesterday.

What was wrong with Bone that he was never satisfied doing what he was doing but always looking forward to doing something else? And when he was doing *that*, he was looking forward to doing something *else*. He wanted to work on his book, except when he had time to do it. He dreaded teaching class, yet it was the one part of the day he'd enjoyed. He looked forward to being with Mary, but when he was, he felt disappointed. She insisted on being so stubbornly, obstinately herself. And life kept insisting on being *life,* with people to deal with and socks to ball up. Did this have to do with Bone's self becoming dislodged?

Mary said it was a purple Jell-O with fresh fruit and a cream-cheese icing that looked beautiful in *Southern Living,* and Bone said it sounded fabulous, reading Limongello's questionnaire.

Jesus, what was Limongello after?

CHAPTER EIGHT

H, h

From the Semitic *khet* (⊟), "fence," **H**'s status has always been borderline. The Greeks knocked off the top and bottom rails, calling it *eta* (H), changing its pronunciation to our equivalent of long /a/. In 500 CE, Priscian claimed that **H** was not a true letter, a position seconded a thousand years later by Geoffroy Tory, who nevertheless included it in the alphabet. In 1712, Michael Maittaire attempted once more to strike **H** from the alphabet; however, by that time the letter had received the imprimatur from Ben Jonson's influential *English Grammar* (1640), so it was here to stay. The name "aitch" is from the French *hache*, "hatchet," the lowercase **H** resembling an upside-down ax: **h**.

Hobson-Jobson, Law of: The tendency to corrupt exotic words to conform to familiar patterns, e.g., "oxycotton" for "oxycontin," "Old timer's" for "Alzheimer's," and "very close veins" for "varicose veins." (See **hocus-pocus**.) British soldiers in India corrupted as **"Hobson-Jobson"** the Arabic cry *Ya Hasan! Ya Husayn!* "Oh, Hassan! Oh, Husain!"

hocus-pocus: A jocular incantation, too foolish-sounding even for Vegas magicians. A corruption by disdainful Protestants, following the law of Hobson-Jobson, of the Latin *hoc est corpus meum*, "This is my body," spoken by the priest at the moment the sacramental bread and wine is believed to be transformed into the body and blood of Christ.

B one didn't need Limongello's questionnaire to know his condition was driving him insane. In addition to his syndrome, there was the ongoing uncertainty about Mary. He tried persuading her to skip the neighborhood cookout—wouldn't it be nicer to just stay home and enjoy each other's company?—but her mind was already made up, and his attempt to unmake it only occasioned one of their little quarrels.

Mary: "We've been looking forward to this all week. I *told* her we would be there."

Bone: Sulks silently.

Mary: "You can stay here and pout if you want to, but I'm going."

It wasn't as if they wouldn't be just as happy to see her arrive without Bone. He could have played the trump card of his condition, said he couldn't get through the door and blackmailed her into staying—"blackmail" was too strong a word; at worst it would be *navy-blue*mail—then he could work on *Words* and have Mary to fetch sandwiches, but his illness infantilized him enough without faking it, so he said nothing. Besides, he had before him the chilling example of Y, who one day had refused to get out of bed.

He felt better after seeing Mary model her new white blouse in the bedroom mirror—profile, full front, profile— she'd bought it the other week especially for the cookout, she explained, a short-sleeved top that showed off her gold- en arms and with a delightful tendency of peeking open to the sternum whenever she turned. Mary's lacy white bra lay unused at the foot of the bed. Bone began looking forward to an afternoon standing next to his wife in that succulent blouse.

"What is Betty's husband's name?" Bone asked, bearing

Mary's purple Jell-O with cream-cheese icing as he followed her to Betty's house. "I forget."

"Jesus, Bone. Steve."

They walked across their yard and passed the boundary of Betty's, entering the smell of cooking meat and phatic warbling: a man's "Yeah!" behind Betty's privacy fence and hand-clapping, apropos of nothing; other "yeah"s and claps responded. Mary's breast in profile played peekaboo through her blouse.

"What's Laurel doing here?" Bone asked, hearing a familiar sardonic laugh above the ambient party sounds. "She's not one of the neighbors."

"I invited her. She's a friend of mine."

Bone was far from happy. He'd always suspected Laurel liked him as little as he liked her.

Betty welcomed them with a command—"You *must* try Charlotte's pasta salad"—and Bone dipped generous lumps for himself and Mary, looking forward to Charlotte's pleasure at a compliment. Excellent, he assured her. Mary said it was wonderful even before she swallowed, and that she must get the recipe. Charlotte, Bone's landlord, the only neighbor he had much use for, slowly being transformed into a question mark by osteoporosis, looked up and smiled.

Out back, Bone pumped beer for them, balancing his plate on the Solo cups, before joining Mary and Laurel at the grill. Cash was also there. What the hell? What kind of neighborhood party was this? Cash lived a whole street away. Was just any old body allowed to come, or did you have to be someone Bone didn't like?

Working clockwise around his Weber, Steve flipped six burgers gray side up, a story in medias res: "Mickey Mouse goes to court, and the judge says, 'I don't understand, Mr.— uh—Mouse. You want to divorce Minnie because she's silly?' 'No,' says Mickey," Steve imitated Mickey's high-pitched voice, "'she's fucking Goofy!'"

Everyone laughed, and Bone said, "That's a very interesting joke. It's a grammatical joke." Cash and Steve looked at Bone quizzically, and Laurel cocked an eyebrow. Mary looked down at her beer. In the silence, Bone felt called on to explain. "The judge thinks 'goofy''s an adjective and 'fucking''s an adverb, but Mickey meant 'fucking' as a verb and 'Goofy' as a proper noun." Everyone avoided Bone's eye except Laurel, who seemed to enjoy a private joke of her own. Steve raised his spatula, saluting a clap and "yeah!" from across the patio. "Of course, part of the joke is we don't expect a Disney character to use the F-word. And imagining Minnie having sex with Goofy," Bone elaborated, his face growing hot. "Goofy is the name of another Disney character."

"Well, somebody's fucking goofy, that's for sure," Laurel said. At that, everyone laughed but Bone. Mary snorted beer through her nose and required Cash to rub her back to stop coughing. Laurel's non sequitur amused them, whereas at Bone, they'd merely stared, when Bone had gotten the joke. What Laurel said hadn't even made sense.

Bone muttered, "I just thought it interesting is all, that it's a grammatical joke."

Sipping her beer, Mary watched Bone over the rim of her cup, trying to choose what reaction to have. Cash looked in the other direction as if searching for a clock.

"We're out of pasta salad," Laurel said. "Why don't you get us some, Bone?"

Bone hesitated. "Would you, Bone?" Mary asked.

Whatever Betty was drinking when Bone came in wasn't beer; ginger ale mixed with something, he guessed. Talking about the party—going well was their mutual judgment—he dipped pasta salad and left. A man by the keg greeted him; he knew Bone, but Bone didn't know him. Who was he? Mike? Mitch? Bone concealed his confusion with a blustery, "Hey! You must think I really love pasta salad." Bone held up the two plates. Mike or Mitch took a drink and said nothing. "Say, have you seen Mary?"

Mitch, we'll call him Mitch, raised his chin in greeting to a plaid-wearing codger coming for a refill. "That Tebow, what do you think about—"

"Mary asked me to get her some pasta salad," Bone explained. "I don't really like pasta salad this much. The other plate's for a friend of hers. She's not a neighbor." Mitch and the codger were in rapt conversation, and Bone addressed only their shoulders. "It is good pasta salad, though," he said, excusing himself. Goddamn, where was she?

He moved among the partiers in their bright summer clothes drinking beer from red plastic cups, talking about nothing and laughing at nothing, and doing both at ever-increasing volume. He stretched his neck to peer over their heads, clamping a smile over his simmering, bowel-clenching anxiety. He did not find her.

Someone told a joke. Laughter. Jokes were stupid: forcing everyone to listen up not to miss the punch line, and if you didn't laugh, if you didn't "get it," you flunked some kind of minor social test.

"Hey, have you seen Mary?" Bone asked Laurel, holding the plates up.

"Hey, no, I haven't," Laurel said. Was she mocking him, repeating his "hey"? He couldn't search her face for an answer because she turned to talk to someone. Avoiding eye contact?

"I got your pasta," he told her, shouldering his way slightly between her and the man she was talking to.

She looked at it. "I really couldn't eat it now. Do you mind throwing it away for me? Thanks." And she turned back to her conversation without awaiting reply.

Through the plastic plates he felt warm pasta in greasy puddles of Italian dressing. A black fly landed but, before he could shoo it, lifted off. He dropped the plates in a trash can by the privacy fence. Bone went inside and, after using the bathroom, furtively opened doors to the other rooms. Nothing. Nothing. Nothing. Mary wasn't in the living room, either. Charlotte sat on the couch. He sat beside her.

"Have you seen Mary?" he asked. Charlotte looked mildly disoriented. "My wife?"

"Your wife," Charlotte said with a peculiar slight emphasis on the *your.* "I thought I saw you walking up with her to look at Betty's arbor."

"It wasn't me," Bone said.

"How's that book of yours coming?"

He said it was fine and left. Outside, shadows lengthened, and party guests swarmed and dispersed, some holding plates of purple Jell-O with cream-cheese icing. Laurel pointedly looked very innocent, oblivious to Bone's miserable rage. (The phrase "impotent rage" is commonly employed in such situations.) Oh, Bone got the point, all right, Bone got the point. But the knowing taunts, the sly insults always stayed just this side of flagrant, nothing he could openly object to. Were they all in on it?

Bone's face heated, and Charlotte's oily pasta salad came up, burning his throat. "Great party," Bone told Betty. He queasily considered leaving. "Have you seen Mary?"

Betty looked at him sharp-eyed, and Bone sensed her making up her mind about something. A dark hope rose in his heart that he had finally found an ally. "I think she walked up to the arbor. Let's check." They went up the stone steps and an uneven flagstone path into Betty's backyard just as Mary and Cash came down.

"We probably need to get home," Bone said, iciness spreading in his gut: not a precursor to another outbreak of his condition, just an ordinary iciness. He made only the briefest eye contact with Betty and could not bear to look at Cash at all.

They left: Mary with the casserole dish, streaked with the

purple ruins of Jell-O, Bone with his dread. After maintaining frigid silence as long as he could bear, Bone asked where she'd been. He'd looked all over the party for her. To her reply, that she'd looked for him, too, and had decided not to worry about it, he snorted in disgust.

Where had she looked?

Well, in the kitchen for starters.

That was not possible, because *he'd* been in the kitchen.

Maybe they'd just missed each other; he couldn't have been there the whole time.

Betty's party wasn't that big. It wasn't possible they'd missed each other.

The discussion continued at home:

What was she doing up there alone with Cash?

She wasn't doing anything.

Why had she gone up there?

To see the arbor, Jesus.

He was trying to believe her; he was trying, but it was so hard. If she could just be honest, whatever it was he could forgive her, but she had to trust him enough to be honest first.

Did he want her to tell him she was having an affair; is that what he wanted?

Was she having an affair?

She stared. "Is that what you want? You want me to tell you I kissed him?"

"If that's the truth."

"Okay, yes, I kissed Cash."

"Oh, God." If fear had chilled Bone before, it now closed him in an iceberg.

"I thought that's what you wanted to hear."

"It doesn't mean I liked hearing it. Why did you do it?"

They were in the kitchen. She squirted yellow soap into the casserole dish and ran hot water. "I don't know why, okay? I just did it. These things happen."

"They don't happen unless you want them to happen." Mary did not respond to this logic. "Are you at least sorry you did it?"

"Yes, I'm sorry, okay? If I hurt you, I'm sorry." She washed out the Jell-O remnants, peeling pieces out of the glass container like purple skin.

"'*If* I hurt you' isn't a real apology. You can't be sorry because I might be hurt. You have to be sorry for what you did." Bone had heard this point made on a TV drama, and it had turned out to be a useful thing to know.

Her face was set in a stubborn frown. "Okay. I'm sorry for what I did. I fucked up."

"I would have given anything on earth if you had not used that particular idiom." Bone began to cry, and Mary put her arms around him. At this point, he realized he was trembling. "Are you going to do it again?"

"No, of course not," she said. She kissed him on the cheek. He could feel the warm dishwater still on her hands as she held them against his back.

"Do you promise?"

"Of course, I promise. It was a stupid mistake, is all."

"In that case, I forgive you, darling, I forgive you," he said wholeheartedly. It was so simple, forgiving. At once he shed twenty dark pounds of dread. The clouds broke, and it was over. They'd settled it. He'd heard the worst and forgiven her. Now they could move on. Confession and forgiveness operated as if he and Mary had renewed their wedding vows.

They did a lot of talking and soul-baring that night. Mary admitted it flattered her that Cash might still find her attractive. She'd tried one kiss, one, and suffered instant remorse and embarrassment. Cash felt the same, she knew. Bone listened without anger or jealousy, proud of his maturity and empathy. Afterward, he and Mary made slippery love in the bathtub—not entirely successful but memorable for its novelty. Later, Mary gave him a smile as she got into bed beside him, his Post-It-noted Fowler propped up on his knees, and kissed his forehead with a new tenderness before turning out her light.

Confession was a good thing, no doubt about it. How wonderful that she'd confessed. Ironic, but kissing Cash and then confessing it might just be the best thing that had ever happened to their marriage.

Then something occurred to Bone that sent his thoughts corkscrewing like squirrels around a tree trunk. Periodic mental shouts, *Shut up, shut up, stop thinking!* availed not; the more he tried to make his brain think less, the more it thought more.

What if Mary were lying?

Preposterous, of course, but what if? What if he'd pressured her into a confession that wasn't true? She'd kept repeating— hadn't she?—"Is that what you want me to tell you; is that what you *want* to hear?" Had she only said she'd kissed Cash because Bone had demanded it, because the only way to stop his hectoring was saying what he obviously wanted to hear? If that were Mary's calculation, she'd calculated correctly; he'd been more reassured than he had been in many a day.

What an odd idiom that was, when you came to think of it. Many a day. "A day" cannot be more than one, let alone "many." Yet the expression was "many a day." Probably a French idiom translated into English. It sounded French. The French were responsible for a lot of nonsense creeping into English. Or pseudo-French. Ever since William the Conqueror, Anglo-Saxons have had a linguistic inferiority complex about the French.

A Joke Illustrating This:

An American couple in Paris ask their host, "Can we go to the Eiffel Tower?"

"*Mais oui.*"

"Okay! Okay! *May* we go to the Eiffel Tower?"

Bilingual puns, a little-exploited source of humor in monolingual America.

Another:

A Frenchman and a Spaniard are on a park bench when a pretty girl walks by, and the wind blows her skirt up.

H, h | 97

The Frenchman says, "*C'est la vie.*" (That's life.)

The Spaniard replies, "*Se la vi tambien, pero no diga nada.*" (I saw it, too, but I didn't say anything.)

Park benches, suggesting conversation and passive spectating, seem made for puns about pretty girls walking by.

Another:

Did you hear about the miracle? Mr. Wood and Mr. Stone are on a park bench, and a pretty girl walks by. Wood turns to Stone, Stone turns to Wood, and the girl turns into a beauty parlor.

(Shut up! Stop thinking!)

One Last One:

A man and his pretty wife sit on a park bench.

"You're lying, aren't you?" the husband says. "Tell me the truth, you're lying!"

"Okay, here's the truth: I'm lying."

YES, THERE IS many a joke about women and park benches. Of course, the last one wasn't so much a joke as a paradox, but then Bone had just come up with it himself.

If your wife confesses to kissing the neighbor, does it make her more or less trustworthy if she didn't really do it?

Finally, he nerved himself to ask the darkness, "When you said you kissed Cash, did you really do it, or were you just saying it?"

The brief halt in her breathing told him clearly enough

she'd heard his question, but she didn't answer. Her rib cage resumed its regular contraction and expansion, and he permitted them both to believe she'd been sleeping.

When my love says she is made of truth, I do believe her, though I know she lies.

But what if when my love *says* she lies, I *don't* believe her?

Bone thought he would never go to sleep that night, but he did, nor did his doubts infect his dreams.

CHAPTER NINE

I, i

From the Semitic *yodh* (ﬖ), "hand." The Greeks pared it to a single stroke, (I) *iota*, which, being their smallest letter, became a metonym for anything tiny or insignificant, "not one iota." The King James Bible translated **iota** as **"jot"**: "Till heaven and earth pass, one jot or one tittle shall in no wise pass from the law, till all be fulfilled" (Matthew 5:18). To this day, **jot** remains a noun, "a small or insignificant thing," as well as a verb, "to write quickly or briefly." Parenthetically, **tittle** refers to a small mark over a letter, such as the dot floating over the lowercase **I**, introduced during the Middle Ages to prevent confusion with similar-looking letters.

ignus and **lignus:** Medieval scholars proposed an ingenious etymology for the Latin words *ignus*, "ignite," and *lignus*, "wood." Wood, they supposed, burned easily because it already had fire inside it. Modern scholars chuckle up their sleeves at this, as they do at the folk wisdom that woman means "woe to man." These naive guesses lack empirical support but are meaningful to anyone who believes them. Who can deny there is evil in the devil?

S unday morning, when Bone started to get out of bed, Mary said, "No, you lie here," and kissed him. Bone lay, telling himself that staying in bed because your wife *says* to is a very different case than not getting out of bed because you *can't*, contentedly listening to the soft clap and clatter of dishes and cookware, savoring the delicious fragrances beginning to emanate from the kitchen, covers snugged up under his chin, toes wriggling in happy anticipation under the taut sheets. Mary brought a tray and laid it on his lap: waffles, bacon, orange juice, and coffee. Before letting him touch a bite, however, Mary gave him a long kiss that caused him to spill some of his orange juice.

Was she buying him off? Did he care? Did it even matter whether she'd really kissed Cash or not when life was so sweet?

She stripped off her summer nightgown, causing Bone to spill his juice again, and carefully slipped into bed beside him. Eating breakfast from a tray in his lap with a beautiful naked woman pressed to his side and licking and nibbling his ear posed difficulties, but it was a problem worth having.

"Let's go to church this morning," she said.

"Yes, let's."

"But first. Finish your breakfast. Then we're making love."

"Yes. Yes."

He ate breakfast, and they made love—somewhat stickily, thanks to maple syrup—and then souped together in the shower before dressing for church.

What a wonderful privilege after the morning's delights stepping into the chapel, cool and dark as a cave's mouth with parables bejeweling the windows—the Good Samaritan, the Prodigal Son—Bone's starched shirt buttoned to his Adam's apple, the unaccustomed pressure of a necktie at his throat, Mary in a demure dress that nonetheless showed her lovely tanned arms, holding hands as they nodded their heads to the altar before taking their pew, two children of paradise innocent and loving and loved.

Bone, voice stretched like a rubber sheet, attempted that

exquisitely awful hymn as acolytes and crucifixes and candles
and choristers followed by Father Pepys himself filed down
the aisle and ascended to the altar. Then came the readings,
Old Testament, Psalm—they had to sing that, too, and dear
Lord, it was abominable, but how joyous and wholesome
and silly!—then something from Letters, then two acolytes
bore the gilt-bound gospel into the aisle and Pepys read from
Luke, an incident when Jesus, asked an impertinent, wholly
irrelevant question by some Pharisee, stops him in his tracks
with a pertinent and holy relevant comeback.

Next came Father Pepys's homily, and how Bone loved
a good long sermon. What a wonderful opportunity it gave
one to think!

Then they confessed their sins, and by golly, Bone meant
every word of it! He *had* sinned against God in thought,
word, and deed! He *hadn't* loved God with his whole heart!
He hadn't loved his *neighbor* as himself! He was sorry and
wanted to do better! And God forgave him, Pepys said so,
with the holy hocus-pocus of a cross made in the air! And
everyone passed the peace, "The Lord be with you, and with
your spirit." They reached hands across the pews and even
across the aisle and greeted each other like beloved siblings
reunited after long separation. *I love you. I love everybody.*

Last they took communion. Ah, to kneel at the rail, shoulder and thigh against Mary's shoulder and thigh, taking the
wafer from his cupped hands into his mouth, where it clung
to the alveolar ridge like a shred of skin. His lips pressed the
same cup as hers, a secret kiss passed along with the sacra-

mental wine like a coded message. After one more godawful hymn and the recessional, Pepys called out from the back of the church, "Let us go forth in gladness and singleness of heart to love and serve the Lord!" Yes, yes! And Bone said, with the whole congregation, "Thanks be to God! Hallelujah, hallelujah!" And everyone began to exit their pews.

Normally, as soon as church ended, Bone preferred to scoot out with all deliberate speed, but today, topped to the eyebrows with the Holy Ghost and Christian love, he just had to speak to Father Pepys. "Something I bet you didn't know about the word 'cretin,'" he said, taking the priest's hand. "You'd probably think it's a derisive term for a native of Crete, but it's not. Actually, it's from the Swiss French, '*crestin*,' which just means 'Christian.' See, they thought of even idiots as s*ouls*." Pepys's smile congealed, and his eyes unfocused. "Isn't that nicer than some clinical term," Bone persisted, "like 'Down Syndrome,' or some complicated euphemism like 'intellectually challenged'? Just identify a moron as a Christian and let it go?" Mary pulled Bone's elbow.

"Yes, yes," Pepys murmured vacantly, still smiling but looking displeased, and finally getting his hand loose as Mary led Bone to the door.

Damn it, they hadn't let him finish. Pepys thought Bone was insulting him, but that wasn't it at all, not this time; he'd been trying to get at the idea that from the vantage of the omniscient, no human has a greater claim to intelligence than another, and someone we mark as a fool was as apt a spokesman for God as anyone, but Bone hadn't gotten to say any of it, and now Pepys was offended.

And then, just as they were about to exit, Bone's condition struck, and he couldn't leave. So now he had to—goddamn it—do-si-do back through the line, bowing to partners and sides, swinging his invisible partner, before he could promenade out the door and escape their thunderstruck faces—Steve Duffy audibly snorting in horror, old Rose Blocker gaping like he'd just dropped his drawers—with Mary blushing so red Bone could fairly feel heat radiating from her face.

After church, Mary didn't mention the incident, but the atmosphere between them had chilled. A cold front had moved in. They spent the rest of the day in relative silence. Mary read her mystery and watched the news. Bone worked on *Words*. Finally, when they were in bed together—and even here, with the roundness of her butt pressed into his back, Bone felt as if a wall had descended between them—Mary said what Bone had been dreading and waiting for her to say all day. "Whatever possessed you to do that square-dance thing in the church?"

"I don't decide when my condition strikes," Bone said. "It hits when it hits."

"And what you said to Father Pepys. Jesus. Did you actually say, Christians are cretins?"

"No. No. It was the other way around. It was the other way around."

CHAPTER TEN

J, j

Originally a variant style of **I, J** did not appear as a letter in its own right until sixth-century Spain, where it was pronounced as /h/, as in *junto*. English adoption was spotty and sporadic; Noah Webster's *Dictionary of the English Language* (1806) included all twenty-six letters, but on the other side of the Atlantic, the **J**-less alphabet had prominent defenders for another fifty years.

jealous: From the Middle English *jelos*, from the Latin *zelus*, from the Greek *zelos*, "zeal."

Jehovah: One of the variant pronunciations, along with **Yahweh,** of the tetragrammaton (יהוה), the ineffable name of God. Perhaps designedly, the word's etymology is as obscure as its pronunciation, possibly derived from a Western Semitic root meaning "to bring into existence" but with equal likelihood coming from a *southern* Semitic root, "to destroy or bring low." Many scholars argue it means simply "to be," an explanation supported by God's impatient retort when asked his name by Moses, "I AM THAT I AM... Thus shalt thou say unto the children of Israel, I AM hath sent me unto you" (Exodus 3:14).

Jupiter: The Roman god takes his name from the Greek god Zeus and the epithet "father," as in "Father of the Gods." Zeus and pater → *zeupater* → Jupiter.

M onday morning, Mary brought Bone his coffee, signaling that the breach was healed again. Later, Limongello called. "There's an exhibit at the Fernbank Museum I'd like to show you. Can you make it out?" Bone said he could, and just before he pressed the button to hang up, Limongello added, "And bring the questionnaire."

As Bone pulled into the parking lot, he saw the doctor, incongruously dressed in shorts and red polo shirt, leaning against his green sedan. Limongello greeted him with his usual carpal-crushing handshake. "You're here. And you've got the questionnaire. I knew I could count on you." Bone glimpsed inside the doctor's car, the floorboard full of wadded clothes and empty Taco Veloz bags. "You like games, right? Want to play a little game today?"

"Sure," Bone said uncertainly.

They walked up the circular drive, shimmering in the sunlight, to the museum. Fourth graders were being herded from a school bus by a pretty but no-nonsense-looking teacher who surveyed her students, the bus, and everything in the world with the sharp-eyed vigilance of a mother eagle.

Limongello called it "The Compliment Game." The rule was they had to take turns paying compliments to people. "Say anything you want," Limongello explained, "as long as it's flattering and true. I'll go first.

"How wonderful bringing your class here," Limongello told the teacher as he and Bone mounted the steps. Limongello spread his arms as if she'd brought them not only to the museum but to Planet Earth. "Must be a lot of work arranging this. You must be a *wonderful* teacher."

The teacher, who, although she looked very much in control, must have often found it taxing being pretty, no-nonsense, and eagle-eyed all at the same time, said nothing but smiled, keeping her vigil and lifting her arms to make little summoning movements in the air with her fingers at the fourth graders.

As they went into the main gallery, Limongello said, "I love this place. Look down." The stone tiles were etched with sea creatures. "Fossil rock," Limongello said. "The floor is tiled with it. Look, there's a trilobite, and there's an ammonite. There's another. Oh, it's fascinating." Limongello put his hand on Bone's shoulder. "I've got some thoughts about your condition, but first—" Limongello picked up something in Bone's expression and asked, "Oh, no, is something wrong? Is something *new* wrong?"

"Mary kissed Cash." They passed through a swarm of fourth graders, or a swarm of fourth graders passed through them, and Bone lowered his voice. "She told me about it. We had a big talk the other night and straightened everything out."

"That's good, right?"

"It's wonderful. Things have never been better between us. Only now," Bone laughed, rubbing the back of his neck, "only now I'm not sure I believe that. I think maybe she might have lied about it just to get me off her back. It's crazy as hell, but I feel like a wreck. And then I had another episode at the church."

"I understand," Limongello said with a solemn sigh. "Your hypothalamus doesn't know how to respond. If this is good news, that is to say, bad—Mary kissed the neighbor, but now you know about it—it needs to excrete oxytocin and dopamine, but if it's bad news—that is to say, good—Mary did *not* kiss the neighbor but said she did—it needs to excrete noradrenaline, so your body's excreting both at once, making you a basket case, like driving with your foot on the gas and the brakes at the same time."

"Exactly."

"Humph." Limongello stared over Bone's shoulder, contemplating this conundrum.

"But you wanted to see my questionnaire," Bone said.

"Right, right," Limongello said. The doctor patted his pockets. "You know, I left the house without any money. Do you mind getting the tickets? I'll sit here and read this." Limongello planted himself on a padded bench next to the wall. "And Bone, Bone." Bone turned. "It's your turn." Limongello pointed the questionnaire like a baton at the man in the glass ticket booth.

Trying to think of a compliment, Bone handed over his credit card. As he accepted the two cardboard slips, he said, "That's some tie."

The ticket seller grinned and lifted it from his shirt. "Yeah, my wife gave it to me." In truth, the tie was a masterpiece of tackiness; it looked as if it had been made from cut-up Hawaiian shirts. "It's watered silk," the ticket seller said, and he and Bone admired it again before Bone brought the tickets to Limongello, unaccountably giddy.

"I did it," Bone whispered, sitting beside Limongello and handing him a ticket.

Limongello looked up and smiled, then returned to reading the survey, from time to time nodding, grinning, and quietly grunting. Bone, having nothing else to do, waited. The fourth graders and their teacher, who already had tickets, filed into the main gallery past another museum worker.

"You probably wonder what all this has to do with getting through doors, don't you?" Limongello murmured, not raising his eyes. Finding something interesting, he elbowed Bone's solar plexus and pointed at one of the responses, as if Bone himself hadn't written it. "You say here that you sometimes feel as if you were a character in a book," Limongello said. "That's very interesting." He fixed Bone with a glittering eye. "Y told his wife he sometimes felt he was a character in a *TV show*." Bone felt his eyes widen. "So you see we're dealing with basically identical symptoms here. Well, let's go in and take a look at this museum," Limongello said, standing up.

As they presented their tickets, Limongello told the lady at the turnstile, "You know, you just have a *beautiful* smile." The lady with the beautiful smile beamed, and Limongello and Bone entered the main atrium, which featured a complete tyrannosaur skeleton next to a spiral staircase leading to the mezzanine. Limongello continued sotto voce, "You know, when your transmission falls out, it doesn't do it all at once. There are signs, signals, if you know what to look for. A funny noise. Your car hesitates and surges. Next thing you know, *wham!*" He clapped. "Transmission's on the asphalt, and you're stuck on the highway gaping like a gaffed fish. Same thing with what we got here.

"As I reconstruct it, this syndrome of yours has three phases. First, you see other people or even yourself as not being real, like you're a character in a book or a TV show. This is accompanied by inappropriate emotional responses: feeling good when you have every reason to feel bad, and vice versa. I call this *Psychological* Dislodgement. In the second phase, the mind or soul, or whatever, the *self*, suffers intermittent loss of motor control. Your self simply loses the power to command the body to do things. For example, you find yourself unable to get out of bed or walk through the door. I call this Neuro-*Physical* Dislodgement. Last comes *Complete Radical* Self Dislodgement. The self dislodges completely, and next thing you know, there is no next thing you know. The person who used to be you is dipping toast into a fried egg in another town somewhere with no memory of being you, and if the self that remembers being you exists at all, no one has any idea where it went or where to look for it.

"Of course, each case has its own distinct flavor." Limongello eyed Bone narrowly, seeming to make up his mind. "Yes, I suppose I can tell *you*," he said judiciously. "One of the more disturbing features of dislodgement is it seems to be contagious. Oh, not like germs," Limongello said, reading Bone's incredulous expression. "Nevertheless, it travels from person to person. I'm not sure why this is. Maybe if you live with someone who's dislodged, you start to dislodge yourself, or maybe if you view others as not quite real, that's what they become. Not quite real."

Limongello took Bone's elbow and spoke in confidential

tones. "I've been making a careful study of Y's wife, and I'm convinced she's thoroughly dislodged as well, maybe more hopelessly than Y himself, but the syndrome is camouflaged by her particular symptoms. It seems years ago, she started saying, 'okely-dokely,' something she'd picked up from TV. Not especially funny, but she seemed to think it was and said it every chance she got. 'Okely-dokely, okely-dokely.' It was her thing. Also, she was very political and picked up catchphrases from commentators and people who think like she does, all about the economy, the war, or whatever, and when she met people with the opposite opinion, she got very impatient—but also kind of excited, right?—like having people to argue with is what makes having strong opinions worthwhile—and around people who think like her, she felt satisfied—but also kind of bored, because what's the point if everyone thinks the same way?—and she had these certain jokes and punch lines she liked to use, and some funny voices she liked to imitate from TV or somewhere, I guess, until finally there is nothing else left. Her *self* is completely gone. Oh, she's still walking and talking and functioning, no one suspects, but her *self* has been replaced by political rants, pet punch lines, and 'okely-dokely.' Her *self* is gone."

"Are you sure?" Bone said. "It sounds like—"

"No," Limongello said adamantly. "She's gone. Dislodged. *Pfft.* It's a not-uncommon manifestation of the syndrome."

Bone now recalled a number of people whose selves seemed buried under a slag pile of catchphrases and canned opinions.

"Now," Limongello said, "come upstairs. This is what I came to show you." They climbed the spiral staircase, leaving the grinning tyrannosaur skull below and passing a fourth grader in a blue Cub Scout uniform already coming down. "I needed you to fill out the questionnaire before I said any more about Y because people are so suggestible. If you knew the symptoms I was looking for, you might imagine you had the same ones, but this questionnaire," Limongello rattled the sheets in the air, "confirms we're looking at the same thing here."

Limongello stopped at one of the glass display cases wrapping the mezzanine level. Pitted gray bones outlined a child-sized skeleton on dark felt: skull fragments, a lower jaw, four rainbow arcs of a rib cage, half a pelvis, an upper leg on one side, and a lower on the other.

"There she is. Or at least a plaster model of her. Lucy. Three point six million years old. The great-great-great-grandma of us all." Limongello leaned, nose nearly to the glass, as if inspecting his family photo album. "Just to think we ever came from anything that small."

A docent passed, giving a mildly curious look at two grown men visiting the science museum in the middle of the day. Limongello lifted his gaze from the glass and tugged Bone's elbow. Putting a finger to his lips before Bone could speak, Limongello pointed at the docent's back. The doctor's wink was slow and deliberate as a shade being drawn over a window. *Go say something nice to her.*

Bone went to her and asked where the restroom was, and

when she told him, he added, "Those are some great shoes. Where did you get those?"

The docent smiled and looked down, turning her ankle outward to see her own shoe in profile. "Thanks, I've had these things forever."

"They look really comfortable, but they're still stylish."

"Thank you."

Because it had been his cover story for paying a compliment, Bone went to the restroom, shaking his head and smiling. It was cheating, two compliments in a row on clothing, and he hadn't been strictly sincere either time. Still, the docent, who hadn't spared a thought for her shoes for years, would think intermittently for the rest of the day what a satisfactory pair they were. And she'd happily think about them again that night when she took them off.

"Mission accomplished," Bone reported when he returned to Limongello's side.

"Good." Limongello stood in front of a life-sized model of a human and chimpanzee holding hands. "You know, humans aren't like other animals. Social animals, like ants, give their lives for a brother ant without a thought. The survival of one ant is the survival of all. And nonsocial animals, like sharks, eat each other soon as look at you, because with them, it's every shark for himself. Then you have humans, the most social and most nonsocial at the same time." They crossed the gallery and looked over the heads of the fourth graders at a mural featuring a lemur-like primate on the left, progressing through taller and more human-looking primates, and ending with a handsome bearded man on the right, totally nude, his right leg striding forward so as to conceal his genitalia. "The first phase of your condition is feeling bad when you should feel good, and vice versa. Or rather, feeling good in the *middle* of feeling bad."

"Yang and Yin," Bone said.

"How's that?"

"The Chinese symbol. Each side has a little bit of the opposite inside. When you're feeling really good, there's a little bit of sadness in it. Like Yang and Yin."

"Yang and Ying," Limongello repeated. "Yes. That's it exactly. Yang and Ying. If I ever get to the bottom of this thing, maybe I'll call it the Ying-Yang Syndrome. I was going to call it the Limongello Syndrome, only then, everyone would call it *Lemon Jell-O*. Why would anyone have a name like Limongello?" The doctor laughed, shaking his head as if his name were a regrettable purchase at Costco. "Anyway, I think the root cause has to do with evolution. Say you're a monkey, and the monkey the next tree over gets a whole bunch of bananas, a windfall. That's good news for you, too, because at least indirectly you stand to benefit. His bananas are your bananas. So your hypothalamus shoots out a little boost of oxytocin and dopamine. But. If you feel *too* good, you may neglect your own self-interest. If he's got a bunch of bananas, maybe you're getting shortchanged, so you also get a shot of calcitonin and noradrenaline to make you a little anxious and keep you on your toes. There's the Ying inside your Yang.

"But now suppose monkey fever goes through and wipes

out all the monkeys. Your friends and family are all dying of monkey fever, but not you. Not yet. Naturally the limbic system gives you plenty of calcitonin to make you feel bad, because if there's monkey fever going around, you could be next. On the other hand, just because they're sick doesn't mean *you* are. You could be the one that lives! You could have natural immunity! And every new case of monkey fever means more bananas, better trees, and more potential mates for you. If you didn't have a shot of dopamine to balance out the calcitonin, you'd be too overwhelmed to take advantage of this potential opportunity. Or even clear the hell out of the jungle before you got monkey fever, too. So your brain is geared to empathize with others and at the same time *not* empathize. Got it?"

"Sure."

"But there's more. As we evolved, somewhere around here, I think, excuse me," making a gap between the fourth graders like Moses parting the Red Sea, Limongello ran his finger over the mural, stopping somewhere between the *Australopithecus* and modern man, "we acquired a new way to use the empathizing/not-empathizing thing. It's not even essential to empathize with *yourself*. This has tremendous survival benefits. In your worst predicament—tsetse flies swarming over the hill, a monsoon knocking down all the banana trees— you'd get a little shot of dopamine and oxytocin in the middle of all that calcitonin and noradrenaline. And there'd be a little part of you that'd think, *Cool*. You have the necessary detachment to cope with the tsetse flies or the monsoon or whatever and not just be a basket case. Likewise, if things were good—loads of bananas, all the females in heat, watering hole full of water, whatever. You can't afford at a time like that to overdose on dopamine. You'd be caught off guard when the next monsoon hit or monkey fever broke out. So your limbic system stirs some calcitonin in the mix so you don't lose your edge. A little free-floating anxiety like you're waiting for the other shoe to drop or maybe the nagging worry that there has to be more to life than a tree full of bananas and an attractive mate.

"Flash forward about a million years. Excuse me," he apologized for stepping on a fourth grader's foot as he ran his finger across the mural to modern man. "The evolutionary trick of empathizing/not-empathizing began to backfire. Now we aren't just worried about our personal monkey pack getting hit by monkey fever. We're worried about all the people in Katrina, those people wiped out by the tsunami, those people in Japan wiped out by the *other* tsunami, and global warming, deforestation, and the rest of it. And on every street corner someone with a sign, 'Will work for food.' You can't possibly empathize with all of it. It'd fry your brain circuits. Your limbic system's busy twenty-four-seven damping calcitonin secretions and squirting out dopamine to keep you on an even keel. But at the same time, we're surrounded by people with *unbelievably* good fortune. We're not just sizing up our mate compared to the monkey in the next tree; we're comparing her to Angelina Jolie. And not if our banana pile's as big as the next monkey's, we're stacking ourselves up next to Warren Buffet. And on top of that, there's just life; there's just freaking *life*. It's not that everything's unreal; it's that it's *too* real. It's just too dang real. It's too much." Limongello trained his patient, humorous, quizzical stare on Bone. "I'm going to ask you an extremely personal question."

"Okay."

"The answer to which may be embarrassing, but I assure you there's no judgment on my part."

"Okay."

"Remember 9/11? The planes burning and smoking where they'd hit, and then *whoom*! These two huge towers going straight down, like they'd fallen in an elevator shaft, one after the other. People screaming, huge clouds of dust and smoke."

"Yes."

"Shocking, wasn't it? Horrible. Appalling. A nightmare come true, and yet," Limongello placed a hand on Bone's shoulder, "was there just a little part of you, and we're not talking about the people, that part was so terrible, of course, but just the sight of those buildings going down, like something in a movie, was there a little tiny part that you never told anyone about and didn't want to admit even to yourself, watching those two towers—*whoosh*! just disappear like that—that you thought, 'This is so *neat*'?"

Bone didn't answer, but Limongello's stare was so compassionate and at the same time so insistent that he finally admitted, "Yes, that's right. I did feel that way. A little."

"And you weren't alone. Millions of people, people who

should have been so loaded with calcitonin and noradrenaline they were nothing but little red dials wavering between suicide and homicide, were secretly feeling *good*. Because at the same time, their bodies were loading them up on dopamine. Imagine that: millions and millions of people having precisely the wrong reaction to a terrible national tragedy, feeling good at the one time they should have been feeling their *worst*. No wonder everyone's self is starting to dislodge." Bone and Limongello were silent after that. "Let's go," Limongello said. Once he'd gotten his explanation out, the wind seemed to go out of him, too; his shoulders slumped, and his eyes became lusterless as a brown Crayola. "That's all I brought you to see."

"So does this mean you know how to treat my condition?"

"Like what do you expect?" Limongello asked, his tone suddenly guarded. Now they were on the staircase, spiraling down around the familiar tyrannosaur.

"I don't know. A medication?"

"Goddamn it!" Limongello said loudly, then, remembering himself and looking up toward the fourth graders, more softly, "Goddamn it. Why is the first thing everyone turns to always a pill?" He took Bone's elbow, and began walking again. "I'm sorry. I'm sorry. It's just—everybody these days always goes running to some chemical to fix them up. Feel like killing yourself? Let's put a little sertacline hydrochloride in you and see if that doesn't help. Balance his meds. All you hear about these days is balance his meds. Balance his meds, balance his meds," he sang in grating make-believe glee, hands flopping as if jerked by wires overhead. "Kid got ants in the pants? Just needs a little methylphenidate, and he'll be hunky-dory, end of story. Balance his meds." Limongello pantomimed a puppet dance on the stairwell. "Can't stop washing your hands? Stir some clomipramine in your coffee every morning, and you'll be okey-dokey, artichokey. Balance your meds. Like we're just bags of chemicals. Like human nature is a recipe that you can just add a drop more potassium and a smidge less sodium and turn out any way you want. Is that how you see yourself, Bone? A bag of chemicals? Is that all you want to be?"

"No."

"Because if that's what you want, I can hook you up. There's plenty of neurologists out there just itching to give you a pill. I mean, if you want to turn your soul over, your very self, to some research chemist in Paducah, I won't stand in your way."

"I don't want that."

"What?"

"I don't want a pill."

"Good. Now, what I'm going to prescribe is slower and, frankly, less certain than medication. I'll admit that. But I want you to try it for me." Limongello stopped to wipe his forehead and with a trembling hand pulled a folded paper from his pocket and handed it to Bone. "I've written three tasks down, and I need you to do them. Two you'll do daily, one weekly. The second one is going out of your way to compliment somebody."

Bone's silence was more expressive of skepticism than words could have been.

"Pretty much," Limongello said resignedly, "what it amounts to is I want you to do good deeds. I know it sounds silly. But we've got to get your *self* back into gear with your limbic system. We're attacking the first phase of the syndrome. We have to retrain your brain in the trick of empathy. When you pay a compliment, what's going to happen? The other person is going to feel pleased but also maybe just a little embarrassed."

"I'm going to feel embarrassed, too," Bone pointed out.

"Exactly," Limongello said. "And you'll feel pleased, too, because it's a pleasure giving other people pleasure. You'll feel pleased and slightly foolish, which is exactly how the other person will feel at that moment. You'll both feel the exact same way at the exact same time. And you'll *know* you're feeling the same way. That's empathy. We're employing a trick to get there, but it's still empathy. Your condition's root cause is a disjunction between how your hormones tell you to feel and a decent human response."

Bone followed the doctor's gaze to the grinning tyranno-saur skull.

"Maybe that's all extinction is," Limongello said. "Once your hormones betray you, make you feel good about things that are bad and vice versa, you've had it. You'll seek out the bad and shun the good. Maybe that's what really happened to our friend here; the asteroid was just a contributing factor. The dinosaurs had already dislodged from their selves. Maybe when it hit, and the sun went behind a big smudge of black smoke," Limongello's hands shaped the plume of a mushroom cloud, and in the back of his throat, he gargled the rumble of a distant impact, "the dinosaurs all thought, 'Oh, cool!'" Limongello sighed. "Anyway, I'll check in on you soon. Follow through with those three tasks, and if you have an episode—"

"I'll just square dance."

"And your wife, you feel pretty bad about that, don't you?"

"Of course."

"That's good; you should feel bad. And you're worried about work, and about your book?"

"Yes."

"And you should be worried. But your condition. You're worried about that, too, but there's a little part of you, the Yang inside the Ying, that feels good about it. That thinks, 'How cool to have such an interesting and maybe even important disease.'"

"Yes, I'll admit it does."

"I want you to try out this treatment. I want you to give it a real shot. I know it's not much. It's only a start, and I can't tell you by any means it's a cure. But the most important pledge in the Hippocratic Oath is *do no harm*. And I'm pretty sure, whether this does any good or not, at least it won't hurt anyone, and I promise you, Bone," Limongello said solemnly, "we'll get to the bottom of this thing if it's the last thing that I do. You trust me, don't you?"

"Absolutely," Bone said.

CHAPTER ELEVEN

K, k

From the Semitic *kaph* (**ﻻ**), "hand," the original Egyptian hieroglyph having already lost several fingers. Since *yodh* (I), from which we get **I**, also means hand, and since **J** is derived from **I**, **K** makes three hands in a row, lined up between the fence of H (**目**) and the ox-goad of L (**ㄥ**).

kiss: Defined by Freud, with characteristic Viennese suavity, as "the sexual use of the mucous membrane of the lips and mouth." Directly traceable to the Old Norse *koss* but unmistakably similar to the Proto Indo-European *kus*. Ernest Crawley (*The Mystic Rose*, 1902) claims erotic kissing was unknown in ancient Egypt, a misconception easily debunked by lines carved in an Egyptian tomb two thousand years before Christ: "I kissed her open mouth and it made me drunker than wine." Song of Solomon employs a similar metaphor, "Let him kiss me with the kisses of his mouth: for thy love is better than wine." The comparison to intoxication is apropos; studies show that dopamine levels during kissing rival those caused by cocaine.

PRESCRIPTION FOR BONE KING

FOR SELF DISLODGEMENT

Prepared by Arthur Limongello, MD, MD

Task One: Each morning, before getting dressed, clap your hands and say, "This is a good day!" *Repeat no more than once daily.*

Task Two: Pay an unexpected compliment. *Repeat at least twice daily.*

Task Three: Do another person an act of kindness when doing so seems inconvenient—when you have something more interesting, more important-seeming, or more enjoyable to do. Neither ask for nor refuse thanks. *Repeat at least once weekly.*

NEXT MORNING, OPPORTUNITY arose to perform Dr. Limongello's third task, courtesy of an anonymous dog who, all unasked, had distributed the landlady's trash with a liberal paw, strewing a glutinous largesse of sodden newspaper, chicken bones, and gummy eggshells up and down the street. Grateful dopamine throbbing warmly into his bloodstream, Bone all but clapped his hands and said, "This really is a good day," before recalling Limongello's admonition against doing this more than once a day. Instead, he pulled a white plastic bag from under the sink and went outside like a cheerful Charlie to gather up the archipelago of garbage.

Bone's willingness to carry out Limongello's peculiar prescription perplexed even himself, but by now he'd gotten in the habit of following the double-doc's dictums, however odd; moreover, following physicians' orders is what twenty-first-century Americans do: *Take this pill before eating, after eating, with water, without water. One pill, two pills, half a pill.*

Golden warmth spread along the horizon—how is it that moisture makes touching an ordinary piece of tissue paper so objectionable?—and prismatic dew hung heavy on the grass. He worked alone, sensing that this increased the potency of the chore's curative properties.

He was nearly finished when Charlotte caught him at it, coming down the driveway in her nightgown and fuzzy blue slippers, clasping her robe closed at the sternum with one hand. "Well, look at you! You are so thoughtful! Thank you!"

"Well, you know," Bone said. Limongello had said he must neither seek nor refuse gratitude. "You're welcome."

"I saw you from the kitchen window and thought you were cleaning up your own garbage, and then I looked again, and it was mine!" She put her hand to her face in good-natured surprise and pleased embarrassment. "It's the neighborhood dogs," she said. "Someone should do something about them, but you can't really blame them. They smelled something good in the garbage. Good-smelling to *them*, ha-ha." She touched his arm at this witticism.

"I guess no dog can resist the smell of chicken," Bone said. A glorious summer day was opening before him like a flower, and he held a bag of freshly gathered garbage in his hand. Beneficence brimmed over onto Charlotte, the dew-laden grass, and the giddy neighborhood dogs whom no one could blame for loving chicken so.

"What were you doing out there?" Mary asked over her coffee cup when he came in.

"Picking up Charlotte's garbage," he said.

Mary studied him with a hard-to-read expression but said nothing.

Gassing up en route to Fulsome, Bone prepaid inside instead of at the pump, giving him a pretext to speak to the cashier. He saw at once she'd be a challenge: sullen, sallow, simultaneously slack-skinned and fat. To buy time, he loitered at the cooler making his root beer selection and then at the snack carousel, perusing the peanuts. Praising her smile was out of the question; she didn't have one. Nor could he admire her eyes, resembling, as they did, twin pools of stagnant water. Nor, judging from her grooming, was hair a special point of pride. He couldn't compliment her wardrobe because, apart from the official blue gas-station vest with its regulation grease stain just below the right shoulder, Bone saw only her blouse—graying white or fading beige?—which, for all he knew, was part of the uniform.

In desperation, he blurted the only thing he could think of. "You have to be a special person to work here." Waggling his eyebrows like Groucho Marx, he held up the root beer and hot nuts to show her the price. She regarded him suspiciously. "Putting up with all these customers," he clarified weakly. The store was vacant save for the two of them. The skin across his forehead tightened. A greeting card on the counter rack displayed a tough-faced little boy of the sort you *knew* never ate his vegetables or washed behind his ears, offering a fistful of ragged wildflowers with the inscription "I like *you*." Maybe buying it for Mary might count as Task Three, a compliment, or maybe Task Two, an act of kindness, but it couldn't hurt either way, and complimenting the cashier wasn't proving especially effective. "And forty dollars of regular on pump number seven." He leaned back to make out the number of the fuel bay and give himself an excuse to avoid her eye.

"Do you want a bag with that?" she asked. He shook his head, and to his surprise, she had broken into a smile. "You're right about the customers," she said. "I could tell you some stories."

"I bet. "

"You don't have to be crazy to work here," she quipped as he shouldered the door open, hot nuts and greeting card in one hand and root beer in the other, "but it helps."

"Ha-ha," he said. Pumping gas, he began laughing for real. He felt like a secret agent exchanging coded messages behind enemy lines, oxytocin and dopamine bubbling through his veins like gangbusters; the cashier would relish the success of her bon mot all evening, and a glow would fill the gas station as if she were seeing it through a prism. In the window, she was still laughing. He was laughing, too. Was it wrong if they weren't laughing for the same reason?

In his car, he tore open the hot nuts with his teeth, twisted the cap off the root beer, and took a meditative dose of each. But what did Limongello's therapy accomplish beyond a temporary mood elevation? Couldn't he get the same result with any extraordinary or unexpected behavior? Didn't college fraternities achieve the same effect by making pledges wear pajamas in public, or a beanie, or sing the school fight song whenever someone said hello? Wasn't that what they were all trying to do—the kleptomaniacs, self-mutilators, alcoholics, sex addicts, compulsive gamblers—seeking some new sensation as a way of holding on to the self, preventing it from dislodging? Wouldn't Limongello's strange remedy lose effectiveness as it became routine?

Bone arrived at Fulsome and opened the door to the familiar musty shadows of his office. Next door, there came a long rasping *scri-i-i-tch* as Miranda Richter stretched strapping tape over the lid of a cardboard box. Her silence dotted the air like an ellipsis compelling him to speak, as her speech would have compelled him to silence.

"Miranda? My God, what's happening?"

"Bone," she said, "can you help? Dope that I am, I put my Klaeber out of reach again." Turning and bumping her knee on a drawer, she pointed to the bookshelves, once stuffed proudly with *The Anglo-Saxon Chronicle* and fat Chaucer, now bare save for an outsized volume of ancient maps leaning on a shiny blue globe on the bottom shelf and the unobtainable Klaeber on the top, tauntingly peeping over the edge at them. On the floor sat two cardboard boxes, one with lips sealed in a prim line by strapping tape, the other gaping its lid-flaps like an obese baby bird awaiting a worm; the teapot and sugar bowl were already in its gullet.

Bone climbed on a chair and brought down the Klaeber. "What's going on?"

"I'm leaving," she said. Her voice was melodic as ever, but her smile was squeezed into a little bow. "This is the end for me. Toodle-oo." Her slim hands went up. "Gordon says I'm not needed. No more Medieval Lit. No more Miranda Richter. It's toodle-oo."

Couldn't she teach Freshman English?

"Too expensive. It's cheaper to hire a grad student from Georgia State." She tried a "Damn it" and made a go of kicking the wastebasket, but instead of knocking it over with a satisfying dead-center bang, her foot sideswiped and slammed into the file cabinet. She took off her shoe and fingered her toes for signs of breakage, defenseless in her unhappiness.

What would she do?

"I'll find something. I'm young yet." She was no more successful at sardonic laughter than trash-can kicking or cussing. "Truth to tell, I was getting tired of all that—" her voice cracked, "Chaucer anyway." Her warm hand touched Bone's. "Watch out for Loundsberry. Watch out for Dr. Gordon." She patted his hand. "*Illegitimi non carborundum.*"

"You're a great teacher," he said. His second compliment of the day.

She only patted his hand and repeated, "*Illegitimi non carborundum.*"

Poor Miranda. Bone was in a funk for the rest of the evening, but, if he had to be honest, in the center of that funk, there was also an unworthy spark of relief: right smack in the center of sympathizing Yin's fattest, blackest bulge shone the white-hot pinpoint of self-interested Yang. *(It wasn't I! I still have a job! Monkey Fever passed me by!)*

He should have spared more time to console her, but what could he have done? He couldn't get her job back. Frankly, she was probably better off, anyway. A tiny part of him began secretly making up its mind that she must've had it coming. Besides, did he even know Professor Richter that well? Was she really even a friend, or just a colleague? Moreover, he had—in the words of a hideously vivid French idiom—

other cats to skin: his condition, his work on *Words*, and his marriage.

But it solved one mystery at least. Bone spoke to Belinda about this after class.

"I'm definitely back fall semester," he told her. As usual, she'd lingered after everyone else, but sullenly, as if for him to prove something to her. She met his gaze without interest. "Miranda—Professor Richter, Loundsberry's letting her go. It's a terrible thing, really. What this department's coming to. Still, I'll be back. So you can take me fall semester."

"Well, that's good." She was standing now, holding her *Norton Anthology* and notebook against her chest, waiting for permission to leave.

What was wrong here?

"Okay," Bone said. "Have you read the Conrad yet?" An opening for her to feed him a stolen opinion that she could fob off as her own, one of her please-affirm-I'm-worthy observations stated in the form of a question, but she didn't rise to the bait.

"Not yet."

"Well, the final exam's coming up."

"Right. Well, I'll read it."

Telling Miranda Richter she was a great teacher hadn't helped Bone's mood one jot or tittle, and the oxytocin boost from his conversation with the Quik-Trip cashier had long since dissipated, leaving in its place the slow-rising dread from calcitonin and noradrenaline swirling up in his blood like mud in a troubled stream. He needed to restore his levels. He tried modulating his hormones by reminding himself that this was how he felt when he was feeling anxious, but contrary to Limongello's prediction, articulating the emotion seemed to increase rather than diminish it.

"I have to tell you something," he said, keeping his voice as cold and scaly as he could manage. "You." Long pause after that word, building the suspense, savoring her apprehension: *What is he about to tell me?* Yes, it was definitely working; Bone could feel his oxytocin beginning to seep back into his bloodstream. "Are a very good student. Truly. It is a privilege to have you in class."

Belinda stared as if a bucket of cold water had dropped on her head, then astonished Bone by bursting into sobs. "Oh, Professor King!" She hugged him, clawing at his sleeves, wetting his astonished shoulder with her tears.

After accepting the card with the tough-faced kid, the clutched flowers, and the "I like *you*," Mary gave Bone a quizzical look and said, "What's this about?"

"It's nothing. It's just a card, and it made me think of you."

"Well, thank you."

"You're welcome."

She kissed him and put the card on the dresser mirror where she would see it every day, and stood there for a time studying it as if it were a clue to a mystery she was working out.

CHAPTER TWELVE

L, l

From the North Semitic *lamed* ($\angle$), "ox goad." A liquid consonant, formed sensuously by pressing the upper side of the tongue to the alveolar ridge.

love: From the Proto Indo-European *lewb.* In the Aristotelian concept of *essential meanings,* **love** means the same whether we say, "I **love** bacon," "I **love** my wife," or "God is **love**," a problematic point because Aristotle himself had four different words for **love**: *storge,* "familial love," *eros,* "sexual love," *philia,* "love of friends," and *agape,* "unselfish love." Wittgenstein, however, argues that a word's many meanings are only family resemblances. If so, **love**'s in-laws and multiremoved cousins could perplex the most patient genealogist. *Overview of Neurology* (Arthur Limongello, MD, MD, New York: Kakos Publishing, 2009) defines **love** as "endorphins and oxytocin creating sensations of emotional bonding." But surely we **love** even when filled with hormones for anger or fear. Does it overstretch Wittgenstein's familial similarity to say animals with other hormones than ours feel a version of **love**? Do chickens, displaying motherly concern for their chicks, know *storge*? Do turtles, companionably sharing a floating log, have p*hilia*? Do they **love** the sunshine on their backs? Is a chicken closer than a turtle to understanding the es*sential* meaning of **love**? Are we closer than a chicken? Can God, who, if He exists at all, has no limbic system or hormones whatsoever, **love** us?

B one wondered if after what had happened at the party, Cash would have the nerve to do their lawn on Friday. Cash had the nerve. Of course, while *Bone* knew Cash had kissed Mary because Mary had told him so, *Cash* didn't know Bone knew because Mary hadn't told Cash she'd told Bone; unless Mary *had* told Cash she'd told Bone, in which case Cash would know Bone knew Cash kissed Mary, but Bone wouldn't know Cash knew Bone knew. Jesus, since when had life turned into an Archie Comics book?

In spite of promising not to "see Cash" again, Mary spent as much time that afternoon with Cash as ever, if not more. "It really hurts me to see you talking to him," Bone said when she came in to get Cash a glass of tea. What was it about that man and *tea*?

"We have to act normal. He lives in our neighborhood. I can't avoid him," Mary pointed out with the infuriating calm of common sense. Still, it cut Bone to pieces seeing them together in the speckled shadows of the Rose of Sharon. What the hell were they talking about? If she were capable of talking to Cash so brazenly when Bone was there, what prevented her from doing something more than talk when Bone wasn't? Or did it work the other way around? Did she only allow herself to be around Cash when she had Bone as a chaperone?

Mary came inside, rinsed Cash's glass, and put it in the dishwasher, then finished off a glass of water herself, draining it in a single swallow—a way she had—setting the glass down and gasping. With a look of having something to say, but waiting for when saying it would seem natural, she stared out the window at Cash lowering the truck gate and a Mexican rolling the lawn mower up it. Bone could see Mary weighing and planning, mentally constructing and demolishing conversational bridges to carry her from the blank wall of utter silence to whatever it was she had to tell him. Finally, she came out with it: she was driving up to the mountains to spend the weekend with Laurel.

When did this come up?, was what Bone wanted to know.

It transpired that she and Laurel had been discussing it for a while now and had finalized the plans at Betty's party.

The same party at which she had kissed Cash?

Jesus, how long was Bone going to keep throwing that up in her face?

Why did she have to go to the mountains? Why couldn't she stay here with him?

To paint. She'd always wanted to paint, and this was her chance. She'd already been to Binders' Art Supply: a bag of wooden stretcher strips, canvas, tubes of Bengal Rose and Cerulean Blue were waiting in her Honda.

Jesus. She was leaving now? Right now?

Yes.

Couldn't he come, too?

She couldn't concentrate with Bone around. She needed to be alone.

But wasn't Laurel going to be there?

That wasn't the same thing.

Was anyone else going to be there?

What was he talking about?

Cash?

Jesus, how many times was he going to throw that up in her face?

Couldn't she understand? He was sick. He had a condition.

"If you don't want me to go," her chin was out, "then I won't go."

"I don't want you to go."

"I already told Laurel I would."

So she went.

OF THE MANY ways to console oneself, diagramming sentences is the rarest; nevertheless, other comforts—walking room to empty room mumbling, for example—don't provide the serene, objectifying distance between ourselves and our self-pity that diagramming does. Ordinary sentences, outwardly so similar, anatomized in a diagram, show the operations of transitive, intransitive, and passive verbs that define our relationships to each other, the outside world, and ourselves.

Bone took a simple-seeming example: There Mary goes.

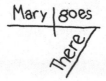

Until you see it diagrammed, you might almost mistake "there" for the subject, but "there" is not doing the going; it is a mere preposition, a dummy subject taking the place of the absent Mary. Ironically, "goes" is an intransitive verb. No object receives the action of Mary's going. She simply goes and is gone.

Unlike "to go," which a subject does by itself, a transitive verb is a vector requiring an object to receive the action. Next Bone considered the sentence, "Bone diagrams himself a sentence."

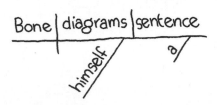

If not for the diagram, we might whimsically imagine that Bone is diagramming *himself*, but the diagram clarifies that what Bone diagrams is "a sentence" and that "himself" is only an object, the person for whom he diagrams it. Identity is fractured here; "Bone," as subject, occupies the primary position, but as "himself" hangs as an afterthought, broken from the main sentence stem like a pencil refracted in a glass of water.

Some verbs, however, do not show action, transitive or intransitive, but a state of being. These are passive verbs. Take, for example, "Bone is all alone." "All" is redundant ("alone" being a compound of *all* and *one*) but permissible for emphasis.

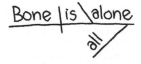

Instead of being perpendicular, the line after the verb totters back toward the subject, signifying that "Bone" is not performing an action, such as "going" or "diagramming"; he merely *is* alone. Unless we supply the adverb "now," there's no reason to infer a time he was ever *not* alone. Unlike a transitive verb, a passive verb stays put, an unmoving link between subject and complement. Since the verb is directionless, the same idea can be expressed in almost any order. While it would be untrue to say, "Bone left Mary," and nonsense to say, "A sentence diagrammed himself Bone," it would be perfectly correct—although unorthodox—to say, instead of "Bone is all alone," "All alone is Bone."

SATURDAY, BONE DROVE out in the rain to buy himself some cut fruit, bread, and sandwich meat and had the good fortune to come across someone stranded with a dead battery in the parking lot of the Skyland Kroger. Having helped the stranger jump-start his battery, sprinkled with raindrops and personal virtue, Bone went to the library to return one set of books and check out another.

That night, Mary called.

"So how're the mountains?"

"Beautiful. I wish you could have come."

"I thought you said I couldn't," Bone said. Mary responded with silence, and for a moment Bone thought he'd lost the connection. "So are you getting much painting done?" This time an "um" was her reply. "Come home soon, Mary."

She said, "That sounds like an order."

"I just meant that I love you, and I miss you, and I want you home."

"I don't like it when you give orders."

"I'm sorry," Bone said. Something had shifted. He felt as if she had stepped behind clouded glass. "Listen, I've been meaning to tell you," Bone leaned on the kitchen wall, forehead to wrist, the side of his face casting twin dove-gray shadows, dark as a rain-sky where they overlapped. The phone mashed into the side of his face. "There was something you were telling me about a year or so ago. It was a day we were out shopping, and I showed you the sign for the attorneys."

"What are you talking about, Bone?"

"The sign for the attorneys, do you remember? It was misspelled. We were just coming back from the library, and I pointed it out to you and said how irritating it was that some people can't master simple spelling. Do you remember that?"

"No."

"You were saying something at the time, you were trying to say something, but I wasn't listening because I was looking at the sign. Do you remember that?"

"No. I can't say I do."

"The point is, if you remembered what you were talking about, you were unhappy about something, I'd listen now. I'm sorry I wasn't listening then, but I'd listen now. You were unhappy about something. Can't you remember? I think it was about me."

"Not everything is about you, Bone."

"I know that. It's just that I miss you."

The call, which Bone had been looking forward to all day, ended with a dismal exchange of "I love you"s, a distance in her voice much greater than from there to the mountains.

Late that night, on a terrible, irresistible impulse, he got in his car and drove to a house one street over. No truck was in the driveway. His stomach clenched so hard, he thought he'd be sick. But that didn't prove anything, right? He was going crazy. Get a grip. He drove home but couldn't sleep. Mentally, he returned over and over to Cash's house, gliding in his mind like a silent manta ray over the wet blacktop to double-, triple-, quadruple-check: no truck in the driveway, no truck in the driveway.

Sunday, Mary came home, and Bone was grateful to have her. She kissed him, but they didn't make love because she had a yeast infection. Cash's truck being gone had been a coincidence. There was nothing to worry about between her and Cash. Nevertheless, Bone couldn't help noticing that after a weekend of painting, not one stretcher strip had been assembled with another, her canvas was unsized, and her tubes of gesso, Bengal Rose, and Cerulean Blue were unopened.

CHAPTER THIRTEEN

M, m

From the Semitic *mem* (**M**), "water." Our modern **M** has the same sharp, steep waves but, rather than cascading, stands on two feet, dipping a beak in the middle to touch the ground, so it now resembles twin mountains more than a waterfall.

metathesis: The transposition of sounds in a word, as in the childish pronunciation of "pasketti" for "spaghetti" or the doltish proclivity for saying "noocular" for "nuclear." **Metathesis** is responsible for some genuine words in English: **sideburns** take their name from the metathesis of **Burnsides**, the Civil War general who popularized the style. Alas, the charming notion that a **butterfly** was once known as a **flutterby** has no empirical backing.

mind: An efflorescence of the nervous system, an unverifiable but undeniable consciousness of one's own consciousness. From the Greek *menos,* "mind," hence **mental** and **mentor**. *Menos* is unmistakably related to *mania,* "madness."

move: From the Latin *movere,* whence also **motion, motor, demote,** and **promote** as well as **emotion** and **motivation**. Movement is expressed as the ratio of distance and time: *miles per hour, feet per second.* We use time to measure movement and movement to measure time—the gliding of a second hand around a dial; the march of numbers across the Cartesian grid of a calendar; a sweetheart's good-bye. Without movement, time would not exist.

L imongello called and said to meet at the Waffle House on the 285 access road. When he arrived, Bone was shocked by the doctor's downcast expression, almost like the cartoon frowny-face the nurse was to show Bone later in the hospital, the far-right expression that represented 10 on the pain scale of 1 to 10, where the mouth bends into a nearly perfect upside-down U, lacking only the ant-column of teardrops marching down the cheek from one eye.

"Are you okay?" Bone asked. "I hope you don't mind my asking. You look like you have the weight of the world on you."

"There's a little something for all of us in this world, I guess," Limongello said. "That's why all this." He nodded toward the plates before him; he'd ordered the All-Star Breakfast, a meal of monstrous glory requiring four plates to serve: waffles, eggs, toast, bacon, and hash browns. "Trying to give my digestive system enough to do so it'll trick the ol' amygdala into not releasing so dang many stress hormones. An old trick, but effective sometimes. I guess I'm going through a rough patch right now. Thanks for asking." He said in a comically dramatic voice, "So the patient becomes the *doctor*. Ha-ha. Speaking of which, how is your own therapy coming, the tasks I gave you?"

"I really think it's helping. Just the other day, I got to help a man whose battery died. Lucky break running into him. I've been feeling a lot better."

"Lucky break," Limongello agreed, as if he considered the break as far from being lucky as a break could get. He stared at his scattered and smothered hash browns as if the bloom had gone off them and cut a bite-sized piece of waffle from the main mass, then further divided the piece with his knife and fork. "That's all well and good, but I want to warn you, at first, the tasks will make you feel terrific, but that wears off. The time comes, and sooner rather than later, when you won't feel so good dishing out compliments and doing good deeds. And when you clap your hands in the morning, you just feel stupid." Limongello cut the recut bite of waffle again, pushing it with his fork through a thin smear of syrup to the side of the plate and arranging the other pieces around it in a triangle. He seemed to be attempting to break his waffle into sufficiently small bits that it would atomize and disappear entirely, saving him the trouble of eating. "You're going to start feeling stupid and resenting the whole process, but that's when you really need to keep it up. We want to get to the point where you do it without feeling especially one way or the other. When you get to the stage where it stops feeling good, you need to keep going. Promise me."

"You almost talk like you're not going to be here."

"As a matter of fact, that's the other thing we need to discuss. I'm going to Leipzig for a neurological institute. I'd like to put it off, but I can't." Spearing his waffle bit on two tines of his fork, Limongello pointed it at the upside-down U of his mouth but did not eat. "I've got some friends there, some colleagues I'm corresponding with, and maybe they can shed some light on your condition." Another sigh, and he reluctantly ate the waffle bit, jaws working slowly as if he were masticating a sponge the size of a supper plate. "I can't tell you exactly how long I'll be gone, because—well, it's a pretty major thing. It's international, you see. But in the meantime, and I can't stress this enough, I need you to follow through with your therapy. Will you promise?"

"Of course."

"It may get pretty unpleasant."

"Actually, I've sort of been enjoying it."

"And I'm here to tell you, that won't last. After a while, you won't like it. It's like jogging." Another bit of waffle was subjected to Limongello's relentless dissection and resection, preparatory to eventual doleful chewing. "The first few minutes are great, and you think, 'I could do this all day!' Then it starts to get hard, and all you can think about is lying on the sofa in front of the TV with a big bag of Fritos and a beer. Believe me, though, just when it starts to get really tough, that's when you know it's doing the most good. Like with jogging. You haven't gone far enough until your feet get sore and your side starts cramping." Limongello looked at his wrist as if he expected to find a watch there and, when he didn't, looked at the Waffle House clock. "I wish I could be here with you, but maybe it's for the best. You need to do the next part on your own. Walk that lonesome valley and all that."

"I guess," Bone said.

"Well, I wish you good luck. I have to go now."

"To Leipzig," Bone said.

"To Leipzig."

If someone had asked Bone what he thought of Limongello's prediction that the remedy would become a joyless exercise—less than joyless, dreary and dreaded—he'd have replied confidently that the double-doc was exaggerating. Bone expected, as most people expect, for life to continue in the stream it has generally run in up to then, neither significantly better nor worse. In this, he was, like most people, horribly, catastrophically mistaken.

As the apricot sky silhouetted the pine trees on the hill, Cash came to discuss—Bone assumed—some issue of lawn maintenance with Mary in the spotted shadows of the Rose of Sharon. Bone had poured himself a glass of tea and was about to join them to ascertain if they were indeed discussing fescue and not matters of more dire import when the phone rang. Bone had tried to reach Grisamore several times over the past three days, but each time had gotten only the secretary: Mr. Grisamore hadn't come in to work yet, Mr. Grisamore was out of the office, Mr. Grisamore was in a meeting, no, she didn't know when the meeting would be over, yes, she would be sure to have Mr. Grisamore return the call, what was the name and number again? Today, however, Grisamore called Bone, an astonishing thing so long after office hours.

"Did you get to read the chapters?" Bone asked. "Have you had a chance to look at it?"

"Well, yes."

"What do you think about the introduction? That part still might need some work."

"Well, yes."

"I know it still needs polishing, but I wanted you to see where I was heading with it."

"Well, yes."

Grisamore's "well, yes," repeated for the third time, began to rub Bone's nerves like a cheese grater; that leaden "well" had an ominous ring to it, a sound like things were not well at all, and in that dull, heavy "yes" was the undertone of something distinctly "no" in the offing.

At the scent of gardenia, Bone looked up and saw Mary; whatever Cash had come to discuss, it seemed they'd finished discussing it. She stood arms akimbo in a I-have-something-to-say-and-you're-probably-not-going-to-like-it pose. Bone signaled to be patient with a raised index finger. "You *have* read it, right? I know it needs polish, but—I mean, you have read it, right?"

"Well, the fact is, I've been pretty busy, Bone." This was when Grisamore let the hammer fall.

"What do you mean?" Bone felt the blood leave his face, his dopamine levels dipping dangerously and his calcitonin climbing. His be-patient index finger, still poised midair for Mary, seemed to belong to another person.

"A different author, Bone. I tried telling you the publisher wouldn't wait forever. Someone else submitted a ready-to-go manuscript, and we've decided to go with it." Rushing waves filled Bone's ear. "It's not your traditional grammar book. It's actually a very interesting approach," Grisamore was saying, "something you might want to look into. The idea is there's no such thing as 'correct' grammar—" Bone silently mouthed several curse words. "—that all dialects have their own worthy grammar. In fact you might know the author. His name is—"

"Oh, please God, don't let it be—"

"E. Knolton."

Bone's numbed arm dropped the phone to the counter, and he put his trembling hand to his brow. When he found the strength to lift the phone again, Grisamore was still talking. "—y excited about him, and our sales team is already getting calls from bookstores. We'll have to put a late notice out as it is, because it didn't make the catalog, but he had a manuscript ready. We're rushing it into galleys now, and we'll have it out by winter. We are using your title, though," Grisamore said as if it were good news. "*Words.*"

Bone tried to stammer an objection, but only a soft clicking sound proceeded from the back of his throat, like one of those dreams in which just when your life depends on screaming your lungs out, your voice comes out as dim as the lifeguard's whistle to a drowning man at the bottom of a pool. Meanwhile, an adjective here, a participle there floated from the phone to Bone's ears: "… refreshing … glad … saved … don't have to be alarmed …" The Kit-Kat Clock on the wall above Mary's head blurred but did not stop smiling or operating; its tail wagged left, its eyes darted right, its tail wagged right, its eyes darted left.

"What was that last part?" Bone said through a throat as dry as thistles.

"Knolton says we don't need to be alarmed about the changes in English. Language can't be corrupted; there is no 'pure' language. Living languages change; they evolve. It's a very refreshing thought when you think of it. All the change we see going on around us is a testament to the vitality of English. Change is natural and inevitable."

Lots of things are natural and inevitable, but we still fight them tooth and nail, and we damn well ought to: soil erosion, rust, food spoilage, death; just because something's natural and inevitable doesn't mean we abet the process or even look on indifferently.

"So when do you want my manuscript?"

"What?"

"My manuscript. The manuscript I've been working on for two years. *Words. Words, Words, Words.* When do you want the completed manuscript?"

"It's not really what you said it would be. We were expecting a book on *grammar.*"

"I can write a book on grammar. I can write a god-damned book on grammar. Give me a chance." Bone hadn't meant to sound so desperate.

"I'm sorry," Grisamore said. "Listen, I've got to go to a meeting."

"Oh, a meeting! Right! A meeting! Anytime you want to avoid me, just go to a mee—" But Grisamore had hung up, and Bone was holding only a buzzing receiver. Muttering a succession of Anglo-Saxon words, Bone replaced the phone in its dock. Mary cleared her throat.

"We have to talk," she said.

"Does it have to be now?" Bone felt if he took his hands from the counter, he might fall. Only by applied concentration could he remember to fill and empty his lungs. "Do we have to talk about it now? I have just had the single worst conversation of my entire life. In one short exchange of words," he gestured to the phone, "someone completely ripped the rug out from under me and ruined my life. Whatever this is about, can't it wait?" Bone believed the worst thing that could happen to him had already happened; again, he was proven cataclysmically wrong.

"I'm not going to spend the night here, Bone. I need a night out of this house."

CHAPTER FOURTEEN

N, n

From the Phoenician *nun* (⑂), "fish." Between the waterfall, *mem* (𝗠), and the lightning-bolt leap of fish, *nun* (⑂), comes the alphabet's midpoint, dividing the most common letters, placed within easy reach, from the least common, shoved to the back. A typical dictionary devotes a hundred pages to **aardvark** to **azygous**, whereas we can get all the way from **xanthate** to **Zyrian** in less than ten.

nonce word: A word coined for a single occasion and never used again. One might reasonably ask if such a thing can even exist. For example, if someone made up the word "gurk" to mean "I'm unable to breathe," could this properly be considered a word at all if it were never repeated? And once spoken, if it were printed in a dictionary somewhere even as an example of a **nonce word**, wouldn't it cease to be one?

After Mary's announcement, the grinning Kit-Kat Clock's tail wagged left and eyes went right, and the refrigerator hummed uneasily, filling the silence.

"You're kidding me," Bone said. The air seemed brittle and thin, and neither of them moved.

"I know you've been trying lately—the card, I know—but you're just too—distant. It's something I've got to do until I work some things out."

"Let it go, man," Cash said. Bone realized their neighbor had come into the kitchen without his noticing. Cash stood, arms folded, biceps slightly flexed, like a defensive tackle blocking the way to Mary, except he wasn't standing in front of her, but behind.

"Jesus, are you spending the night with *him*?" Bone had the sensation that if he looked down, he would see his knees shimmering as if they were behind a waterfall. Did he even have knees anymore? He felt as though he weren't standing on the floor. In situations like this, weren't you expected to fight your rival? Should he do that now?

Mary left the kitchen, and Cash said, "Don't try to stop her. This is something she's got to do."

Bone said, "Christ, you're spending the night with him? Right in front of me? God, are you *crazy*?"

What Cash said next was, "She'll be back when she's done," but what Bone *heard* was "when I'm done," at which every individual corpuscle in his brain went off like a hand grenade, and his ears roared like a train crash.

"You—" Bone began, unable to add anything worse than the bare pronoun. His vision blurred, and he swung his fist. Then everything went white, and his knees buckled, but he didn't hit the floor; a second later his tardy brain caught up with events: his misaimed fist had brushed Cash's face, and Cash had moved forward and seized Bone in a position as impotent as it was perplexing and exasperating. Bone's arm was pressed against his ear, and his other hand was seized in Cash's; the crook of Cash's elbow squeezed Bone's Adam's apple. Bone tried explaining that he couldn't breathe, but the most he could get out was "Gurk." Meanwhile, he was doing his best to claw Cash with his free hand, but given his predicament, his arm was as feeble and ineffective as a tyrannosaur's.

"Just let her do this, man," Cash advised calmly. He repeated, "She'll be back when she's done." Done with *what?* was Bone's riposte, but it only came out as a gastric gurgle.

"Will you please try to be mature about this?" Mary's voice said.

"He started it," Cash said. "If I let you go, you promise not to try anything? I don't want to hurt you, man." You seem to be doing a pretty good job, Bone thought, but he nodded. His vision cleared. "You ready?" Cash released his hold, and Bone tottered. Drool broke from his lower lip and wet the ceramic tile. Bone rose and realized Cash was talking to Mary.

She had her blue overnight case. Christ, while he'd been lollygagging in the kitchen getting manhandled by the neighbor, she'd been casually packing her things. Bone hadn't even followed her to see what she'd put in there! "Is your diaphragm in there?"

"You always think everything's about sex," Mary said. "Everything's not about sex."

"Let her go, man," Cash said. "Just let her go." With both hands, using only his fingertips, he gently pushed Bone back.

After they left, Bone stormed room to room, cussing, hollering, howling, laughing, and sometimes doing all at once. How could he lose both his book deal and his wife in one evening? It had taken her only a day after her "mountain trip" to announce she "needed to stay over with Cash" to "work some things out." Goddamn, what a fool Bone was.

Mountain trip! She needed to do some "painting"! The walls reverberated with maniacal laughter. He ought to throw something, punch holes in the Sheetrock, overturn bookcases. He grabbed *Misplaced Modifiers* and hurled it, but the pathetic thud it made was so anticlimactic, he did not care to repeat the experiment and instead sat on the sofa, wringing his hands between his knees, rocking, roaring, and moaning. This couldn't be happening. God, he would go insane! He would!

He jumped up and went outside. It was too deliberative getting in the car and turning the ignition, as if he were off to the Stop-n-Go for eggs and milk; the only fitting response was storming over on foot. A man can storm on foot, however, three to five paces at most before beginning to feel foolish, and long before reaching the end of the street, Bone felt exceedingly foolish indeed, but by then it was too late to turn back.

He held his thumb on Cash's doorbell until it went numb.

The door opened, and light filled the front stoop. "What the hell do you want?" Cash blocked the threshold, one hand holding the top of the door, still wearing his shirt and jeans. Good Lord, was it possible Mary was telling the truth? That they were only talking? But wait. Cash was barefoot. For some reason those ten little piggies made Bone tremble as violently as if Cash had come to the door wearing only jockey shorts and a sheen of body oil.

"I want my wife," Bone said, trying and failing to keep the tears from his voice.

"Go the hell back home, man; go the hell back home. Don't ring my doorbell again." The door closed.

Bone stood, shaking in spite of the evening warmth.

It was too early in the season for the cicadas to set up their stupefying roar; instead there was just the mindless *bri-i-i-c, bra-a-a-c, bri-i-i-c,* bra-a-a-c, of the crickets. On any night but this, Bone would have thought it was beautiful. Fireflies rose in sparks from the lawn, and the luminous backs of the magnolia leaves shivered in the full moon's light.

Bone didn't linger by the kitchen window but climbed the chain-link into the backyard, piercing his hand on the tines and tumbling ignominiously to the other side, twisting his ankle and getting a piece of bark in his eye—if he'd gone the other way around, he realized belatedly, he could have used the gate. He crouched, gathering his breath and vainly trying to subdue his trembling. It hadn't rained recently, but Cash watered his lawn religiously, so the English ivy dampened Bone's ankles as he crept up the hill where he could look down at the back of the house through the picture window and into Cash's living room.

The lights were on, but there was no sign of Bone's wife or neighbor. *They're already in the bedroom!* his thudding heart exclaimed, and delaying only long enough to trip on a root and roll three feet through the wet ivy, Bone went to the bedroom window—easy to locate since Cash's house was the inverted twin of Bone's—ominously dark but too high for easy surveillance. He grabbed the brick ledge, jacking himself to the window in a shaky chin-up, knees scraping and the wound in his hand throbbing against the rough brick. He hung, panting, shaking, elbows on the ledge, toe-balanced on a seam between brick tiers, cheek so near the windowpane, he felt its coolness. He saw nothing, but did he hear something? Was it his imagination, or was there heavy breathing?

"Oh, God." He recognized Mary's voice. "Oh, God."

It wasn't coming from the bedroom, but behind him. He started to fall, but not before someone grabbed him by the belt and pulled him away from the bricks.

"You are the biggest butt-hole I ever knew," Cash said. He still wore jeans and a tee shirt, but he'd slipped on Docksiders to come outside. Mary stood behind Cash in her night robe, light from the full moon and picture window illuminating her in her beauty and fury. "If you come here again, I'm gonna—" Cash didn't finish, but his silence was filled with insinuations of humiliating and painful ass-whippings. Cash pushed Bone again, and for the third time that night, he fell. "Don't come back again," Cash warned, and Bone, the pain from his wound vying with his jarred carpal bones, rose and left, letting himself out this time through the gate.

Bone had already learned that the distance between his house and Cash's far exceeded the maximum range for storming on foot, but he made a go of it, tears blurring the moon-washed streets. Goddamn her, anyway. Goddamn her. Who needed her?

Next morning Mary, flush-faced, returned to the kitchen where Bone was waiting, white-faced.

"How could you?" he asked. He'd pulled a chair up to the

kitchen door and sat in it all night so he'd know the moment she came in. "How could you?"

"I have to see if this thing is going to work out. Between me and Cash. I'm confused right now, and I'm figuring things out."

"You're a bitch."

"Nothing happened between us, if you really want to know. We just stayed up and talked."

"Oh, like I believe *that*."

"Believe whatever you want. It's true. Are you going to let me by? I have to take a shower."

"What, to wash him off you?"

"Jesus, Bone. I told you nothing happened. And anyway, it was already over between us. We both knew that."

"*I* didn't know that," he protested and, sitting in his chair like the pathetic cuckold he was, did the one thing he'd sworn he would not do: he began to cry. "I love you. God help me, I love you. You can't be doing this to me. Not now. Not on top of everything else."

"These things happen, Bone. Just … these things happen." She opened the refrigerator door and plucked out a square of watermelon from the bowl of cut fruit and ate it. "It's nobody's fault. It's just something that happens."

"It doesn't happen unless you *want* it to."

She eased around him on her way to the shower.

He should just throw her out. Take all her things and just throw them into the yard. Let her be with Cash if that's what she wanted. The hell with her. He could hear the shower running as he passed the bathroom door on the way to the bedroom. He yanked a dresser drawer open but, facing the froth of her lacy bras and panties, couldn't bear to throw them out. Instead, he went back and stood at the bathroom door, listening to the shower. He tried the door, but it was locked. So he pounded. "I'm going to throw your goddamn stuff out of the house! Do you hear me? I'm throwing out all your goddamn stuff."

The shower stopped, and a minute later, the door opened. Mary stood in a towel. Even now, even after everything— seeing beaded water on her smooth shoulders, her thick, wet hair pulled back like a heavy rope, her dark eyes bright with contempt—if she had put her arms around him, he would have forgiven her in an instant. He fought an impulse to drop to the floor and clasp her knees.

"Bone, please don't be immature about this."

"Don't be immature?"

"It was already over between us," she repeated. "I never mattered to you as much as that damn book."

"I've lost the book," Bone said, his voice rasping. "The deal fell through."

"And what hurts more? Me or the book?"

Bone would never forgive himself for the fatal pause before he framed a reply; he should have cried out instantly, "You, of course!" but instead his chin dropped as he considered his answer.

"I have to get ready for work," Mary said, pushing past him into the bedroom, and before he could stop her, she locked the door behind her, so he was denied even the glory of watching her pull the towel from her shimmering skin and put on her clothes. Her hair dryer came on.

"God, God, God," Bone cried. He could pick the lock if he had a safety pin. There were paper clips in the office. The first paper clip he tried to straighten, his trembling fingers dropped in the crack between the desk and the wall. On his knees, he pulled out the desk but couldn't reach his arm behind it. To hell with this. He shaped a second lock-pick and ran to the bedroom door, clumsily working it around in the hole. Before he succeeded, the knob turned, and Mary came out. "I'm going to work now. We'll talk about this later."

Bone spent that day in a lather of anxiety, and when the afternoon rolled around to evening without Mary's return, he walked to the house one street over. With heart-leaping horror, he saw her Honda already parked in Cash's drive. Cash's truck, however, was gone. He knocked and rang the doorbell. He reconnoitered the house's perimeter, peering in windows under visored hands. He saw nothing. He walked foolishly to one end of the street and then the other in the forlorn hope that he might catch sight of them. Finally, around eight o'clock, Cash's truck pulled up. Bone was sitting on Cash's front stoop. Cash slowed to a stop at the curb, but then the truck started up again, heading for Bone's street. Bone followed, and when he was almost home, Cash's truck passed him again, this time heading the other direction, no Mary in the front seat.

"Where have you been? I've been waiting for hours!" His voice was ragged.

"We went out to dinner," Mary said in a not-that-it's-any-of-your-business voice. She bore a faint aroma of kung pao. Bone's throat constricted.

"So that's how it's going to be?" Bone demanded. "Every night with him and just come back in the morning to change your damn clothes?"

"No," Mary said. "I'm getting a change of clothes so I can get dressed over there tomorrow. I'm tired of dealing with your drama."

CHAPTER FIFTEEN

O, o

From the Semitic *aiyn* (O), "eye," but it is an Orphan Annie eye, without iris or pupil; in the modern alphabet, it resembles an open mouth pronouncing the letter. Its simple shape has not changed in thousands of years. The Greeks called it *mikron*, "small."

onomatopoeia: A word that, strangely enough, does not sound the least bit like what it means.

orgasm: The kinship to **organ** is more distant than we are first tempted to believe. **Organ** derives from the Greek root *organo-* and ultimately from *erg*, "to work," and **orgasm** from *orge*, "urge," and ultimately the Proto Indo-European root—*uerg*, "to swell." Partridge notes that the *-asm* ending, while associated with abstract nouns, seems to connote more vigorous activity than *-ism*: to wit, **orgasm, enthusiasm, spasm**.

Osiris: The green-skinned Egyptian god of eternal life, killed by his evil brother, Set, but resurrected by his faithful wife, Isis.

oxymoron: A self-contradictory phrase such as "pretty ugly." The word itself is an **oxymoron**, from the Greek *oxus*, "sharp-witted," and *moros*, "stupid."

S aturday morning, Mary came over to announce another decision: "I'm moving in with Cash." Bone faced her, unspeaking. "Did you hear what I said? I'm moving in with Cash."

Bone just shook his head at her. "Christ, Mary. Have you even thought what the neighbors will say?"

"I guess they'll say I moved in with Cash." She didn't seem to appreciate that it was the *way* they'd say it. She took the cut fruit from the refrigerator and fixed a bowl. "Want some?" she asked. Bone didn't answer. She sat at the living room table and ate, expressionless as a marble goddess. "I'm sorry if I hurt you, Bone. I never meant to hurt you. I think—"There was a rehearsed-feeling pause as she looked out the picture window. She was gearing up to launch into a difficult, personal, and deeply honest self-analysis, like a character in a television drama. Bone felt like gagging. "I never knew my father, and my mother was irrational and alcoholic, so I grew up always missing a stable father figure. My friends all had daddies, and subconsciously, I think I believed my life would have been happy if I had a daddy, too. When I began dating, I was looking for someone to be sort of a surrogate father. Looking back on all my early relationships, I always chose men that represented that to me."

"Is that what Gordon represented?" Bone asked, his jaw tight. "Your daddy?"

Mary looked disapproving. When you're in the middle of difficult, personal, and deeply honest self-analysis, you don't appreciate people chiming in with snide remarks. "I think that's what you represented to me. A father figure."

"Christ, Mary. I'm the same age you are."

"I mean spiritually, emotionally. You're a college professor and an author. You're very intimidating. You're distant. You're always filled with your own thoughts. Lately you seemed like you were trying to change, but—the world isn't quite real to you. I don't mean in a bad way. But in my insecurity, I thought you could fill a gap in me. The missing piece of my childhood. I'm ready to move forward now."

"So. Fill a gap in you. So now Cash is filling your gap?"

"I'm sorry you're taking it this way," she said. She ate the last bite of melon, rose from the table, and left the room with the empty bowl. He followed her to the kitchen, where she put the bowl into the dishwasher, and then to the bedroom, where she opened a big suitcase on the bed and began taking her stockings and panties from the top dresser drawer and laying them in it.

"How you can do this? After everything? You said you loved me."

"I'm sorry, Bone. I didn't want to hurt you. It's just something that happened. It's nobody's fault." Her gaze turned to the window as if she'd spotted her own ghost walking in the backyard and was watching not with alarm, or even surprise, but with understandable interest. "One of the most wonderful memories I'll ever have is standing beside you in the front of the church, waiting to take my vows to love forever this wonderful, intelligent, handsome man." She spared him a smile, like flattery would make him feel *so* much better. "To realize I just don't love you anymore—that I can't love you anymore. It's awful. Tragic."

"My God. You want me to feel sorry for *you*. What book did you read this in?"

"I'm just trying to make sense of it all. These tumultuous, confusing emotions."

"Did you just say 'tumultuous'? Who the hell says 'tumultuous'?"

"I don't think I ever really loved you. Not really."

"How can you say that?" Bone asked, but she was too preoccupied packing and dealing with her tumultuous, confusing emotions to answer. "You'll be sorry." Goddamn it, he couldn't stop from issuing these clichés She was playing a breakup scene from a TV drama, and he was trading line for line like they were reading from the same script. "You won't ever find anyone as good as I." He couldn't help saying this stuff. At least that last one was so moth-eaten, it sounded almost original.

"I'll bring the suitcase back when I'm done with it," she promised.

Bone took her elbow. "Everybody's going to know what you did. Don't you care what other people—" It seemed bourgeois to finish "what other people think," but at the moment, this seemed the most monumental objection imaginable.

"No one in the neighborhood likes you, Bone," she said, suddenly cold, her eyes the color of a gun barrel. She pulled her arm from his grip. "No one likes you. I'm sorry, but it's the truth. They all think you're a kook and a creep, and they wonder why I even stay with you."

"Goddamn you, you goddamn whore," Bone said, shaking in every part of his body. He went to the kitchen and poured himself a furious glass of water from the sink. He drank a third of it, spilled half on the floor, and poured out the rest. No, he thought, a whore takes money for sex; she's a common slut. He stomped back to the bedroom to add a few more "goddamns," "whores," "sluts," and home truths, such as that he'd find another woman better than she in a week—his mind shot to Miranda Richter—but he was blocked at the hall door by an untimely bout with his condition and had to endure the infuriating necessity of square dancing to get through. Mary came by with her suitcase just before he reached "*prah*-menade" and said, "I'll be back for the rest of my clothes; this is going to take more than one trip."

When Mary came back, Cash came with her. Bone glowed with fury; his skin felt like it was stretched over a heat lamp. He deliberately stood in his path and said, "You're a bastard."

Cash put his hand on Bone's shoulder and nodded solemnly. "I understand why you'd say that."

Later that evening, there was a knock, and when Bone opened, it was Cash. "I need to get Mary's furniture," Cash explained. "She says there's a dresser of hers and a loveseat. Can you help me?"

"You're a bastard."

"I completely understand why you feel that way," Cash said. Bone detected Mary's coaching in these bland, nonconfrontational responses.

"Goddamn it, quit acting reasonable about this, you bastard."

Cash did not respond but said, "Can I get her stuff?"

"What the hell. Sure, why not?"

In the bedroom, Cash, fists on hips, made a quick apprais-
al. "If we push the bed against the wall, it'll be easier moving
the dresser." Cash pushed the bed, its feet groaning against
the hardwood, as far to the side of the room as it would
go. Then he took all the loose items off the dresser—Bone's
hairbrush, the snapshot of Bone and Mary on honeymoon
in Jacksonville, the box where they kept the nail clippers and
spare change, the card with the little boy and fistful of flowers, "I like *you*"—and placed them on the bed. When he was
done, he said, "Can you help me with this?"

"You're a bastard," Bone said. Cash nodded without
making eye contact, touching the dresser top as a silent
reminder that it wasn't going to move itself. "You're a complete bastard. You should fucking go to fucking hell and
fucking get fucked." Bone, inexperienced with cursing,
sensed he wasn't doing it correctly, but hearing himself talk
this way, liberation fizzed in his veins, and he began trembling uncontrollably again. "You fucking fucker, fuck you,
fucking fuck."

"I completely understand. Really," Cash kept saying, lifting one end of the dresser. "Can you help me with this?"

Bone took the other end, still maintaining a steady stream
of "fucks," "bastards," and wishes for Cash's and Mary's
prompt deaths and everlasting torment, following as Cash
backed through the bedroom door. Bone paused his mono-
logue when they reached the hallway, however, partly because his voice was tired, partly because the explosive rush of
angry hormones had drained from him, and partly because

maneuvering the dresser into the hallway entailed solving a riddle of applied geometry that required both his and Cash's full concentration.

They took the dresser through Bone's front door and loaded it in the back of Cash's truck. "I'll need your help over there, too," Cash said. "Climb in; we'll drive over." So Bone had to play the role not only of deceived husband but also of assistant furniture mover. The drama of his life had a small cast, and everyone had to take two parts.

★ ONE TIME ONLY ★
SPECIAL EVENT NOT TO BE MISSED:
CUCKOLD HELPS WIFE'S LOVER
MOVE DRESSER

They brought the dresser through Cash's front door and to the room corresponding to Bone's bedroom. Through the door corresponding to Bone's office door in this mirror house, Bone watched Mary watch them walk by with the dresser. She was folding her things and putting them away, just as she would have at Bone's house, and Bone imagined they were inside of one of those toys where you roll a BB through a plastic maze of hallways and little niches, and how making the BB and its target destination coincide seemed to take hours of Satori-like patience to do something not worth doing, and which the slightest jostle would undo, sending the BB caroming back to the start.

Cash's house and Bone's were palindromes, those words that spelled the same thing backward and forward.

Live on no evil.

"Wait a minute, wait a minute."

"What's wrong?"

"I can't get through the door," Bone muttered, his eyes cast down to avoid looking at his rival. With a dresser blocking the hall, there was no room for a proper square dance. Bone tried improvising a sidestep to get around it, but it was no use. Square dancing requires more than one foot of space. "You have to pull the dresser back." Cash stood perplexed, unmoving. "Pull the damn dresser back so I can square dance," Bone repeated. Cash pulled it back, and Bone completed a truncated sort of square dance, only barely getting through the door.

The room, Bone's mirror room, still had Cash's things, though these were in the process of being rearranged to make space for Mary. An electric keyboard. What was Cash doing with an electric keyboard? They pushed the dresser into position, and Cash studied the effect.

"Well, let's go back and get that loveseat."

Moving Mary's furniture, and the other items Mary had left behind, took all evening and what remained of Bone's righteous rage. He got home that night, no longer even angry, just weary: weary with moving furniture, weary with love and jealousy, weary with himself.

His bed was still pushed to the side of the room, and his

hairbrush, change box, and other things were still on the covers where Cash had put them. The little boy on the card still offered his fistful of flowers.

Bone had been through so much, and so quickly. How could things possibly be worse?

This is not a question a wise man asks.

CHAPTER SIXTEEN

P, p

From the Semitic *pe* (**7**), "mouth," a letter that must have been frequently mistaken for the third letter, *gimel* (**7**). The Greeks avoided confusion by propping up one side to make the stool-shaped *pi* (Π). The Romans transformed it to an upside-down **b** by twisting up the right leg, so now **P** stands poised on one foot, like a pensive heron at the water's edge.

paradox: A seeming self-contradiction. "If you don't get this message, call me." From the Greek *para-*, "apart from," and *doxa*, "belief."

phatic communication: Social language stripped of content, coined by Malinowski in *The Meaning of Meaning*. For example, in the exchange "How's it going?" "Great, how're you?" no information is sought or given, question and response being ritualized. So prevalent is **phatic communication** that many people, talking nearly non-stop all their lives—pausing only to chew, swallow, use the bathroom, sleep, go into comas, and die—are buried, having said almost *nothing*.

psychiatrist: From the French *psychiatrie*, first used in 1890 to replace the uneuphonious "mad doctor." Literally, "healer of the soul," from Greek *iatreia*, "heal," and *psykhe*, "soul" or "butterfly." We can see the butterfly's wings in the Greek letter *psi* (Ψ).

S unday, after Mary moved out, promising himself he wouldn't let his life sink into disorder, Bone made a pot of chili.

This was the last actual meal he prepared.

Bone spent not a second longer at Fulsome than necessary, skulking on and off campus like a trespasser. Tuesday, when he got hungry, he ate tablespoons of cold chili straight from the pot, leaving in the spoon. He left the pot, scraped clean except for a few brown smears, in the sink.

He did not sleep but on Wednesday slept late. A paradox. He fortified himself against the ordeal of Wednesday-night class—thank God, this was the final—with Kelley's Korn Flakes, a knock-off of the national brand—the box bore a cartoon rooster with the predatory beak and furrowed brow of a bald eagle—pouring cereal being the maximum effort justified by eating. A bowl joined the chili-crusted pot in the sink, both filled with water: one a translucent, milky pond and one brown.

On the way to class, Bone got a strange look from Loundsberry passing in the hallway, and Bone ducked into an empty room to avoid talking.

Coming home with the dead weight of ungraded finals in his leather case—God, but his voice had squeaked in class; what was happening to his voice?—he eliminated the step of pouring cereal into a bowl, instead stuffing fistfuls of dry flakes into his mouth, washed down with milk chugged straight from the jug; this approach, however, with all the time-saving it had to recommend it, lasted only one feeding before the cereal ran out.

The option of calling Limongello's office, Bone rejected on three counts: (1) Limongello was in Leipzig, (2) neurology offered no help in his present crisis, and (3) Bone didn't want to be *that* patient. Bone wondered, why, if life were so miserable, he didn't simply take a good stiff rope, knot one end to the chimney, the other to his neck, and jump off the roof—a thought that recurred later with a stab of regret nearly as agonizing as a broken ankle: that he hadn't exited when it would have been convenient and relatively painless—but Bone hung in there, nagged by the hope that dogs the human race: that someday, things might get *better.*

He drove to Skyland Kroger Thursday night for supplies. Cereal and milk seemed a logical and nutritious choice, as well as ground beef for more chili, and maybe some frozen dinners, bread, jelly, and peanut butter. He pictured himself striding through the checkout, shopping cart abrim with satisfying and easy-to-prepare items, feeling competent and in charge in a way that he had not since Mary left. This was the turning point for him; he sensed it.

He detached a cart from the centipede next to his parking place and, counteracting the requisite wobbly wheel always striving to veer off course, rolled up to the grocery store's bright glass maw, but when the unseeing electric eye sensed him and opened the sliding glass doors, Bone could not go in. This was not an episode of his condition; he simply couldn't bear facing the aisles ranged in columns before him, filled with blue-white fluorescence, boxes, cans, and Muzak. He pushed the cart's nose into the anus of another at the door, hoping if a cashier witnessed it, she'd assume he was returning a cart, not cravenly losing the nerve to enter. Other carts stood silhouetted in the glaring dark of the parking lot and spotlighted in fuzzy halos falling from the parking-lot lights, scattered forlornly where shoppers had abandoned them, carts that an underpaid bag boy would have to go and collect.

Goddamn. Goddamn. Goddamn.

Bone needed to get his act of kindness out of the way, per Limongello's instructions, so for twenty minutes he rounded up strays and returned them to the cart corral. The double-doc had certainly known his business, predicting the three tasks would lose their joy. But surely Limongello hadn't foreseen *this*? How long since Bone had performed his morning ritual? In the car he clapped his hands, saying, "This is a good day." But he only felt worse. Since he was avoiding people, paying his daily compliments would also be a challenge. He'd get back on his regimen, but in the meantime, he didn't have the intestinal fortitude to face the inside of the Kroger, so *this time* instead of grocery shopping—the adverbial "this time" a necessary rationalization, implying a *next time* that would be not only successful but effortless—he got a three-piece from the Kentucky Fried Chicken drive-through and ate in the car, tipping the Styrofoam cup of coleslaw into his mouth at the red light instead of using the spork in order to keep one hand on the wheel. He left the KFC bag with its greasy paper napkin and sucked-clean chicken bones in the car, taking only the enormous plastic drink cup. (Drink *pail* would have been more apt than *cup*, given its bladder-busting volume.) He'd finished it, but the ice, still having Pepsi residue, would provide further, if diluted, refreshment once melted. Besides, why waste a perfectly serviceable cup with many useful days before it?

Friday, he ran down the mailman, waving his arms and calling, "Wait! Wait!" because he'd missed him when the truck had come to the box. The mailman, who anticipated an envelope of suspected anthrax or at the very least an urgent package to mail, was taken aback when he learned all Bone wanted to say was "Thanks for the great job. I really appreciate the way you bring mail the same time every day."

God, what was wrong with Bone's voice? What a strange, rusty squeak!

After the mailman fiasco, Bone hit on a way to follow through on Limongello's regimen without the unpleasantness of dealing with actual people. Every day, he'd write a letter to a person he had reason to be grateful to; this way he could simultaneously take care of tasks two and three.

Hunger struck at odd hours, and sleep lost correspondence to sunrise and -set. He ate three meals in a row—going to Taco Bell as soon as he finished his KFC three-piece, and thence to Krystal, the last bite of burrito grande still in his mouth; paper bags, napkins, sporks, unused ketchup and hot-sauce packets, and fast-food receipts mounded on the passenger-side floorboard. He slept fourteen hours in a row, then stayed up 'til dawn, watching Spanish-language soap operas and infomercials on amassing real estate fortunes and direct-marketing household cleaners and pure positive thinking. He cast a queasy eye on the students' finals, piled on his sofa. He finally gave everyone an A without checking them and was done with it. He'd go back to being a real teacher next semester.

Saturday.

Bone made up his mind with an I'll-show-them intensity to throw himself into *Words*; fanning up fresh hatred for Knolton's skullduggery would banish the drabness and flabbiness of life without Mary. Even if Grisamore didn't want the manuscript, so what? Someone was bound to want it. Besides, he needed to complete it for his dissertation. He worked into the afternoon, amending the introduction for a book that might never be published, until he became uncomfortably aware that he needed to use the bathroom. Predictably, the office door blocked him. His condition always struck when getting through was especially urgent. Impatiently—his bowels were insistent—he began square dancing, skipping the formality of bowing to his partner and his side and the preliminary do-si-do, starting with a brusque promenade, and unwisely, in spite of Limongello's advice against thinking too much, permitting himself a moment of self-consciousness: This is the way I get through doors.

The door wasn't having it; Bone could not get through.

He tried again. Surely, this time would work.

Damn.

No time for a third try: he had to go *now*. For a makeshift toilet, he dumped out a box of paper, turning and squatting just in time. Disgust, shame, and relief—plus a little gratification at his quick thinking—mingled in him, but now that the crisis had been dealt with, he shouldn't have any trouble getting through; it was only needing to go so badly that'd stymied him in the first place. Printer paper was not as soft or absorbent as the two-ply in the bathroom but was good enough under the circumstances. He put a lid on the box and gently pushed it into the hallway with his toe. Once he got through the door, he could dispose of it.

He square danced again, this time going through all the careful preambles of bowing to his partner, bowing to his side. It was a square dance without brio, however, a pensive and a meditative square dance, the square dance of a man concerned with getting things right. Dancing and stamping contemplatively, he thought of Mary's words: "They never liked you." Why did he think of that now? It turned into the caller's singsong, chanted to fiddles and clapping: "They never liked you. They never liked you."

He came to the door and again couldn't get through. Damn.

He stood nonplussed, and then a solution hit him, so simple it was surprising the Wonderful Double-Doc Lemon Jell-O hadn't thought of himself. He couldn't walk through, but surely he'd be able to crawl. He'd attend to the box of feces once on the other side; then he could get back to work. He shook his head. The things he went through, coping with his absurd condition. He got on hands and knees to crawl out, but when he got to the door, he froze.

Well, what do you know about that?

He stood. Now, this was definitely inconvenient. Okay, but

no big deal. He'd write a little longer and try again. The condition was sure to abate on its own if he ignored it.

He sat, fingers poised at his computer, but didn't touch the keys. At his wrist was a letter he'd written and addressed but not yet stamped. Care of the Cook County Library, it was written to Laurence Hobbs, the librarian, letting him know how the interest once shown in a hayseed bookworm had changed Bone's life, and how grateful Bone was. Was the condition striking because Bone had been remiss in fulfilling the three tasks? But he'd *intended* to mail it, and look at all the trouble he'd already gone to to Google the address, taking his laptop into the bedroom to hook up the cable. (Bone deliberately denied himself an Internet connection in the office to prevent cyberspace-lollygagging.)

What was the point of working on his manuscript? Outside the window, a bird angled down through the oaks and disappeared into the Rose of Sharon. *Words* would never be published, not with Bone's name on it. How could Grisamore turn to Knolton, that quack? Because Bone hadn't met the deadline, that's how. He had only himself to blame.

Without warning Bone's pulse beat with longing for Mary. It wasn't making love he thought of, or her beauty, or even her companionship; it was the way she drank water. That long, uninterrupted swallow, plonking down the empty glass with a gasp, devoting herself to the experience of an ordinary glass of water even to the exclusion of *breathing*. That fact seemed wonderful to Bone, but maybe part of the reason it seemed so was that he was starting to feel pretty thirsty himself.

When you got down to it, all Bone's separate problems—his syndrome, his unfinished dissertation, losing his publishing contract, losing Mary—his flubs, failures, and false starts—the Yin and Yang of his life, mostly Yin—were all aspects of one big problem: not following through. The cardboard box, sitting and reeking and possibly seeping on the other side of the door, was a metaphor; he let things slide, hence they got worse. But no more. This was it. He'd make changes starting here and now. It wasn't the end of the world. Mary didn't love him. She never had. Sure, it hurt like blisters, but he was better off. He'd show her—if he'd looked in the mirror just then, he'd have seen his chin thrust forward in determination. Meanwhile, he had his manuscript. He'd finish it and have his PhD. He'd find another publisher. Hell, resubmit it to Grisamore. Why not? Grisamore would be sure to want it once he saw how well it'd turned out. Bone was taking charge of his life again. He pressed the save button, went back to the top of the page, and reread his introduction.

He had a bit more water tinged with brown cola in the plastic cup at his elbow, and he drank it. Now another way out occurred to him. If he sat on the floor in front of the threshold, facing into the room, and allowed himself to fall backward, his upper torso would land in the hallway, and surely once his top half crossed the boundary, the rest of him wouldn't offer any trouble. He imagined witnessing the plan in action as if he were a video camera mounted on the ceiling, pleased at the prospect of elegant success, the satisfaction the Coyote must've felt studying the dotted line on a blueprint, charting a dislodged boulder's trajectory to the X-marked intersection with the Roadrunner.

Bone sat on the floor, hands on his knees, scooting his butt across the hardwood until his back was to the threshold. Man, that box really stank. He'd gotten used to it, but this close it was something awful. How had it come to this? A car filling with fast-food receipts and containers, a house filling with plastic cups, dishes sitting a week without washing, and feces in a cardboard box. He released his knees and let himself fall back.

Only he didn't fall.

Now, this was too much. He pushed on his knees to make himself fall, but it did no good. Was something wrong with his plan? He turned the other way, facing the door now, to see if he could fall in the other direction. He let go of his knees and fell with marvelous success, banging his head on the open drawer of a filing cabinet he'd forgotten to allow for.

Leaving the office began to assume the dimensions of Job One. Not that it was a crisis; he'd definitely be out before matters progressed as far as that, but his manuscript could wait until he reached the other side of that door.

His faux-leather rolling office chair presented itself as the next obvious solution. It wouldn't fit through the door, but when it jolted to a standstill at the frame, the momentum ought to eject him into the hallway. Starting at the desk to build up speed, he launched toward the door. Unfortunately, the manufacturers of rolling office chairs, not considering them transportation devices, don't design them for building up speed. The instant Bone pushed off, the chair lost momentum. It stopped a little past the starting line.

Trying to maintain velocity by giving additional pushes with his feet did as much to retard his progress as improve it; moreover, as he discovered, rolling chairs are designed with as little thought to maneuverability as to speed, at least with distances greater than scooting up to or away from a reasonably nearby workspace. Whereas a conventional grocery cart comes equipped with a single rogue wheel with its own notion of where the cart should go, his rolling office chair had five such wheels, each as independent as a hog on ice, and even then a hog of an infuriatingly distractible and inconsistent disposition, a hog greatly in need of a good dose of Ritalin.

On the third attempt, Bone smashed his hand between the wall and the arm of the chair. Naturally, it was the same hand he'd pierced on Cash's chain-link fence. If he had a broomstick, he could use it as a pole to propel himself, but then, as he considered it, the rolling-chair concept was doomed to failure. Even at maximum rolling-chair speed, he'd never attain enough velocity to overcome the friction of the faux-leather cushion and slide into the hallway. No, he'd have to come up with another method.

CHAPTER SEVENTEEN

Q, q

From the Semitic *qoph* (𝚽), "monkey." The monkey's tail curves like a contented cat's in the uppercase and in the lowercase hangs as if a lead weight were tied to it. Of all the ideographs in the Semitic alphabet—the oxen, pegs, houses, doors, weapons, eyes, hands, and mouths—only little *qoph* refers to nothing of practical value, except the delight we have always taken from our funny little cousins and the pleasure of an ancient scribe discovering that with one elegant downstroke, he could signify tail as well as butt cheeks.

quack: Onomatopoeia for a duck call, also any irritating noise. A healer who boasted or **quacked** about his salves was called a *quack-salver* (a pun on quicksilver, mercury being a common ingredient for medieval medicines?), hence **quack** as a term for a bogus physician.

Bone awoke, cottonmouthed and headachy; it had been late afternoon, and now it was night. He needed to leave the room now, and no more fooling around. He arose and square danced, once, twice, three times for good measure. Each attempt as useless as the one before. He tried crawling on all fours and on his belly. He tried sitting on the floor and falling backward again. Somersault. No luck. He did not resort to rolling the chair again.

Naturally, the one thing he needed, an office phone so he could call somebody, he didn't have. His cell phone was in another room. He cussed his perverse obstinacy in not permitting Internet in the office. What he'd have given to tap out a quick "Help, Get Me out of the Office" e-mail. To whom would he have sent it, and what would they have made of it? Would the recipient of a message like "This is very embarrassing, but I'm trapped in my office. Please come at once to release me" have thought it a new identity-theft scheme, like the e-mail saying a friend is marooned in Zimbabwe and needs a moneygram? No matter. These questions were moot.

His head hurt too much to go back to sleep. He was very thirsty now. Remembering a trick from his Tennessee childhood of sucking something to work up spit, he put a pen cap in his mouth and, sure enough, got some relief.

Might as well work on his manuscript and try again later. He couldn't manage to write anything new, so he made do with revising, adding a phrase, taking out the same phrase, polishing and unpolishing the same few lines and getting nowhere until sunrise.

The neighbors would be up now. He made another futile attempt to square dance through, then cranked open the window and shouted, "Help!" And again, louder, "Help!"

They never liked you.

They wouldn't be able to hear him, he decided.

"Well, I'll just have to go through the window," he said, rolling up the shirtsleeves of his imagination.

"If you use something as a means of exit, that makes it a door," he imagined E. Knolton's mellow accent interjecting, "and, as we know, you can't go through doors."

"Shut up," Bone retorted. "A thing doesn't change identity

just because we use it for a different purpose. If you wear a frying pan on your head, it doesn't make it a hat. And anyway, you're just imaginary."

"Touché," he imagined Miranda Richter chiming in supportively. "*Illegitimi non carborundum.*"

"Thank you," Bone said. "You're the one I should have married." Bone's knee was on his desk, and with a final push up, he was standing. The office windows were high jalousies, and even cranked out to their fullest extent offered little room for a full-grown man to squeeze through. "I can't go straight out," Bone pondered aloud. "The best way to do it, I reckon, is lie on my back and go feet first, so I can bend my knees. Once I'm to my waist, I can wriggle around onto my stomach, lower myself as far as I can, then drop into the holly bushes." Bone studied the sill, the distance to the ground, and the holly bushes below, estimating the cost of his escapade in cuts, scrapes, abrasions, and bruises. Outside, the air darkened, and the Rose of Sharon leaves shivered and turned in the wind of an approaching storm. He moved his pen holder to the edge of the desk, as well as his computer, several spiral-bound notebooks, and an unabridged *Devil's Dictionary* that Mary had given him during their courtship. He opened it and looked on the inside cover.

To the man in love with words, Love Mary.

"Here's an interesting word," he said, like a man abruptly changing the subject of conversation. "'Defenestrate.'" He put the dictionary beside the unmailed letter. "Throwing something out of a window, from the Latin, *fenestria*, 'window.' I will now defenestrate myself." He lay on his back and pushed his feet toward the open window.

His feet would not move.

For the first time, something like genuine panic flared in Bone's stomach. Goddamn it, why did it have to occur to him that windows are just another type of door? Goddamn Knolton anyway; the man was a menace even in the imaginary state.

He climbed off the desk. Now he was really in a fix. Soberly, but knees trembling, he did one last square dance, bowing, do-si-doing, and attempting to promenade through the door. It didn't work. He knew it wouldn't work. He couldn't go through the door, and he couldn't get through the window. What other way out was there, unless …

He climbed back on the desk and with his good pair of red-handled scissors jabbed the ceiling, gratified and horrified by how easily they punched through. "This is silly," he told himself. "I'm really overreacting. I'm sure I could have gone through the door on my own if I'd just waited a little longer." Nevertheless, he kept jabbing, hot attic air brushing his face as a black wedge took shape in the white ceiling. Presently he was reaching through the smooth white ceiling to pull down a hunk of Sheetrock, at which a confetti of shredded-paper insulation, dust, and no doubt rat turds fell into his eyes. Outside, wind whirled and whipped the Rose of Sharon in the approaching thunderstorm, and a serrated leaf ripped from its branch, pressed briefly to the windowpane, and passed on, while on this side of the window, Bone's heel, unaware, stepped on the letter he meant to mail and knocked the dictionary Mary had given him to the floor.

He looked down, wiping his face against his arm, batting his eyes. He reached up to pull down more Sheetrock, keeping his eyes closed this time against the rain of debris.

After blowing grit and grime from his nose and picking it from his eyelids, he studied his handiwork: an irregular starburst hole of jags and obtuse angles and a corresponding heap of Sheetrock on the desk. Someone's going to have a time cleaning this up, he thought, and vaguely guesstimated the cost of repair, but the headache blossoming behind his eyebrows slowed its growth just a little bit. Above the Sheetrock, a yellow joist rose in the attic darkness, illuminated like a moon crater's inner wall.

Now for the acid test: "A ceiling hole is really just another kind of d—" Knolton's imaginary voice began, but Bone silenced it by grabbing the joist—standing on his desk, he didn't need to jump to get his hands over it—and, in spite of his sore palm, chinned into the dark attic heat, choked on his pen cap, and lowered to spit it out before lifting himself again.

He saw little but his head's shadow floating on swirling dust, but he hung a few moments, savoring his first success after a long drought of failure before lowering himself to the desk. So much for Knolton. A ceiling hole was clearly a different matter than a door. Still, it needed to be a good bit bigger if he intended to pull himself through, so he set to work with gusto until a hole, Tennessee-shaped and man-hole-wide, exposed two joists. It would still take some doing to wriggle through; the joists were only about a foot and a half apart, but Bone figured he could do it.

He did another chin-up and realized he couldn't.

It wasn't that the joists were too close together; they were fine, nor was it another bout with his condition—*that* had elected to exclude ceiling holes from its jurisdiction—it was that he'd knocked out the hole too close to the side of the house. The roofline here was so low, he could lift his head no more above than nose-level to the joist. If he'd chinned-up higher on his first reconnoiter, he'd have bumped his head and spotted his mistake before going any further. As it was, he'd made an unnecessary mess, not to mention wasting time and energy and working up an even greater thirst—he was terrifically thirsty, he realized—for nothing.

And nothing now remained to do but to begin the game anew.

He dragged the desk to the center of the room—God, but it was heavy—stood on it, and gave the ceiling three jabs. It turned out that scissors are not meant to be gripped by the blade when used to pierce Sheetrock, and he managed to give himself a nice gash on the hand. Was there a risk of tetanus? When was his last shot? God knows, with all the crap falling from the ceiling, he was liable to catch measles, mumps, and rabies with shingles and scurvy tossed in for good measure. He tenderly wiped his hand on his pants and studied the wound running along his lifeline from his pinky to his ring finger, wondering how deep it was and wishing he had some water to wash it. It would probably need stitches, he decided. Damn, yet another thing to deal with if he ever got out of this room.

When he got out of this room, he amended.

Removing his shirt to bind his wound seemed melodramatic, but this was precisely what he did, figuring better melodramatic than sorry and feeling absurdly macho, covered with grime, bare-chested, his shirt wrapped tightly around his hand.

It was harder and less effective jabbing the ceiling with his left hand, but he succeeded in starting a decent hole as well as gashing *that* hand, but not as seriously. His shoulders ached from reaching overhead, so he stopped and rested often, dropping his arms by his sides to shake the soreness out and get the blood circulating. His right hand throbbed no matter what position he held it in, distracting him so badly that not only did he forget to close his eyes against the rain of debris when he tore free the Sheetrock, but he allowed his jaw to hang slack, getting a good mouthful of dust and insulation into the bargain. He picked pieces and tatters from his teeth and dug a plug of dust from between his cheek and gum, but without water to rinse, the chalky Sheetrock taste stayed in his mouth.

Outside, the swaying trees brightened in a flash of lightning. Maybe he should give another try at shouting at the neighbors from the window. No, the die was cast; he'd already made a hole in the ceiling and a wreck of his office.

Besides, he'd sufficiently demonstrated that the neighbors weren't close enough to hear him. They'd never liked him, Mary said. But she'd also written, "To the man in love with words, Love Mary."

At last the new hole was big enough, and he grabbed the joist, chinning himself up. It was much harder than before. He'd used up a lot of energy and couldn't bear to put too much weight on his right hand, which was wrapped in a tee shirt with a crimson chevron of a bloodstain.

There was more overhead clearance in this section of the attic, but not much, and the roof beam scraped Bone's bare back as he tugged himself into the heat and darkness. With a sudden move that shot pain from his hand all the way up his spine, he released the joist and grabbed for the next one over. He lay for a time unable to summon the will to move, the joist pressing his rib cage, the migratory pain from his hand tingling in his forearm. Then, more slowly, he grabbed the joist with his other hand and hauled himself the rest of the way up.

He rose tottering on all fours. The narrow joists gouged his knees and made the wound on his hand sing. He rested on his forearms to take the weight off his injured hand. He had made it. It was going to be okay. Two glowing holes in the ceiling below lit the interstitial triangles of support beams, and the narrow seams of light outlined the rectangle of the attic door; silhouettes of Christmas-ornament boxes, boxes of old clothes—his past with Mary—ranged themselves around him, and not only those but also leave-behinds of the family before them: shoe boxes and baby toys, fossilized under decades of attic dust. He crawled to the attic door, squeezing between support beams, ignoring the clamoring pain in his hand and head. Then he was on the rough floor planking in the center of the attic, and though he still couldn't stand straight, he could walk in a crouch, and what a relief to get off his poor hands and knees!

The air was heavy with dust and the attic insufferably hot, but he did not perspire. Almost there. He pushed down on the attic door, but powerful springs held it closed. It would need his full weight to open.

"How do you expect to get through?" Knolton's voice asked. "The attic door is still a door after all."

"It's really more of a ladder," Miranda Richter's voice amended. "In any case, all he has to do is put his weight on it, and gravity will take care of the rest. It'll open by itself, and he'll just drop to the ground."

Bone could imagine Knolton wondering, but not mentioning, what would happen when the attic door opened. If the metal ladder unfolded, as it seemed certain to do, where would Bone end up? At what angle would he hit? Could he control his fall? The prospect of ricocheting against a wall or getting painfully tangled in a collapsible stair was not a pleasant one, but in for a penny, in for a pound was Bone's motto by this point. He took hold of the ladder as tightly as he could bear, grimacing at the pain from his hand—the bloody stain on the tee shirt had stopped growing, at least—but he hesitated before bringing his knees onto the attic door.

"Toodle-oo," Miranda Richter suggested helpfully.

Bone brought both knees up, and instantly the door swung down out of the darkness into the lit hallway below. "Wait!" he shouted. The ladder extended, unfolding, knocking Bone's skull against the frame, and stopped. "Wait!"

Iron bands clamped his head. He strained the nape of his neck against the frame, holding himself in place, trembling at the effort. What a hideous blunder he'd nearly made: wasting all this work escaping the trap of his office only to drop himself into the trap of the hallway, where his exit would be barred by not one but five taunting doors. His head slipped from the frame, and he went down. The ladder did not unfold the rest of the way, thank God, and Bone perched and panted.

"You need to get back up that ladder," Knolton pointed out unnecessarily.

Bone scrabbled up, holding his body low against the ladder to keep it from unfolding.

Back in the attic's safety, he crouched and panted until his trembling subsided. No harm done. He'd just keep going toward the back of the attic until he was safely over the living room, break through the ceiling there, and go down. No need to turn on the attic light; it was bright enough to see where he was going without it. The rough plank floor of the attic gave out after a little distance, and he crawled on knees and wrists—it hurt less than resting his hands on the joists. Above him the roof tapped and pattered in the falling rain. Then, contrary to expectations, he discovered that the light penetrated the opaque attic air only a little way after all, and he passed into darkness as if going through a curtain. His hand was throbbing less, though, or at least he no longer noticed it as much. His head, on the other hand, felt like something was crushing it. And his throat…

To the man in love with words, Love Mary.

Perhaps the "Love" was neither the object of a preposition—"(with) Love, Mary"—nor a present indicative verb "(I) Love (you), Mary" but a command, or at least a recommendation, offered to a man who'd unwisely given his heart to words: "Love Mary."

Far enough. He must be clear of the hallway by now. Probably over the living room. He balanced himself on the joists. With his less-injured hand, he pressed against the Sheetrock through the fluff of dust and insulation. It was going to be harder breaking through than he'd anticipated. If only he'd thought to bring his scissors. He definitely wasn't going back for them. He pawed back the insulation until his palm pressed smooth Sheetrock. He pushed down. No good.

"You're going to have to put your weight on it," Miranda said.

Sitting on one joist and bent forward to brace his hands against another, Bone put his feet on the Sheetrock, powdery insulation almost up to his ankles. He tentatively lifted his butt, and at once there was a hollow tearing sound and the Sheetrock gave way. His butt hit the joist before he went through. Powder floated in the air, and he gave a dry, useless sneeze. Leg hairs cast shadows up his white calves. The hole wasn't big, but he could see a corner of the rug that lay in front of the sofa, and there, unless he mistook, was a bit of the dining table. He was above the living room.

The jagged Sheetrock reminded him of broken ice over a pond, and for a moment Bone imagined it actually was ice, that the builders had prudently constructed the ceiling from a special ice that didn't melt at room temperature but would dissolve in the mouth. He instantly pulled himself back from the brink of this dangerous fantasy. He wasn't that far gone. Soon he'd be drinking a glassful of actual water from the sink. He'd drink the first two glasses, he promised himself, with no ice at all, and then the third and fourth glasses he'd put ice in. Then he'd reward himself each day for the rest of his life by driving to the Quik-Trip and buying himself a giant cherry slushy.

Maybe he'd have the first three glasses without ice.

He lowered himself through the ceiling, holding onto the joist, the Sheetrock cracking and falling as he pushed through, slowing his descent. While his elbows were still bent at ninety degrees, his feet touched something solid. He was standing on the edge of the dining table.

Bone let go and, in that speeded-up thinking you get in a crisis, realized a nanosecond too late that the table's edge was not the sturdiest possible place to rest his weight. The commotion that followed came in a flurry of sensations: first his feet were touching the heavy oak table, then the table was under his arm, then he was on the floor, the table on top of him. All of this accompanied by the loudest possible knocks and bangs.

Then it was over.

There wasn't even an echo in the stillness. Added to the crushing feeling in his skull and the all-but-forgotten throb in his hand was a magnificent shooting pain in his ankle. Blue and red spots flashed in his vision.

"I will have broken my ankle," he told Miranda and Knolton, employing the little-used future perfect tense to indicate that in the fullness of time, it would be *discovered* that he had done so.

Bone rolled the table off his legs and turned sideways so his broken ankle rested on top of his good one. He allowed himself—and instantly regretted—one look back to check if it could possibly have swollen as elephantine as it felt, as if it were ripping open the shoe from the inside. A white cotton sock bloated over the canvas rim of the tennis shoe like a muffin, but the thought of gripping the heel and pulling off the shoe made everything go swimmy.

Bone shut his eyes against the sight and began crawling to the—

And this was when he wasted a perfectly good bellow on his own misery.

Door.

CHAPTER EIGHTEEN

R, r

From the Semitic *resh* (◀), "head." The Greek *rho* faced the opposite direction. The Romans added a leaning-post under the nose to prevent confusion with **P**. In the lower-case **R**, the entire bottom half of the face is amputated: **r**.

rage: Fury to the point of madness, from the Latin *rabere*, hence **rave** and **rabid**.

real: Almost incredibly, this monosyllable is a compound. From the Latin *re* "thing" and *-al* "real." **Real** is not **real** by itself. It must be a **real** *thing*.

redundant: Needless repetition, as in "extreme emergency" or "final outcome." It would be as **redundant** listing redundancies here as listing clichés under the heading "cliché" would be cliché. From the Latin *redundans*, "overflow," the *unda* meaning "water in motion, wave," whence **inundation**, **undulate**, and **surround**.

regret: Anguish over the past, from *re* (again) and the Old Norse *grata*, "to moan or sob" from the Proto Indo-European *gher*, a root with a wide range of meanings from "bellow" to "scrape or scratch."

rescue: To deliver from confinement or danger. From the Latin *ex* (out) and *cutere* (to shake), i.e. , "shake free of chains"?

He had done it again. He had done it again. He-haddoneitdoneitdoneitagain.

He had managed to land in the *one place* besides his office or the hallway that did him no good whatsoever. If he'd come down in the kitchen or the bathroom, there would have been water. Even if he'd let himself down in the bedroom, there would have been a phone to dial 911. But here he was in the living room, with nothing to drink and every faucet, every spigot, every drop and gallon on the other side of a mocking threshold.

He did not look back but slithered resolutely to the door.

Surely his condition could not block him now.

It could.

It did.

There were two entrances to the kitchen from the living room; he dragged himself around and tried the other. No good. He tried the back door and found the deadbolt bolted. Goody. And of course he didn't have a key, so even if he *could* have opened it, he still couldn't.

Okay. Nothing to do but go back up through the ceiling. He had to get up on something, broken ankle or no, and lift himself through. Outside the picture window, the criminal rain tormented the dogwood and pummeled the knockout roses. Strangely, the broken bone was not as painful as his headache. Or his thirst. His tongue glued to the roof of his mouth. He tried swallowing but could work up no saliva.

He dragged himself to the couch and took a cushion.

"What are you going to do with that?" he imagined Knolton asking incredulously.

"You'll see," he replied. He unzipped the cover and pulled out the stuffing. Tearing the cover was harder than expected, but once a rip started, it gave way easily until that last stubborn shred that just didn't want to separate. But with the application of additional grunting and groaning, that tore too, and Bone had two strips of cloth.

"You're making a splint, aren't you? But what are you going to use for a brace?"

"You'll see." He wormed over to one of the ladder-back chairs he'd knocked down when he'd fallen from the ceiling.

"You'll never be able to break that, you know," Knolton said.

"Who said anything about breaking it?" Sitting beside the chair, he began strapping a wooden leg to his leg. He pulled the cloth as tight as he could bear, but it loosened before he knotted it, and he had to sit for a while, hands resting on the floor behind him, waiting out a dizzy spell before trying again. "Please, God. This had better work."

There's a saying that there are no atheists in foxholes. Other places without atheists include ordinary living rooms where someone is dying of thirst. If he ever got out, Bone swore the first thing he'd do was mail that damn letter to Laurence. Beyond the picture window, the backyard sloped. Angled trees grew in strange geometries in the roiling rain. Having tied the chair leg to his calf and thigh, Bone realized the tall ladder-back still wouldn't be stable enough. It was awkward crawling with a chair tied to his leg, so he undid his straps. He laid these across his neck, then crawled, dragged the chair after him, crawled, dragged the chair, crawled—astonishing the distance between table and couch when measured out this way—dragged the chair, until he was close enough to the couch again to pull off the other cushion. He unzipped the cover and removed it, but for some reason the upholstery proved even sturdier than before. He tugged and yanked, gritting his teeth in a rictus of effort, but a rip refused to start.

"The strange thing is," the Knolton in his mind commented, "you're not sweating. All this effort and the pain from your broken leg, and you're not sweating a drop."

Bone knew why he wasn't sweating but tried not to think about it. With one more Herculean pull, a rip began, and he tore the cover down the middle. He could not tear it completely in two, but he didn't need to. Now came the time to stand on his own two feet. His own two feet plus the chair's four.

He pushed up from the sofa, keeping the weight off his broken foot, until he was able to sit. Cinching it as tightly as he could, he tied his chair-splint to his leg, starting midway between his knee and his ankle, the second tie just above his knee, and the last between the first two rails of the ladder-back at his waist. He rose, pushing himself up against the arm of the couch, pulling his makeshift splint after him. Even through the headache clamping his skull, there was a smack of triumph at how well the arrangement worked—still some Yang in the Yin, no matter what. The ladder-back served admirably not only as splint but as crutch and walker, too. By resting his weight on it, Bone took almost all the pressure from his bad leg, which was turning numb, and with its four legs, the chair was supremely steadying.

With his good leg, he nudged the coffee table to the ceiling hole and, after considering alternative ways to get up, undid his splint and knelt on the table with the knee of his bad leg, pushing himself up on his good foot. After a monstrous expense of pain and effort, he discovered he was too low; standing tottering on one leg, he could barely touch the hole's rim. He'd never be able to get his hands over the joist.

Lowering to his starting position, he lost his balance and put his weight on his broken ankle. His scream was so loud he was sure the neighbors would hear him after all and come to investigate. He waited, panting, in front of the shimmering couch for someone to knock. He passed out for a little and in his imagination heard someone ring the doorbell and call his name.

When he came to, the post-rain world was silver and glass. He heard the telephone ring and then Mary's voice saying to pick up. Yes, he needed to pick up.

How much time had passed? A blue puddle on the hill mirrored the sky above the dripping trees. "Get me a glass of that," he asked Miranda.

"What is that ticking sound?" Miranda asked. "Do you hear it? Something soft and ticking?"

"Good Lord," said Knolton, "it's his tongue! He's so dried out, his tongue is tapping against his teeth like a stick!"

Meanwhile, he had to make another effort.

The upended table waved and rippled behind blue and red flashes like a reflection in a puddle. Bracing against the tabletop, he bent until his hands were under the rim, then, supporting himself on his right foot and putting as much weight on his left as he could bear, he began to lift. His arms were too sore and shaking to budge it. Why had he wanted to lift it? To get to the ceiling. In any case, he didn't have the strength or willpower to try standing.

"Listen!" Miranda said. "There's someone in the room with us."

A bellow, a strange hoarse noise, so unexpected that at first no one in the room knew where it came from.

"Who is it?" Knolton asked.

Another weird bellow, and Miranda said, "It's Bone."

Bone did not blame them for their confusion; had it not been for his chest's soreness after making it, he might have thought the bellow belonged to someone else, too.

Bone could see perfectly through the dancing lights too, the white ceiling, gaping at him where he'd fallen through. The ceiling was made of special ice, he remembered, and he regretted not having a chip of it to suck on. But there were also water pipes under the floor. He bellowed again. The dryness had a voice of its own. He told it to be quiet so he could locate the rushing water under the floor.

CHAPTER NINETEEN

S, s

From the Semitic *shin* ( ), "tooth," the original letter looking a good deal more fang-like than its modern incarnation. The Greek *sigma* (Σ) was a sideways *shin*, but the earliest incarnation was a backward **Z**. The Romans gave us our current **S**, perhaps because the serpentine shape matched **S**'s hisses and fizzes better than the jagged incisors of the original *shin*. S is the only letter to become a US president: the **S** in Harry S Truman does not stand for anything; his middle name is only an initial.

space: The interval between things. (See **time**.)

spork: An appropriate portmanteau of **spoon** and **fork** for an object that itself is a portmanteau. Hearing the word for the first time, one knows precisely what it will be, and that it will be made of white plastic.

Bone dreamed of lifting hands, straps across his chest, sirens, a straw in his mouth, sips of water. In his dream, alternating dark and bright rooms moved above him, and between rooms, wheels squeaked below him like a grocery cart. There were no voices, but he knew things were being done for him and that he was being discussed by concerned people.

He did not wake up but slipped smoothly from the stiff, clean sheets of a dream bed into an actual bed with stiff, clean sheets at Northside Hospital.

"Would you like an ice chip?" a woman asked.

Bone nodded. Yes, an ice chip would be lovely.

The nurse tucked an ice chip between his lips, fluorescent light gleaming on the silver cross lying nearly horizontal on her bosom, and Bone sucked: a superlative ice chip, possibly the best ice chip Bone had ever had in his life.

"My name is Rachel," the nurse said. Her vivid lipstick contrasted with her skin like ketchup on a white plate. "Do you have any pain?"

Bone shook his head. No, no pain. But then he changed his mind and nodded, yes, there was some pain after all.

Rachel held up a chart of cartoon faces progressing from a smiley face on the left to a face with a deep frown and rolling tears on the right. "Can you point to which one you are?"

Bone nearly pointed to the middle, neutral face with its perfect straight-line mouth but then pointed to the second face from the right, next to the crying face that represented the most intense pain of all. His ankle and hand throbbed, now that he thought of it, and his head hurt like someone had jammed a bucket of rocks into his skull. The hand he pointed with was wrapped in gauze.

"They set your bone," Rachel said. "Fractured ankle. And they sewed up your hand. Four stitches. You are one lucky camper. Can you do some talking for me?"

"Yes," Bone said, and at first didn't recognize his own voice, so thin and weak it was.

The sheet exposed his right foot, which was in a cast. A plastic tube led from his arm to a bag hanging on a metal pole. A tube from his other arm led to a hollow plastic socket. A watercolor of a stone cottage and vague red flowers hung next to a door helpfully left ajar to disclose a bathroom. The other wall was a curtain. Bone twisted his neck and saw that the headrest of his bed was a regular cockpit of dials and nozzles.

"I wish we could give you more for the pain," Rachel said, "but there's only so much we can shoot you up with until you get your fluids back. I'll go tell the doctor you're up. Do you want another ice chip?"

A long while later, or else a very short while—hard to tell—Mary came.

"Hi," she said. She stood in the door, wearing a smile where the teeth come into play but the eyes have no part. For a moment, Bone feared she was less beautiful than he'd remembered, or even that he was not grateful to see her—but this doubt lasted only the space between one quavering breath and the next. She gave Bone's forehead a sisterly kiss. "You really had me worried."

"I had me worried, too," Bone admitted.

Before she could stop herself, her jaw dropped in shock at his weak and squeaky voice. Recovering, she held up a canvas tote. "I brought you some things." Announcing each treasure with a drawn-out "*aaand*," she arranged the contents on his bedcover, half in the shadow cast by his right leg's mountain range: pens, pads, Post-Its, and the final gift, his annotated copy of Fowler, which Bone picked up but set down at once to subdue his foolish hand's thankful trembling.

"Someone got new play-pretties," Rachel said, coming into the room. "Time to take your blood, honey. You don't got much to spare, but them vampires downstairs don't live on potato chips, you know." She pushed a purple-capped tube into the socket, and blood burbled into it. "Who's your friend?" When Rachel had filled the tube without getting a reply, she said, "Looks like someone's got a secret." She gave Bone a hard glance. "I don't mind secrets, but she could at least bring you something more interesting than—" She tilted her nose at the books and papers in his lap. "What, Mommy's making sure you do your homework? Next time bring him something worth getting, or sneak in a corned-beef sandwich or something, something I'd have to take away from him." Rachel filled two more tubes and put them on her tray. "They'll be testing your sugars and whatnot, see how your levels are coming, and Dr. Quick will check on you. She's not as big a dumbass as some of the others, but if she don't show up pretty soon, you let me know, and I'll light a fire under her."

A woman in the doorway said, "So I'm not a dumbass. Thanks."

"I said not as much as the others," Rachel corrected, giving Bone a quick, unsmiling wink before exiting with her blood samples: an exchange intended for his therapeutic entertainment—the hardworking, tough-talking but kindhearted doctor and her sassy, no-nonsense nurse swapping one-liners and comebacks like a medical sitcom, guest starring Bone himself as the quirky patient with a strange diagnosis.

Dr. Quick looked over notes on a blue clipboard and gave Bone the rundown: that dying of thirst was no joke, that his hand had been stitched and didn't show any sign of infection, that he had a lateral malleolus fracture—there is no ankle bone, per se, any more than there is an Eskimo language—that would take ten to twelve weeks to heal, that they were monitoring his electrolytes as he rehydrated, and that they needed to rule out kidney damage. Bone listened, giddy to have landed in this lemony-smelling hospital with its nice, bright sheets and blue bowls of ice chips, the weight of books between his legs, Mary at his bedside, listening to a trained medical professional whose only job was to help him get well.

"So what I want to know is what happened? What'd you do?"

"Attic," Bone replied in his strange weak voice. "Fell through."

"And after that—you couldn't move?"

"Doors. I can't."

Dr. Quick cocked an eyebrow.

"He's got a neurological condition," Mary supplied. "Sometimes when he comes to a door, he can't go through."

Taking frequent breaks to gather breath, Bone related his strange saga, and where he left off Mary picked up, supplying a scrap or two to round out the epilogue. It was she who'd discovered him.

"Good Lord," Dr. Quick said. "No one was around?" She looked at Mary, who looked down at the annotated Fowler. "Have you seen someone about this?"

Mary said, "Dr. Limongello."

"Oh. Well, he's wonderful," Dr. Quick admitted. "He has you on dopamine?"

"There's no medication," Mary said.

"*What?*"

"Dr. Limongello says when Bone gets stuck at a door to square dance," Mary explained.

The novelty of the approach dumbfounded the doctor.

"Self." Bone turned his palms up. Lord, talking was hard. Where was a damn ice chip when you needed one? "Dislodging."

"*What?*" Dr. Quick's face looked as if she'd strolled through an unforeseen cobweb. "Well, we'll be getting in touch with Dr. Limongello for you right away."

"Can't. Leipzig."

"*Leipzig?*"

"Conference."

"Leipzig?" Dr. Quick repeated. "Are you saying Dr. Limongello's in Leipzig?"

Bone nodded. "Couple weeks."

"Well, we'll get in touch with him anyway. Meanwhile, you rest and get better." As she was leaving, Dr. Quick turned and repeated, "Leipzig?"

It transpired that Bone owed his life to Mary's favorite handbag, the tan one with the leather strap. Mary had discovered it was missing, half believing that Bone had deliberately hidden it, but she'd resolved to put it out of her mind and be the bigger person. The missing handbag, however, as missing handbags will, engorged on personal grievance, ballooned to fill her mind completely; this was a handbag of a sort no longer manufactured, uniquely suiting her in style and function, holding not only keys, wallet, and makeup but pleasant associations too deep for words. A one-of-a-kind handbag, in short, and Mary's life was materially diminished by its lack.

She went to get her property, and when Bone didn't answer the doorbell, she left a note on yellow paper stuck to the door. Later, she called and left a message. At this point, she concluded he was maliciously holding the handbag hostage. The following afternoon, Bone having acknowledged neither phone call nor note, Mary returned, determined to give him a piece of her mind, and not a stinting piece, either, but a great big granny-slice, and this time, by God, she wouldn't leave without her handbag on her shoulder. Then she saw, stuck to the door where it'd been for twenty-four hours, like a tot unknowingly relaying news of a traffic fatality, the sunny yellow flag of notepaper.

In confirmation of a terrifying and rapidly forming

hypothesis, Mary ran to the mailbox, finding it aglut with uncollected junk mail. She ran back down the driveway, afflicted by that slow, aqueous locomotion that afflicts one in dreams. She'd never have forgiven herself, or Bone, either, if he'd committed suicide. But of course, he hadn't.

She kept Bone company during his supper of spongy meatloaf and pallid broccoli, then explained meekly that she had to get home to Cash. Bone replied in his weak voice that it was quite all right and not to give it another thought. Promising a visit tomorrow, she kissed his forehead and left him, truth to tell, glad of her absence because by this time he was monstrously tired and wanted only to sleep.

In his dream, he was crawling through the attic, his ankle already broken but conveniently set in a cast. The wound in his hand was likewise stitched and dressed. Sometimes Miranda Richter and Knolton were with him, sometimes Mary, sometimes Rachel the nurse. Sometimes he was by himself. Almost eagerly, he crawled on hands and knees from joist to joist, heart pounding, through an attic transformed into a labyrinth of twisting corridors and unexpected alcoves. He came to a familiar spot and pushed back dusty and fluffy insulation between the joists, knowing something bad was about to happen but with an overriding sensation of swooning impatience to get it over with. Sitting carefully, he rested his feet on the Sheetrock.

This was when he woke. The Jamaican nurse who came at night said, "You were having a bad dream." In the blade of light coming through the door, her face was an oval moon. But the only thing that made it a bad dream was the frustration that it ended just before the bad thing happened.

Next morning, Rachel said, "Okay, chief, doctor wants you to walk today. You don't have to go far, but you can't just lay there." He tried not to think of the woozy purple horror of his calf, on which his unsuspecting eye had fallen when she'd pulled back the covers. *Note to self: Don't look at that again.* With her help, he got out of bed and worked crutches under his armpits. His foot puffed instantly into a basketball of agony, but with Rachel bringing the IV stand alongside like a portable sapling, he jerked his way to the door and back. He dropped onto the mattress, huffing and shaking as if he'd spent the day scaling crevasses. His foot felt ready to pop like a grape in a vise, but Rachel seemed satisfied. "We'll try again after lunch, and you'll go a little further each time. You'll see."

Charlotte visited and brought the *Journal* and a slab of lemon pound cake in aluminum foil. "You're in the paper," she said, pointing at the story as if his printed name made him more real, which, in a sense, Bone felt it did. Among things you can count on to relodge a self at risk of dislodgement are solicitude of others, temporary fame, and extreme physical pain. Bone was blessed with all three. "You were Action News, too," she said, patting the arm without the IV as Bone happily ate fingersful of lemon pound cake. "You're famous!"

"That's more like it!" Rachel said approvingly when she saw the yellow cake. "That other woman just brought *books*." She put the blood-pressure cuff on Bone's arm and, spotting the newspaper, said, "Say, look who's in the paper," coolly contemptuous but absorbed nevertheless, silently skimming as the cuff whirred and bulged around his biceps, then, with an abrupt click and slow hiss, released.

After lunch, Dr. Quick looked in, and Rachel took Bone on another walk: first stop the restroom, where she gave him a translucent plastic bottle. "Think you can manage this for me, chief?" His face in the mirror was tomato-red from exertion, but sure enough, after filling the bottle, he walked on his own right through the door of his room and as far down the hall as the nurse's station before turning back. Instead of a basketball, his foot only felt like a soccer ball. On his return trip, he conserved his breath, but outward bound gamely huffed greetings to hospital staff and fellow patients.

His voice wasn't his own yet—it was still high and reedy—but modal verbs, pronouns, and prepositions came back along with his health, and now he spoke in full sentences, which he'd been unable to do the day before. He walked in a three-part rhythm: hop forward on his good foot, swing his crutches up as Rachel dragged the IV pole abreast, and pause to rest: hop, swing, rest—hop, swing, rest. "Hello! Hello! Nice day!" Waving his fingers as much as he dared, dripping with bonhomie to beat the band, but his voice still a tinny trickle, like water through a long, galvanized pipe. Two custodians interrupted their Spanish discussion of soccer, smiled, and glanced sympathetically at his soccer-ball foot. In spite of the agony of walking, Bone felt gloriously happy, as if he'd been reborn.

Mary and Cash visited, and Mary told him she'd cleaned the house; she didn't mention what she'd found in the box outside his office but couldn't help asking about the torn couch cushions. Bone said he didn't remember doing anything to the couch cushions, but Mary's eyebrows made a tilde and a circumflex (˜˘) suggesting she thought he was too embarrassed to tell the whole story. The truth was, though, he really couldn't remember.

"Were you able to scrub the Chaucer off?" he asked, a joke between them.

"No," she said. "Still there. The one place, the *one* place," shaking a finger at him, "I expected to get some privacy from your damn projects." But she wasn't complaining, really; it was a joke complaint. She was ribbing him.

"I was studying that passage," he explained, a prompt to continue her routine about the Chaucer he'd written on the shower wall. "Sister Eglentyne." The mock argument was as comfortable as a terrycloth robe fresh from the dryer.

"We *both* learned it." She closed her eyes to recite, "'Ful weel she soong the service devince, entuned in hir nose ful seemly, and Frenssh she spak ful faire and fetisly.' God, I'd close my eyes to shut it out of my head, and I'd still see it. 'Frenssh'? *'Frenssh'*?"

Bone was too weak to laugh, but he shook his head and smiled. Cash stared, puzzled, an outsider to the joke and not sure how to react. Cash's presence was as awkward as you might expect, but Bone supposed that his wife's lover thought it was the right thing to do and, moreover, on reflection, that it *was* the right thing to do. Still, it was, as already noted, awkward, but it was how their mothers had brought them up: when someone's in the hospital, you visit. Nobody's mother ever foresaw connections such as your lover's estranged husband, but you navigate the best you can with what guidance you've been given.

Bone obliged his rival with a blow-by-blow account of his diagnosis—extreme dehydration—the risks to kidneys and other organs, his gradual reinflation with liquids via IV tube, the physical and occupational therapy, and his general prognosis. Cash went "uh-huh, uh-huh" at each detail with the palpable lack of interest of a nine-year-old at a seminar on irregular verbs. After Bone finished his rundown, Cash stayed until he could decently leave and then stayed an additional five minutes after that, conscientiously inflicting a generous portion of his valuable time on them, his eyes shifting around the room as if hoping to find some new topic of conversation in the wall-mounted TV or the watercolor cottage, looking like a cat mistakenly invited to a wedding among a large family of mice, who has nothing to say to any of them but for the sake of decency is abstaining from eating one.

CHAPTER TWENTY

T, t

From the Semitic *taw* (✝), "mark," a meta-letter unique in the Semitic alphabet; instead of a monkey, or a house, or an ox, or a throwing stick, it is a mark that represents nothing but a mark.

time: The interval between events. (See **space**.) From the Old English *tima*, also meaning "tide," the seafaring Anglo-Saxons not differentiating the ocean's swell and sink from the abstraction they embody. From the Greek *kairos* and ultimately from the Proto Indo-European *di-mon*, a compound using the root *da-*, "cut to pieces."

tmesis (tə me' sis): A figure of speech in which a syllable or word is inserted into another word, often for dramatic or rhetorical effect, as in "a whole nother" or "in-freaking-credible." From the Greek *tmesis*, "cutting," or "cut," thence the Proto Indo-European *da-*. (See **time**.)

By the third day, Bone had adapted to the hospital routine where friendly, helpful people brought him food, gave him pain medication and ice chips, and took his blood and where his only duty was to get well and take nonsensical strolls down the hallway in his hospital gown and boxers. He learned the trick of feeding his IV bag through his bathrobe sleeve before rehanging it on the pole so he could stroll with his bathrobe decently belted instead of in his unclosable hospital gown, parading his underwear in front of God and everybody. Fulfilling his role as quirky patient with strange diagnosis, he gossiped with the staff: Jenny, the Jamaican nurse, had a ten-year-old in a gifted program; Dr. Quick was getting her pilot's license; and Carlo the custodian played in not one but three different soccer leagues. Think of that: three.

In his room, he worked on *Words*, feeling inexplicably that this, too, was part of his role—playing the part of a man working on *Words*. After lunch, Rachel took him to the sunroom, which was filled with donated toys cheerfully abused by recuperating youngsters: crayons scrubbed down to molars, Lincoln logs in insufficient numbers to construct so much as a lean-to, a jigsaw puzzle missing a butterfly-shaped piece with blue sky and the tip of a sail. Famished for a glimpse of the outside, Bone brought his face close to the scratchy Plexiglas window, peering at an adjoining wing of the hospital and a stingy trapezoid of sky, but the window was about as transparent as a shower door, so he had no more idea of the weather than a goldfish in a bowl.

That afternoon, Rachel wheeled him to the elevator to visit with the pretty physical therapist who flexed his knees, massaged his calves, and made him lie on his back and raise and lower his legs while other people pedaled stationary bikes, pulled giant rubber bands, and walked in slow lunges across the floor. A sign said, "Stop if you feel faint or pain."

Bone pointed this out to a fellow patient. "You can't use 'feel' as transitive and intransitive in the same sentence," he said. The other patient gave him a funny look, and Bone apologized. "God forgive me. I'm a recovering grammar teacher."

The other patient chuckled and offered Bone a winter-green Life Saver. He was in for a hernia, he explained, but didn't live in Atlanta. He was only down for a conference when "*Bam!* Rupture."

"Still," Hernia said cheerfully, "you got to be grateful." He kept running his fingers over his yellow hair, delicately touching pinkie finger first, then each finger in turn, as if playing a musical scale. "You got to be grateful, am I right or am I right?" Hernia seemed very grateful.

"Yes," Bone agreed sincerely, "you got to be grateful."

Mary came each day. Bone didn't expect Father Pepys to visit, but he did, having read about Bone in the *Journal*. After praying for Bone's return to full health, amen, the three of them made ill-fitting conversation, cluttering but not filling the silence. Bone listened with unfeigned delight to Pepys, who for some reason wore a contrite expression each time he looked at Mary.

Bone asked her, "Could you give me an ice chip, please?" Mary slipped a sliver between his dry lips with her cool fingertips, a sudden ecstatic confluence of warm, cold, soft, hard, dry, and moist. He attempted an elaborate witticism to keep her eye: "This hospital has the best ice chips I've ever had; we must get their recipe" but only came out with a quiet "Good."

After Pepys left, Bone said, "He is a nice man. Coming to see me."

"He's an idiot," Mary said. She looked at her hands. "He fired me, you know."

"No!"

"He didn't even do it himself. He left me a letter. Some of the blue hairs on the vestry found out about, well, about me. They fired me."

"Son of a bitch. What will you do for money?"

She half-shrugged. "Cash is taking care of it. And I'll find something."

"Yes. Meanwhile, as you say, Cash will take care of it."

"Listen, about everything." She looked down at her folded hands. "I'm visiting you because, you know, you're in the hospital. Nothing's changed between us."

"I understand."

"I didn't want you to get the wrong idea. I'm still with Cash."

"I understand, really."

"We are adults, after all. These things happen."

A sturdy, stifling silence hung in the room. "I know," Bone said. "Nobody's fault." He wanted to tell her he had no expectations and was simply happy to have her there. As Hernia said, he was grateful. He ran his fingers one at a time over his hair, as if this private gesture would communicate his gratitude.

"Do you want me to adjust your broken foot?" Mary offered. "It looks uncomfortable like that."

"Actually, do you mind putting it up on a pillow? It is getting a little stiff."

"Certainly."

Bone asked, if it weren't too much trouble, would Mary

deliver some end-of-semester paperwork to Fulsome for him. She said she'd be glad to, and Bone was effusive in his thanks: passing the conversational ball back and forth as if it were shatter-prone alabaster, like the two hyperpolite chipmunks from the Warner Brothers cartoons: "After you, my fine fellow." "No, after you." "I insist." And like that.

"I'm sorry, wouldn't you like to watch the news?" Bone asked.

"Oh, thank you," Mary said, "but you don't like the news, do you? I'm sorry."

"No, it's okay. I'd like to watch the news if you want to. Really."

"Quit apologizing to each other." Rachel stuck her head in the door. "We can hear you all the way out in the hallway."

Mary turned on the six o'clock news. No rain in the forecast. Then Bone's own name was mentioned, and his face came on the screen, at which point he realized he was no longer watching the news but had fallen asleep and was only dreaming about watching the news; then he was in the attic again, crawling joist to joist.

While at the hospital he slept neither well nor poorly but was always on the verge of dozing when awake and the verge of waking when dozing, and every time he fell asleep, he had the same dream of crawling through the mazy attic of his unconscious. He believed if he could break through the ceiling just once and find out what happened next, he wouldn't need to have the dream anymore.

When he woke, he found Dr. Quick and an unfamiliar doctor by his bed. You'd spot the man as a doctor the instant you saw him, even though he didn't wear a lab coat; snow-white hair stopped cleanly at his head's equator like a tonsure, and from there up, his northern hemisphere was not only bald but gleamed as if buffed with Minwax. His chin receded slightly, and he had a mannerism of emphasizing this by tucking it against his Adam's apple when he was being doctorly and concerned, as he was being now.

Bone asked, "Are you here to look at my ankle?"

"I've never seen you before," the doctor said, his hands folded across his belly—not a big belly, but Bone thought he might be sticking it out a bit for the added measure of solemnity and solidity it gave him.

"And I've never seen you," Bone confirmed. An accurate but odd conversation. "Who are you?"

"I'm Dr. Limongello."

CHAPTER TWENTY-ONE

U, u

Like **F**, from the Semitic *waw* (**У**), "peg," with the bottom stem lopped off. **U** is the immediate ancestor of **V** and **W**, which up to the sixteenth century were represented by the same symbol, so that **evil** was **euil**, **love** was **loue**, and **wife** was **uuife.**

un-: Appropriately for a prefix that reverses or negates the word that follows, the **-n** is an upside-down **u-**. Compare with Greek and Sanskrit, *anti*.

Uranus: Roman sky god, husband of G*aiea,* "earth," from the Greek *ouranos*, "heaven," possibly akin to the Hittite *wara*, "to burn," therefore, "giver of light."

utopia: Coined by Sir Thomas More in 1516, a pun on the Greek *eu-topia*, "good place," and *u-topia*, "no place," so the word contains the wry wisdom that hunt though we will for a land of peace and harmony, we won't find it. More, once a favorite of Henry VIII, fell from grace and was beheaded in 1535 after failing to attend Anne Boleyn's coronation. Boleyn herself was beheaded less than a year later.

The real Dr. Limongello performed an examination almost identical to the impostor's, after which he assured Bone that, although presenting with unusual symptoms, the illness itself was not unheard-of. Bone lay cheek to pillow as the double-doc sat by his bed, telling about some very important chemicals called neurotransmitters that come from *other* chemicals called precursors, while from the hall rose and fell the muted bustle of nurses and doctors making their rounds, discussing patients or something funny someone's husband said, and coded messages chimed up and down the ward.

There was one precursor, Limongello explained, that everyone had ignored because everyone had thought precursors didn't do much but wait around to turn into neurotransmitters. Only they'd been wrong. The brain has a purpose for everything, even the smallest and most insignificant tittle, like this particular precursor. Sure enough, it turned out that while no one was paying attention, the humble precursor was unobtrusively going about its chores, one of which was getting people through doors. It so happened that Bone's brain didn't make enough of this precursor, and without it there to man the switch, certain messages couldn't get through, which meant *Bone* couldn't get through. "Good news is, it's easily treatable with medication. We just have to give you a synthetic version of the precursor that your body should be producing naturally."

"Isn't that risky?" Bone asked.

"Risky compared to what?" Limongello asked, silently inviting Bone to compare the possible side effects of medication versus dying of thirst with a broken ankle in his own living room.

"So that's all I have to do? Take a pill?"

"Well," Limongello said, "the doctors here have to get your levels restored, and then we'll take it slow and monitor you until we get your meds balanced, but, yes, that's really pretty much all there is to it. Take a pill."

THE NEXT MORNING, Rachel explained to Bone and Mary what had happened. She wheeled in a cart laden with a basin, sponges, and a little tower of towels, announcing in an unnaturally carrying voice, just like a wisecracking but no-nonsense TV nurse, "Are we ready for our sponge bath, Mr. King? You stay, too, honey," she told Mary, who was getting up to leave. "You won't see nothing you haven't seen before, I don't guess. Close the door and make sure no one comes in. Now, Mr. King, let's see if we can slip off that gown."

When the door was closed, Rachel said in her normal voice, "I need you to listen up. This is real important. I needed you here," she told Mary, "because I figure you're the smart one." She disconnected Bone's IV and helped him pull off his gown. He felt the warmth of his blush all the way down to his chest. "You got a regular harem here, don't you, chief?" she asked. "Just a sec, we'll cover you with a blanket so me and her can do our job without getting all distracted. Meanwhile, scoot up. We got to get this towel up under you." She got the towel up under him and covered him up, tucking the blanket under his shoulders, then began with his face, soaping lightly and rinsing with a moist sponge. "I got a friend in Limongello's office who says there's been lawyers in and out of there like nobody's business. Now, you absolutely cannot tell where you heard this." She pointed the sponge accusingly in Bone's face. "I know *she* won't blab, but I don't know how much sense *you* got. This would lose me and my friend's job both. Got it?"

"Got it," Bone said.

Rachel leveled the sponge at him two more seconds for good measure, then took a towel from the cart and patted his face dry. "Limongello had another patient, a regular loony tune, who's been AWOL a couple of weeks now, but he exactly fits the description of the man who told you he was Dr. Limongello." With Bone's tingling face dry, Rachel pulled the cover and began softly and studiously sudsing his chest and arms, giving special care to the crinkles and creases at his elbows and armpits. "This guy, the other patient, went missing once before, and they thought they had him fixed, but he must've gone off his meds, because now he's gone again. Anyway, that guy must've been the one who said he was Limongello. Their records show both of you checked in for an appointment on the same day, but neither of you stuck around to see the doctor." Rachel's sponge dabbed up three prismatic bubbles caged in Bone's sternum hairs, then, with two parenthetic sweeps of her towel, she dried his chest.

Mary's "Hunh" at this was a thoughtful hunh and a pondering hunh, the hunh of one on whom a light has broken.

"Poor devil," Bone murmured. "So that explains it. He was

mentally ill. Still, you know, I think he was honestly doing his best for me. He really was a nice man."

"Jesus, Bone," Mary said. "Shut up."

Shaking her head at Bone, Rachel told Mary, "I knew there was a reason I wanted you here." She said, "Here, lift your arms and we'll get your pits." Rachel washed, rinsed, and toweled his torso, then pulled the covers back and did his legs. "Now you need to roll over, boss, think you can do that?" Bone rolled on his side, and Rachel pulled the covers up to his hip and soaped his back. He wondered if and feared that she'd go so far as washing between his fanny cheeks. She did. Nothing escaped this woman.

"So Dr. Limongello," Mary said, "is partly responsible for this mess."

"Check," Rachel said. Bone could tell Rachel was addressing Mary, not him, and although he avoided looking at Mary while he was being bathed, focusing instead on the sheet under his nose where a wrinkle forked and set off in two ridges over the side of the mattress, he imagined Mary's nods of agreement and attentive frown of comprehension. "Now, if you know what's good for you, you'll listen up. The doc's got his panties in a wad you might sue. Maybe they were negligent letting patients poke around in supply closets, putting on lab coats and stuff, and Limongello's office never bothered checking why y'all both ran off before you saw the doctor. If you ever want to see a doctor's blood pressure go through the roof, just *whisper* the word 'malpractice.' My boyfriend says it's not the gold mine it used to be since tort reform, but Limongello's still in a pretty tight fix because it's not just a matter of a settlement, it's Limongello's whole reputation if it gets out his patients run around pretending they're him. The last thing Limongello wants is that getting out. Compared to that getting out, malpractice is just chicken feed.

"Now comes the good part." Rachel pulled the covers back again and said, "Lift up your butt some; we're going to put some extra towels underneath." She spread his legs and began, with the same gentle but thorough and meticulous detachment, to wash his scrotum, which was not the least bit erotic but yet—apart from the complicated embarrassment of having his privates scrubbed by another woman in the presence of his estranged wife—indisputably pleasant. "You can take over this part if you're jealous," Rachel offered Mary, and—though Bone did not suspect this—irrationally, Mary was a bit jealous. Bone kept his eyes trained on the ceiling during this process as the women discussed how to handle Dr. Limongello, like conspirators planning a surprise for Caesar on the Ides of March: *Here, as I point my sword, the sun arises.*

"They wrote about you in the *news*paper, you've been talked about on *TV,* it's been on the *radio.* You can't buy that kind of publicity. Limongello sure as hell doesn't want his name pulled into this. At the very least—at the very least," Rachel said, "you ought to get free medical treatment for life out of this. And—" a pause, during which Bone felt some coded transmission pass between the two women—"maybe some additional compensation for being out of work."

"I have a job," Bone protested.

"This would just be extra," Mary said quickly. "In case you want a year off to work on your book and maybe look for another job. How do we make this happen?"

"I knew you was the practical one. You got to proceed real careful, because if we spook him, you won't see dime one until the thirty-first of Neverary." Rachel gave the future plaintiff of *King v. Limongello* a final soft touch of the towel, which she threw into her bag of dirties. "For starters, you can't talk to anyone about this. I mean En. Ee. One. No press, no newspapers. En. Ee. One. Okay, all done. Let's put your gown back on and cover you up before you catch cold."

That afternoon, Rachel's lawyer-boyfriend came, timing the visit when Rachel was on break; without going so far as to deny that he was a lawyer or somebody's boyfriend, they'd deemed it politic to let everyone assume he was an ordinary visitor come to see Bone. The boyfriend wasn't the sort of person to whom the word "boyfriend" is normally applied. For one thing, he was a lot older than the typical boyfriend, but then Rachel was a lot older than the typical girlfriend.

The lawyer took in the cockpit of dials and nozzles on the headboard, the IV, and the watercolor cottage with an appraiser's eye, sat, took three pens out of his shirt pocket, and began writing on his yellow legal pad: to start with, there were medical expenses, to which Mary replied they had no idea how much the hospital stay would be, but the lawyer-boyfriend said he had a pretty good notion and wrote a string of digits, and then there was money for loss of work.

"Listen," Bone said.

Mary said pain and suffering, and the lawyer wrote that number.

"Stop."

The lawyer said reupholstering the furniture, repairing the ceiling, and incidentals and wrote another number, and Mary said punitive damages.

"I don't want to sue," Bone said.

The lawyer-boyfriend's lower lip drooped, not in dismay but in surprise, as if Bone had broken in to ask them the capital of Nebraska. The lawyer explained that they weren't going to sue. "We're going to show him these numbers, and he's going to write you a check."

When Bone said he didn't want to do that, either, the room got as still as a stone, and as cool, but the lawyer's face had no more expression than a mannequin's. "It's not Dr. Limongello's fault. It just happened," Bone explained. The lawyer eyed his legal pad, as if expecting the numbers to speak up on their own behalf, and looked up, his face impassive as before. At that moment, if someone had *thought* of dropping a pin, the crash would have resounded like the fall of a bowling ball. "I'm not doing this," Bone said. His voice, which was almost back on all cylinders, stalled. "It's not his fault, and I don't want his money. I know it's expensive, the hospital and everything, but I've got insurance—"

"God, you dope," Mary said, and Bone was astonished to see her eyes shining.

"I think," the lawyer said, and stood, returning the pens to his pocket, "I should let you think about this. I don't want you to rush into something." He looked at Mary and back at Bone. "I'll wait for your call." He put his hand on Bone's shoulder in lieu of a handshake and gave him a brief V of a smile, but no impatience in his voice, no nothing. He left.

"Mary, I just don't think—" Bone began.

"You are such a dope." Mary put her fist to her forehead. Her chin trembled the way Bone recognized meant she was about to cry.

"Everything will be okay," Bone promised. "I have a job."

"You don't have a job," Mary said. "They're not renewing your contract. I found out when I turned in your end-of-semester stuff. There was a letter in your faculty mailbox; it must've been there for weeks."

It took a moment for Bone to exit the former topic and find the turn lane for the current one. "But Gordon said he wouldn't fire me."

"Not for your disability. They didn't fire you for that. It said it was an economic decision. It said they'd already made the decision to let you go before they learned about your condition. It mentioned something about a document. Bone, did you sign something about your condition not being a disability?"

"What?" A shadowy recollection glimmered at the threshold of memory, and under the covers, Bone's legs tingled and prickled in a way that seemed illogically connected with the fluorescent light overhead (*fluorescence*, "essence of a flower," what a glaring misnomer, but never mind that now), and in the hallway someone wheeled a cart and called out for Juan. "I—I might have. Yes."

"Don't you see? You don't have a job. You don't have insurance." She rubbed the wet from her cheek with the heel of her hand and seemed about to kneel beside his bed but changed her mind, instead crossing her arms, one elbow clutched in the opposite hand, and turning her head to the door, upper lip stretched down to prevent her nose from running. "This isn't the time to go all noble and principled. You can't walk away from this."

Bone was in a quandary: on one hand there was his Tennessean work ethic that dictated you don't shake people down for money; on the other hand was raw, staring necessity. After delivering her bombshell, Mary collected her purse with busy officiousness, as if she'd like to stuff Bone in it, and left without giving him his customary kiss on the forehead.

Rachel's expression, when she came to wheel Bone down to physical therapy the next day, looked like five miles of glacial ice. They were angry with him, but Bone didn't know the right thing to do.

That afternoon in physical therapy, he shared his dilemma with Hernia.

Hernia temporized, giving Bone a wintergreen Life Saver, then taking one himself, holding the pack to his mouth and pushing it in with his thumbnail. He sucked and nodded, directing his stare perpendicular to Bone and puckering his lips as if kissing something in the air.

"Well," he said slowly, "I know how you feel. But it sounds like God's been playing pretty rough with you up to now. Maybe He's finally deciding to cut you a break. I think you ought to take the money. You got to be grateful, am I right, or am I right?"

Bone took the money.

CHAPTER TWENTY-TWO

The direct descendent of **U**, with which it was once used interchangeably. Johnson omits **V** from the first edition of his dictionary, although conceding it "ought to be" considered as a separate letter. The Latin **V** was pronounced /w/, so that Caesar's famous boast, "Veni, vidi, vinci," came out "Waynie, weedy, winky."

Venus: The Roman goddess of love and desire takes her name from the ancient Proto Indo-European *wen-*, "to desire," a fertile root with many shades of meaning, such as "respect," hence **venerate**; "wish," hence **wish** and **winsome**; and "hunted or sought-after," hence **venison** and **win**.

very: Commonly used to mean "to a great extent" but originally "true," as in "the very thing." From the Latin *uerus*, "true," whence **veracity**, **verdict**, and **verify**.

On the morning of the fifth day, just as Bone had begun to think he would never leave the hospital, he did.

First Rachel and Mary performed a brief pas de deux about steering the wheelchair; as Rachel arranged Bone's crutches on the armrests, Mary maneuvered behind and took the handles, at which the nurse did not look altogether delighted but made no objection.

"I can push that if you like," offered Cash, standing just inside the door.

"No," Mary said, "I'm good."

Poor Cash. Who could blame him for feeling out of place? Something useful to do might help, but Bone's suggestion that he'd like Cash to push the wheelchair only made things worse: Mary repeated she was good, and Cash said he'd just as soon carry the suitcase, sounding as if he expected to find it coated in sticky seepage.

Rolling down the hall toward Carlo, Bone bade him farewell. How many soccer tournaments did he have that weekend? Carlo shyly held up three proud fingers, and Bone chuckled admiringly as he rolled past.

After a silent wait at the elevator door, Rachel remarked on Cash's kindness to take a day off for this, and Cash said he was his own boss and could take time off anytime he wanted. Rachel said that must be nice, and Cash said it was. Rachel had pressed the down button, but Cash pressed it again. Cash said Rachel didn't have to come down with them if she didn't want to, but Rachel said that was all right, and besides, it was procedure. Cash nodded, frowning first at his smeary reflection in the elevator door and then at the fist clutching Bone's suitcase.

"There's something I don't get," Bone said. "When I had my first attack, I kept hearing all about this wonderful Dr. Limongello, and—" The pause at the end of the statement expressed the letdown of the real deal after having encountered the unreal one.

"He *is* wonderful," Rachel said, "in spite of everything. I know a lot of bad stuff went on, but you're lucky to have him. He's, like, famous. You're lucky to be in his hands."

"But people said, you know, he had this really eccentric bedside manner."

"He does, didn't you notice?"

"What?"

"He says 'goldurn.' He said it today when he came to check on you. 'How's this goldurn condition of yours?' How many neurologists go around saying 'goldurn'?"

"That's it? He says 'goldurn'?"

"Well, it's part of it."

The doors shushed back, followed by a small commotion as Cash worked past Rachel and around the barrier of Bone's crutches to stand in the back beside Mary. The elevator counted down in yellow numbers above the door. Now they exited into the hall, and Bone's chair cornered left, then right—Bone's pounding bloodstream foretelling the approach of something momentous—slowing at the automatic glass doors before bumping over the borderline between the hospital's whispering cool and the outside's abrupt warmth, slowing once more at the shoreline between the smooth white concrete sidewalk and the pimply blacktop of the parking lot, and blue sky rolled into sight under the concrete awning.

Sky!

Clouds!

And beyond the car roofs, on the other side of the street, the ragged green heads of trees!

Desist with the exclamation marks; enough is enough. But, he asked himself, what do you do if your heart is become an exclamation mark? Had the aperture of his mind's eye widened to include *birds*, he might have burst.

After hesitating curbside, as if half-hoping for the truck to drive up on its own, Cash explained unnecessarily that he was going to get it. Rachel and Mary helped Bone onto his crutches.

"Dave said you came this close," Rachel pinched a button of empty air in front of Bone's face, "to turning down that money. I don't know if that makes you a saint or a dumbass, but my money's on dumbass. Well, good-bye, Bone. Take care. And you take care of him." She leveled a pointer finger at Mary. Atop his crutches, Bone reached clumsily to the nurse, but while pretending not to notice, Rachel sternly shook her head at the vacancy to his left: nurses don't hug. She turned and the glass doors parted before her, and then, changing her mind, came back and gave Bone a peremptory embrace. "Take care," she ordered again before going inside and leaving them to wait for Cash.

Bone wound up sitting between Mary and Cash, since they'd loaded him into the cab before laying the crutches in the back. Touching Mary's cool, bare midriff, his elbow jerked back, after which he sat, arms docilely pinned to his abdomen, hands clasped between his thighs as if he were praying in a bathtub. Buildings and signs passed outside in brilliant glare, and then overreaching trees glided by, sheathing the passengers in darkness and coolness.

The truck pulled into Bone's carport under a "Welcome Home" poster whose flowers and butterflies must have depleted an entire pack of Sharpies. "Mary did that," Cash explained. "I'll take it down for you. I guess you two need to talk over terms and conditions."

"Right," Bone said, a tad too quickly. The solution to looking after Bone during his convalescence, handling the excess dough bloating his bank account, and what Mary could do after losing her job had been found in one convenient stroke. Lucky them.

Mary held the kitchen door and, fortified by Dr. Limongello's precursor pill, Bone had no more trouble entering than naturally occasioned by going on crutches. The house had the unfamiliar-familiar feel of a home you've been away from: no smell of must or dust but no warm, faint aroma of human habitation, either. Mary had cleaned and straightened so that the house resembled the dwelling of a reasonably tidy professor rather than the lair of a nutcase who rode a pogo stick indoors wearing a spiked helmet. It surprised and inexplicably dismayed Bone to find no hole in the living room ceiling, and Mary explained that Cash knew father-and-son contractors who'd repaired the holes, but not wholly repaired: they still needed to paint. The couch hadn't been reupholstered, either. Two cushions sat naked.

Bone raised his crutch and, with a delicacy of which he'd have thought himself incapable, gently touched the spot with an appreciative rubber tip, ice-smooth though unpainted, and his fingers imagined the powdery surface, reliving with a horrid thrill an ordeal he could neither recall nor forget. He still had his dream, but as it penetrated that the same spot would stymie him every time, the moment just before putting his weight on the ceiling and breaking through, his interest waned, and the dream came less frequently, spaced by more mundane imaginings: explaining the etymology of "cynic" to a disbelieving dachshund, showing up to his elementary school reunion in tighty-whities

Bone said he guessed he'd better make out a check. Mary got the checkbook from a dresser drawer, and Bone filled it out. "I'll pay you the month in advance. Is that good?" Mary said it was good, and he wrote it out and gave it to her. She stared at it—the account still had both their names—before folding it crisply in the center.

"Oh, and you got this." Mary handed him a letter. "Who's Laurence Hobbs?" It delighted Bone to get a letter from his old friend, unretired after all these years. Mary, cleaning up the house, must've found Bone's letter and mailed it for him.

"The librarian where I grew up." He tore the envelope and skimmed the reply. Later, he'd take time to read more closely and savor. "I'm writing letters to everyone who made a difference to me. I've pretty much gone through my schoolteachers; next I'll write some of my undergrad

professors. It's easy getting addresses on the Internet."
He didn't mention this was due to the fake Limongello's
prompting.

"You do that a lot?"

"Well, maybe not *every* day," Bone confessed.

Mary smiled and shook her head. "You're really something. I can't even get Cash to call his own mother."

Cash entered with Bone's "Welcome Home" poster
rolled into a big white ball. "I'll throw this away for you,"
he offered.

The next morning, Mary reported for duty, making
him a light breakfast of yogurt and fruit and seeing to it
he took his precursor: a small dosage, the doctor had explained, an innocuous white tablet smaller than an Advil.
Would there be side effects? Limongello had made Bone
read over and sign a veritable *Who's Who* of potential
negative reactions—*No taking chances with you anymore, Mr.
King!*—before writing the prescription.

Had Bone suffered any of these? Strange dreams? (Yes,
but no stranger than usual.) Uncontrollable sexual urges?
(No. Phoo.) Thoughts of suicide? Mood swings? Dizziness?
(No, no, no.) Bone didn't even have dry mouth, the com-
monest side effect of all. Strange that this was all there
was to it: nearly die of dehydration in your own house,
desiccated victim of an imposter doctor madman, and all
they had to do was patch the ceiling and give you a white
pill to fix you up as if nothing had ever happened. The
contractor and his son would come and paint the ceil-

ing, and Limongello would monitor Bone until he got his meds balanced.

Mary left after breakfast, saying she'd check in at lunch. Consoling himself over her absence, Bone went through his e-mails. Oglethorpe University was looking for a humanities professor. The campus, which Bone drove by almost daily, was an oasis of medieval-looking stonework amid the uniform background of gas stations, fast-food joints, and dry cleaners along Peachtree Industrial, furnished with turrets and battlements, somebody's notion of how a college ought to look, a notion with which Bone wholeheartedly concurred. The job was right up Bone's alley, but he saw little likelihood of landing it. Nevertheless, he brushed up his vita and sent in an application. No harm in trying, after all.

He poured himself a second cup of coffee, then went back to his manuscript. Returning to *Words* after an extended absence was like tugging on a cold, wet bathing suit. His entries had been growing increasingly—eccentric. Jesus, the butter must've really been slipping off his noodles; nevertheless, there was some interesting, valid research here. He realized how close he was to finishing, and then he'd have his PhD even if he didn't find a publisher. Throwing caution to the winds, he e-mailed Dr. Susik, his dissertation chair, to set up a final review. Meanwhile, wrinkles needed ironing.

To wit: the Middle Dutch *wreed*, *wrac*, and *wringen* gave us **wrath, wrest, wrist, writhe, wreathe, awry, wry** (a "bent" sense of humor), **wreck, wreak, wretched, wrench, wrangle,** and **wrong.** In all of these—it both disappointed and elated Bone that Partridge left this unstated—*wr-* is clearly a morpheme for "twist." Pronounce **wrestle** as it's spelled, and you can not only hear but feel the consonants tangle at your alveolar ridge and tumble down your palate. This much is obvious, but a few words defy the pattern. **Write,** for example, descends not from *wringen,* "to twist," but *reissen,* "to rip or rend," but doesn't **writing** have more to do with *twisting*—a pen tip forming sinuous S, gaping G, undulant U—than *ripping*? And **wraith,** Partridge relates not to **wreathe** or **writhe,** which it so closely resembles, but **ward** and **warn,** though surely the metathesis, the sounds twisting so that *r* roughly rubs the *w,* is because no wraith stands flat-footed like a warden delivering a warning but spirals from its crypt in a corkscrew of milky smoke.

    Wren presented another mystery. "Of obscure origin," Partridge comments, and obscure is right. The Old Norse is *ridnill,* but why the intrusive *w* in English? To suggest the swiveling movement of wings? Because wrens make nests of twisted straw and twigs? Onomatopoeia for its convoluted song, described in Betelweis's *Guide to Birds* (1999) as "a rich bubbling chatter of churring and chitting, falling in a cascade of notes"? Parenthetically, *Guide to Birds* itself was the most twisted reference work Bone had ever come up against—arranged not alphabetically nor by genus but by *color.* "Birds that are mostly black," "Birds that are mostly white," "Birds that are mostly black *and* white."

Bone spent the morning doggedly and joyously pursuing **wraith** and **wren** down old trails and cold trails, losing the scent and picking it up again, and around 10:15, he was conscious that something happened—what, he didn't know, but something, a noise in the room, a flash of movement in his peripheral vision.

"What the hell," Mary said that afternoon when she came to look in on Bone. "Bone, you spilled coffee all over the floor. Didn't you see it?"

Sure enough, the coffee mug she'd given him—"I are a grammar teacher"—lay in pieces in a brown puddle of arabica on the floor beside the desk. Moist brown footprints showed where he'd walked through coffee on the way to the bathroom.

"It must've spilled." Bone deduced the obvious.

But he didn't recall spilling it.

There were other mysteries. While talking to the contractor and his son the next day, Bone glimpsed another flash in his periphery, at which the contractor gave a peculiar look and then exchanged a glance with his son. Had they seen it, too?

That same morning, a wobbly, elongated toothpaste ampersand appeared on the bathroom tile beside the sink, the explanation for which Bone could not surmise; ditto for the scrapes and bruises his knuckles didn't remember getting. But all of these were minor affairs: his health was improving; doors—thanks to Wonderful Double-Doc

Lemon Jell-O's precursor—posed no further problems; and his work on *Words*—he had sent out a fresh barrage of queries to agents and publishers—was proceeding apace. There was also the sweet torture of Mary's daily visit to look forward to, when she came to look in on him and take him to physical therapy and doctor's appointments. Moreover, he had his daily letter of gratitude to write. The mystery would solve itself. And so it did.

CHAPTER TWENTY-THREE

Originally, as the name suggests, co-joined **Us**. (**V** did not exist except as a variant of **U**, which is why the letter is not named "double-vee.") In some typefaces, such as Garamond, we can still see the overlapping tops (W). Along with **Y**, **W** is one of two consonants that is sometimes a vowel, as in the archaic Welsh, **cwm**, "a steep hollow."

wed: From the Old High German *wetti*, "to pledge," similar to the Gothic *gawadjon,* from which also come **engage, wage, wager**.

word: From the Latin *verbus*, whence also **verb**. Capitalized, it refers to the Bible, "the Word of God," as well as the Son of God: "In the beginning was the Word, and the Word was God." (John 1:1)

work: Effort undertaken for pay. From the Proto Indo-European, *werg-*, one of the earliest words ever spoken. Originally, the past participle of **work** was **wrought**, with each letter voiced— commencing with twisting *wr-* and culminating with *-ght's* gnash—tough to pronounce, as if it were hard steel that had to be wrestled into shape.

wren: Of obscure origin.

C oming back from having a walking cast put on his foot, Bone exercised the astonishing misjudgment of placing a hand on Mary's knee. Mary lifted it by one finger as if it were a banana peel and returned it to Bone's lap without comment. Bone stared at the windshield through a sudden humidity filling the car, and Mary pulled into the Publix parking lot, where she got out to buy groceries. Alone in the car, Bone repeated the word "stupid" to the dashboard a number of times. When Mary returned with her cart of sensible purchases, the world seemed to go black before Bone's eyes, and he found himself unable to stop his garrulous chattering, babbling for them all the way home, like the little piggy of the poem.

When she pulled into the carport, Mary opened the glove compartment and took out an envelope, which she handed to Bone. Divorce papers. Bone began to say something and coughed, discovering a sudden dry patch in his throat. She hated to do this now, she said, but Bone said, no, they might as well get it over with. This way they knew where they stood. These things happen, Mary said. Yes, Bone said, they might as well be mature about this; they should go into the kitchen, ahem, and sign them. As dutifully as Mary was tending to him, she'd made it crystal clear that they were kaput, that it was over, that she was with Cash now. Sometimes in these situations the phrase "painfully clear" is employed, and seldom have pain and clarity joined in sharper juxtaposition. Bone, as willing to give Mary her freedom as any other thing in his power— an armful of fresh-cut flowers, his heart—resolved not to show how he hungered for her daily visits and from then on, just as one avoids looking at the sun, not to let himself stare in her direction.

His discomfiture was in no way lessened by a change of

heart by Cash, who'd become seemingly unable to get his fill of doing helpful chores for Bone: the driveway had been edged to within an inch of its life; the lawn had endured all that weeding, feeding, and seeding could do for it; the box-woods looked as if they'd been served out with an ice-cream scoop. When Mary and Bone pulled into the carport, Cash and two of his employees were even then installing japonicas in the front bed.

To distract from the afterglow of humiliation as well as the intermittent reappearance of Cash's watchful face in the kitchen window, a sight that sent a centipede's chilly legs running down Bone's spine, Bone carefully read over the papers, commenting that they were much less complicated than he'd have expected. Mary explained that she'd print-ed them off the Internet. She didn't want any money, Mary said. He'd gotten in serious trouble signing papers before, but Mary wanted to assure him that it wouldn't happen again. The process would take about thirty days for an uncontested divorce.

He signed, and as he gave the papers to Mary, she said, "What was that about?"

"What was what about?"

"You just stuck your arm up in the air. You didn't notice?"

"No. What?"

"You stuck your arm up, like this." She jerked her hand over her head and let it fall. "You didn't notice it?"

"No, I—" Then he realized he *had* seen one of those flash-es of movement, like the others he'd glimpsed at odd intervals. Could this explain the minty white squiggle squeezed on the bathroom wall, his busted coffee cup, his bruised and bloodied knuckles?

Limongello's diagnosis when they told him about this new symptom the next day was dyskinesia, "bad movement," from the Greek, *dys-*, "bad," and *kinein*, "move," delivered with a physician's simple confidence that people feel better about an illness if they hear the word for it in Greek, the same way a mechanic will display for you a tailpipe half-eaten by rust or a greasy handful of sheared lug nuts in the expectation that this will resign you to the body blow your bank account is about to suffer.

It turned out the same precursor that helped Bone manage doors could also cause sudden involuntary movements, in this case, sending Bone's arm up into the air. The side effect was listed alongside strange dreams, thoughts of suicide, compulsive gambling, sexual addiction, dry palms, sweaty palms, mood swings, irritability, night sweats, day sweats, dry mouth, headaches, nausea, vomiting, hair loss, and itchy skin. How had Bone overlooked it?

"Is there anything I can do to stop it?"

"We'll try to get those meds balanced and see what happens."

NEXT MORNING, MARY asked, "You know all that mint that's growing in the side bed? Dorothy at Nuts 'n' Berries says if I make mint jelly, I can sell it there." Bone said to knock herself out but opined that the clientele of Nuts 'n' Berries was not much for eating lamb. "Some of them do. And any we don't sell, I'll give away for Easter."

Mary ran to General Hardware to get some half-pint jars, and Bone hobbled to the utility room to fetch the big canning kit. He filled the pot with water and set it on simmer.

What was he doing, Cash wanted to know when Bone came outside with his split-oak basket and green-handled garden shears. Trimming mint for Mary, Bone said, regretting instantly the inclusion of her name. Cash, lips pressed together until they nearly formed a duckbill, looked westward toward Peachtree Industrial, where Mary had gone, and asked if he needed any help with that, and Bone said no, he could manage, and then Bone said, "Whoa!" because at that moment his arm chose to rocket up, launching the shears out of the basket into the air.

Cash returned to his crew, filling in a raised bed in the side yard. Bone didn't ask but thought Cash's business must suffer from all the work he was doing pro bono for Bone. In the last month, the original crew of five stalwart, clean-cut Mexicans and true had dwindled to a sketchy pair: a gray-bearded man with an eye patch and a dirty Braves cap, which had been jammed on his skull as though fastened with rivets, and a Hispanic who looked like he'd been molded out of softened lard, for whom walking entailed a side-to-side roll like a ship on heavy seas, his pink lips moving in what Bone believed was a silent prayer that angels not take him home to Jesus en route to the wheelbarrow.

Bone knelt, carefully extending his broken foot in its outsized padded tennis shoe behind him, scissoring the green fragrance into the air from the feathery stalks. A yellow butterfly bobbed at eye level and darted by. Mint is shockingly easy to grow and, once started, shockingly hard to stop, so Bone was able to harvest a heap sufficient to jelly every lamb between there and New Zealand. Inside, he rinsed it, checking the pale undersides of leaves and picking off a solitary spit bug, white with foam, the only insect able to endure the touch of mint oil on its tender belly. When Mary clinked in with her box of half-pint jars, she found the mint waiting fragrant and water-beaded in the sink, the pot of water bubbling on the stove.

"Thank you," she said. "You didn't need to do all that. Don't you need to work on *Words?*"

Bone said he'd already gotten in some work this morning and would work some more that evening. He was nearly done. Really nearly done. "I went ahead and contacted the dissertation committee and set up my defense."

"Wow. That's great. Well, we don't need to start the canning yet," Mary said. "First I need to make a mint infusion."

"Ah, and how do you do that?"

"I'll take care of it," she said. "You go and work on your book."

And so Bone went to the office to work as Mary prepared to infuse.

There comes a point after even the most arduous writing process when the author realizes with numbed awareness that the long trek is over and the book is finished. So he leans back from his keyboard, in Edmund Hillary–esque stupefaction, saying, "I'll be dog. This is the end, huh? Guess I might as well print it."

Bone's final entry was **zzz**, the cartoon onomatopoeia for snoring, which *The Oxford English Dictionary* traces to H. G. Wells's *Tono-Bungay*, 1909. But Bone believed it went back a quarter of a century earlier. He'd searched the Net and pored through massive hardbound folios of collected cartoons at the main library, hunting the first cartoon with those three lightning bolts inked over a sleeping body, to no avail. He was certain it'd been Thomas Nast, the cartoonist who gave us a fat rather than skinny Santa, the donkey and elephant as political symbols, and lanky, goateed Uncle Sam; somewhere a cartoon pictured Boss Tweed, dimpled fingers laced over a bulging checkered vest, a balloon with a Z oozing through puckered lips. And Bone was as certain as certain could be that that Z had been suggested to the German-born Nast by *schnarken*, "snore," which starts with *s-*, but sounding more like an unvoiced *z-*, besides which, had Nast used S, it would have appeared that Tweed had sprung a leak or was trying unsuccessfully to whistle; had it been SH, it would have seemed Tweed was telling someone to "sh"; and SHN would have been merely perplexing. So Nast hit upon Z, instantly to be imitated by lesser followers, a genuine addition to American idiom, lost in the pile of Nast's many other contributions.

But lacking the cartoon itself as the first link in the chain of evidence, it came to nothing but conjecture, and after researching hours and weeks at home, on the computer and in the library, wondering if he'd have to bear it out even to the edge of doom, Bone came to a realization.

It didn't matter.

It didn't matter whether Nast came up with Z or someone else did, perhaps Hogarth—but it couldn't have been Hogarth; Hogarth never used speech balloons!—in any case, it didn't matter. The thought of this made Bone laugh, and he went into the kitchen, where even then Mary was ladling translucent green syrup into jars.

"I'm done," he told her, surprised to hear himself speak the words. "I'm done with *Words*."

"Wow," she said. "Bone, that's terrific."

"If I meet with my dissertation committee in October, I can squeak under the wire to have my hooding ceremony in January. I'll be a PhD."

"You must feel terrific."

"Really, I don't feel anything at all," Bone said, but he was smiling as he said this. "It's like I've been dipped in Novocain. I don't know how I feel."

Still somewhat dazed, Bone walked to the mailbox and looked through the mail, smiling to find another response from someone he'd written in gratitude. One letter was a postcard picture of the Atlanta skyline. Bone's blood chilled when he turned it over and saw these words.

Your life is in terrible danger.

Do not tell anybody about this message, but meet me

at the Waffle House on the I-285 access road

at 7:00 A.M. tomorrow.

CHAPTER TWENTY-FOUR

X, x

Scholars dispute whether the Greeks invented **X** or adapted it from the Semitic *samek* (𐤎), "fish." Compounding the puzzle, *samek* looks *nothing* like a fish but seems derived from the Egyptian *djed*, a scaffold-looking hieroglyph representing the god Osiris's backbone. Western Greek pronounced **X** /*ks*/; Eastern Greek, however, which became the dominant dialect, pronounced it /*kh*/. English is the loser by adopting the Western pronunciation. Had we done otherwise, **XING** would not be a bastard expediency of signage but a legitimate abbreviation, and **Christ** and **crucify** would begin with a cross.

x: In math, the unknown, an abbreviation of the Arabic *xei*, "thing."

Though not officially supposed to drive in his walking cast, Bone left the home before Mary's arrival and at 7:12 was sitting facing front in a booth at the back, the All-Star glistening in grease and heavy white plates before him—he felt akin to a fool to sit without ordering *something*—when warm air gusted in, and the waitress and short-order cook called out in unison, "Welcome to Waff—" before their greetings died at slight intervals in their throats. A man in a dirty gray-streaked beard and greasy baseball cap stood by the jukebox, his gaze panning the restaurant, until one eye—an ominous black patch covered the other—fell upon Bone like a chill.

The waitress cast Bone an anxious and protective look as the man sat opposite him.

The stranger leaned his beard over the coffee cup. "You don't recognize me?" He pulled off his cap and lifted his eye patch to reveal a right eye as clear and bright as the left. Bone's arm shot up in terror, upsetting his plate of hash browns.

Limongello.

Or rather the man who'd once impersonated him. The fake Limongello assured Bone he had no intention of alarming anyone, reaching under his back collar to pull out the little pillow that had formed his hunchback and making a whisking motion of his fingertips over his dirty, colorless wardrobe. "All this is just a disguise." Bone suspected *some* of it wasn't just a disguise. "I can't let anyone guess my real identity."

Bone snorted before he could stop himself. "This is your idea of being *inconspicuous*?"

The fake Limongello chuckled and shrugged. "The main thing is I'm not recognized."

"How'd you ever get a job with Cash?"

"He needed someone to speak Mexican." Fake Limongello indicated himself with a thumb.

"Goddamn it, that's not even a language. You mean Spanish. Do you even speak Spanish?"

"High school. I can count one to twenty, and I know the words to 'La Cucaracha.' I can ask where the sister of Pedro *trabajas* at. I say that sort of stuff to Jorge and gesture what to do. Mostly he gets the idea. Mostly." Fake Limongello stared into the middle distance. "I knew all along I wasn't the real Dr. Limongello, but as soon as I heard about your condition, I was sure I could help."

Bone's fingers spread on the table as if it were a keyboard. He was heavily conscious of the need to speak slowly, calmly, and soothingly and above all to make no sudden movements. "Don't worry. It's okay. We can get you help."

"I don't need help," he said. "I am help. Don't you get it? I'm back."

"I see that."

"I don't mean I'm back here," he said. "I mean I'm back. My *self* is back."

"Y'all need anything?" the waitress asked. Not lifting his eyes from the madman across the booth from him, Bone transmitted thought rays: *Call 911, call 911, call 911.* Limongello waved her off and said, "No, we're fine," his tone calm and pleasant, his expression the same quizzical, humorous one he always wore, his dark eyes sparkling. "My name is Mulligan Wye. My friends call me 'Flash.' I'm a used-car salesman down near Stone Mountain. I knew all along I wasn't Limongello, but I didn't know who I was. I knew who they *told* me I was, but that's not the same. They kept telling me who I was, and I tried pretending. The meds made it easier, but I was still just pretending. I didn't feel like me. But I do now. I got it back. I got my self back. I'm

Flash Wye. I'm a used-car salesman. I live down near Stone Mountain."

"Good for you," Bone said. He tried to keep his smile from wavering, but it was no use. His arm shot up. He began giggling. Mustn't giggle.

"Fortunately, I got a plan," Wye said, "and you got an ace in the hole Cash don't know about." Flash waggled a thumb at himself. "Me. He don't know he's got a double agent on his yard crew. And I'll tell you something. You got Cash worried."

"Me?"

"Why-oh-you, you," Wye affirmed. "He says to keep an eye on you and Mary whenever we come to do yard work. Haven't you noticed how often Cash comes around? No yard needs that much work! Look at your knockout roses—they've been watered and fed and mulched and trimmed to hell and back! Cash's whole business is going to wrack and ruin keeping an eye on you."

"Why's he worried about me?"

Wye gave Bone an exasperated look. "You really are dumber than ditch water. I mean, you're walking around with a dictionary in your head, but you don't got the sense God gave a stick. Meaning no disrespect," Wye mused and picked up a bacon slice, which he chewed. "In any case," he leaned forward, "now we can start on your cure."

"I'm already being treated," Bone said.

"And a lot of good it's doing you," Wye responded sardonically with a nod at Bone's rogue arm. "We already talked about this. You don't want to just be a bag of chemicals, do you? You're more than that, aren't you?"

"It's not like that."

"It's exactly like that," Wye said. "I found the cure, Bone. Not a treatment. Cure. The cure to Self-Dislodgement. I worked it out on my own. I was on the right track with those tasks I gave you, but it was just the start. I've been working out some more intensive therapies."

Bone did not like the sound of that. "You nearly killed me."

"What?"

Bone well understood the folly of alarming this graybeard loon, but he didn't care; squeezed in a vise of fear and anger, he shook until silver ripples shivered across the black coffee in the cup by his fingertips. "That damn therapy of yours nearly killed me. I was stuck in my house for—" the next word was spoken in a half-sob—"days. I couldn't get through the door. I nearly died of thirst, thanks to your goddamn therapy."

"I don't understand." Wye took a toast triangle from Bone's plate and chewed, ruminating. His eyes dulled, and he looked down at the table. "Did you try square dancing?"

Now Bone really had to laugh. "Oh, I tried square dancing! I tried square dancing! I tried going on all fours, squeezing through windows, I ended up crawling through the attic and breaking my leg. I tried square dancing!"

"And the therapies I gave you. The three tasks, you were doing those?" When Bone didn't answer, Wye looked up, the mild, quizzical, humorous glint back in his eye. He nodded, shook his head, nodded again, and took a bite from the buttery center of the toast, chewing as he spoke. "The therapy doesn't work if you discontinue it, Mr. King."

"It isn't a therapy!" Bone said loudly. His arm went up like an exclamation mark, and an empty plate—*pakkatta-pakkatta-pakka*—did its own little rotating dance. Then Bone repeated more softly, "It isn't a therapy."

"It is," Wye asserted calmly. "It is a therapy. But you've only just started. I've developed a whole new set of tasks."

"Do your treatment, and suddenly I'll be happy. Right."

"Happy? I never said you'd be happy. I'm crazy, but I'm not a quack! I never said you'd be happy. I just said you'd be your *self*. That's all I said."

"If you're going to tell me something hokey like think nice thoughts and do good deeds for the neighbors—" Bone began.

"There's a lot more to it than that," Wye said peevishly. His brow creased and lower lip stuck out, but he regained his composure as soon as he'd lost it. "It goes a lot deeper. As soon as you undergo the full treatment—" He leaned back, displaying himself—his dirty, gray-streaked beard, his hair mashed down as if the baseball cap were still crammed on it, the Halloween-pirate eye patch flipped over his eyebrow. "Well, look at me." The personal testimonial was not as compelling as perhaps he imagined.

"All right, so what's the next phase of this 'treatment'?" Bone aimed for a sardonic note but missed the mark, sounding, in spite of himself, curious—curious almost bordering on hopeful.

"Ah!" Wye said, and "ah!" again. He leaned forward, fingers laced. "That's the thing. The next part of the treatment won't work unless you figure it out for yourself."

"What?"

"It's a custom-made treatment. You have to figure it out on your own. It's part of the deal. You have to relearn to empathize with yourself. You have to see yourself as a person who's worthy of having what you need. You have to know there's things that matter, that you can say, 'This matters. It's important.' You have to find something to say, 'I need this.'"

Bone tried being stern, but an irrepressible sunny bubble of Yang was rising in the heart of midnight Yin. "You left me to die," he said, returning to what seemed the crux.

"I had to go to Leipzig."

Bone slapped the table in his anger. "There is no Leipzig!"

Of course, what he meant was there *is* a Leipzig, only Wye had never been there. Wye seemed to understand this. "There is a Leipzig," he retorted calmly. "There's different kinds of Leipzig. There's a Leipzig of the *self.*" He tapped his forehead meaningfully.

Bone gathered his breath and said slowly and precisely, as

if he were translating word by word from semaphore flags, "It's okay. It's going to be okay. Just wait here and I'll get help."

"You doubt my methods," Wye said. "You don't trust me."

"I'll get you help. You're sick. Oh, God." Bone leaned back in the booth. "I actually believed there was a plague out there—an epidemic of selves dislodging from people's brains. Oh, God, how did I ever fall for that?"

At this Wye became upset. "I wasn't the only one. We weren't the only ones. You think I'd have bothered you if I was the only one? There's others. Radical Self-Dislodgement is real! You remember the woman I told you about who said, 'okely-dokely'? I've seen her; when she's ranting about politics, there's this weird light in her eyes, and you know, you just know, that's her *self* trying to get out, it's pulling at the bars, but it can't because it's trapped inside all these catchphrases and sound bites. That's what I'm talking about here."

"Oh, my God, I just realized. You're talking about your own wife, aren't you?"

Wye turned his head away and looked somberly out the window. "It's too late for her. I tried to help her, but the syndrome went untreated too long, and now she's totally dislodged." He turned back to Bone. "You want that to happen to you?"

In spite of knowing better, the prospect of dislodgement horrified Bone. But he merely said, as calmly as he could, "You are very ill, and you need professional help."

"You aren't going to use my therapy."

"No. I'm not." He was almost sorry to tell him this.

"You'd rather take a pill," Wye said as if the word itself were a pill, "that makes your arm go up and live without the woman you love than put yourself in my hands."

"It seems preferable."

"I wish you'd listen to me. We're on the verge of an epidemic here. A plague. This is serious. Americans are ninety percent dislodged from their selves from the start." Wye shook his head. "But if you don't believe me, you don't believe me."

"That's right."

"I can't force you to undergo therapy."

"Damn straight you can't."

"And that's your right. But will you at least acknowledge my right to seek my own mental health in my own way?"

"You need serious help," Bone protested.

"And from where I sit, you need serious help," Wye said, smiling and turning up his palms. "We're at an impasse. We both have our different ways, and we both think the other one's making a mistake. I wasn't kidding with my note. You are in terrible, terrible danger, but even so, I say you have the right to make your own mistakes, even if they're very serious. Will you acknowledge I have the same right?" Bone's arm went up. "You got to admit," Wye said, "there's something to be said for my position." He jammed his baseball cap on his head and stood, flipping his eye patch into place, retrieving his hunchback pillow, and snagging another piece of bacon from Bone's plate. "At least admit I have the right to choose my own path." Wye gave one of his long, slow winks, where the eyelid traveled as steadily down the eye as a drawn shade—the dramatic effect of which was marred by the eye patch—then closed the door, leaving the waitress and short-order cook staring as if Elvis had just left the Waffle House.

"Oʜ, ᴍʏ Gᴏᴅ. You've got to call the police immediately," Mary said when Bone recounted seeing the madman formerly known as Dr. Limongello. "Where is he?" Jars bobbled against each other in a sterilizing bath of simmering water, and the kitchen was filled with the pleasant steam of orange zest and sugar syrup; Mary and Bone had embarked on canning marmalade.

Bone scratched the end of his nose. "I couldn't say." A subtle obfuscation, meaning *I've decided not to say*.

"It's not just you," Mary said. "Think what he might do to other people. And for his own sake. He's a danger to himself."

"It—" Bone said but didn't have anything to add and left the naked pronoun hanging in space. Any defense would have been a lie: that Flash hadn't nearly killed him, that the catastrophe might have happened anyway. Why he'd mentioned seeing Flash at all, who can say, unless it was the irresistible temptation of such a toothsome piece of news to report to a woman whom he still loved. But having admitted Wye *existed*, Bone didn't divulge that he was, so to speak, right under her very nose, in a greasy baseball cap and an eye patch filched from a Halloween pirate costume.

Let Flash try to work out his own cure in his own way; let him uncover, if he could, the secret to prevent the self from dislodging.

"You could have died," she said, and the rest of the day, at irregular intervals, she caught Bone's eye and mouthed, "You could have died."

Mary wasn't the only one displeased by Bone's meeting with Flash Wye.

"He's a very dangerous man," Dr. Limongello said when Mary told him at their next appointment. "There's no telling how much harm he could do if he's willing to pose as a physician."

"But he doesn't say he's you anymore. He knows who he is now," Bone said.

"And it's not just other people," Limongello went on, ignoring Bone's protest. "He's a danger to himself."

"That's just what I said," Mary said.

"And not just that," Limongello said, "by shielding him, you might be an accessory. In fact," he tucked his chin against his Adam's apple, "your crime might be more serious than his. He can't *help* it." Bone shifted miserably on the examination table. Was that a gleam of vengeance in the doctor's eye?

THE MORTON LIBRARY on the seventh floor of the General Classroom Building was a library only in the broadest and most general sense of the term. It had perhaps a hundred or so books arranged behind glass-doored bookshelves. The principal library occupied twin buildings next to the concrete square laughingly known as the "quad," with a glass-walled bridge spanning Decatur Street to "Library South." But it was in the Morton Library that Bone met his dissertation committee for the final time. There was the requisite amount of chaffing.

"You may have set the record for the longest time completing a dissertation," Dr. Susik said.

"I've been going through some personal issues," Bone explained. But Susik was only ribbing him. She was a grammarian herself, one of the old school, and famished for recruits.

"This dissertation of yours," said Dr. Moore, the only one who bordered on hostility; a theorist and specialist on Derrida, she whiffed eighteenth-century mustiness in Bone's proposal and had been against it from the start. "It's really nothing but a list of words. And not a very complete list."

"It's really more of an appreciation," Bone said. "After all, what're definitions but an attempt to find meaning?" He realized he was quoting Limongello. No, he corrected himself, he was quoting Flash Wye. He coughed, and his arm went up.

The committee exchanged glances, and Dr. Vinsonhaler asked Bone to wait outside while they discussed him. Bone sat in the hall on a bench with a padded cushion. To his right, a ponderous thunderhead in the window began to bloom in the summer sky. How long before Vinsonhaler opened the door and let him in? It was nothing to be concerned about—just what they put you through before signing off on your dissertation, a last piece of hazing before admitting you into their little club.

He suddenly realized the dissertation wouldn't make a difference. Not really. People wouldn't see him differently. He wouldn't *be* different. He'd accept the degree, of course; he'd earned it and would accept it. It meant more opportunity. But it wouldn't change anything that mattered. There was no sadness in this thought; that was the peculiar thing: no sadness or sense of loss or anything like that, just a realization, like looking out the window and seeing it was going to rain. At that moment, Vinsonhaler opened the door to invite him in so the committee could congratulate him.

"That's great, man," Cash said when Bone told him later. "You finally did it." He didn't sound especially enthusiastic, and the "finally" felt aggressive, a little snipe the yardman couldn't resist. Cash asked, "Is Mary in there?" He stood in the kitchen door, leaning against the jamb, his elbow jacked above his ear. He didn't look at Bone but at something along the ceiling, above Bone's head and to the left.

Cash and Mary stood by the stump of the Rose of Sharon, Cash doing most of the talking. Mary, one arm folded across her abdomen, the opposite hand on her hip, watched Bone go up in his walking cast to the mailbox. Bills and an outsized letter on card stock: an engraved invitation from Georgia State to his own hooding ceremony.

"They're talking about you." Flash crouched in the English ivy near the mailbox, spraying poison ivy with Roundup. The conversation between Cash and Mary ended. Cash went to chew Jorge out about something and Mary to the kitchen door.

In Bone's periphery, two cars parked at the curb. He registered that the second was a black-and-white patrol car even as the door opened and an officer got out. Bone's arm shot up, banging his knuckles against the mailbox lid. Dr. Limongello, the real one, got out of the other car. Things weren't making sense. Had Limongello run a stop sign? What were the odds of his getting ticketed in front of Bone's house? The doctor spared Bone no more than a glance, staring instead at Flash, bent down amid the poison ivy.

"That's him," Dr. Limongello said. Only now was Bone piecing together significances. "She can identify him." Mary came up the driveway, not running but in long strides.

The officer said, "Are you Mulligan Wye?"

Here Flash faced a conundrum: admitting his identity would result in being taken off in a squad car, but denying it would substantiate his mental illness, resulting in being taken off anyway. If he weighed these considerations, he hesitated no longer than any man after an unexpected question. "That's me."

"I'll need you to step into the car for me," the deputy said. Helping him into the backseat, the deputy cupped the top of Wye's baseball cap, not pushing, just lightly touching, like a priest's blessing, as if out of solicitude lest he bump his head. All this time, Bone stood slack-jawed. The entire episode had taken less than two minutes.

"I knew who it was as soon as you said you'd seen him," Mary said. "What a getup! He really is crazy." So Mary had snitched.

Limongello stood, arms folded, clutching his elbows, his chin tucked against his neck, yet somehow his head still level.

"What's going on here?" Cash asked with restrained impatience, believing all this was somehow about him. And why shouldn't he think that? One of his two remaining workers had just been abducted by the law. But Bone had been thinking that he, Bone King, was the focal point of this tableau, and Limongello—the real one—had been thinking *he* was. Mary thought she was, too, and so, no doubt, did Flash, and the deputy. Bone looked down the driveway. Even Jorge, with shy eagerness watching hidden behind his rake's insufficient concealment like Greek letter *phi* (Φ), had something to tell his family that night: *my life among the crazy Anglos.* Yes, Jorge, too, like each of the rest of them, was thinking, This is about me, this is another episode in the story that is about what happens to me.

Now the deputy gave a signal, and Limongello, raising his chin in acknowledgment, then tucking it back against his Adam's apple, got into his own car, rumbled it into motion, and followed the patrol car out of the neighborhood.

"What happened?" Cash asked again. "What's going on?"

"I'll tell you about it later," Mary said in a fatigued voice, already heading back to the house. The show was over here. "When we get home."

CHAPTER TWENTY-FIVE

Y, y

Derived, like **F**, **U**, **V**, and **W**, from the Semitic *waw* (**Y**), "peg," and the one that most closely resembles its ancestor. In addition to its familiar pronunciations as vowel and consonant, it is on rare occasions pronounced /th/. Typesetters used **Y** in place of a defunct Old English letter, the *thorn* (Þ), which represented the /th/ sound. The "ye" in kitschy signage such as "Ye Olde Gifte Shoppe" does not mean "your"; it is prosaically and unromantically pronounced "the."

Yang and Yin: From the Mandarin, "light" and "dark," or possibly "sun" and "moon," depicted as interlocking black and white whorls, each with a dot of the other in its center, symbolizing unity or the cosmos. Compare **alpha and omega**.

yoga: Vulgarly a system of exercise but more accurately "discipline." From the Sanskrit *yogu,* "yoke" or "harness." The three types of yoga are **Karma Yoga**, the discipline of action without attachment to results; **Jnana Yoga**, the discipline of understanding what is real and unreal, permanent and temporary, and **Bhakti Yoga**, the discipline of loving devotion to the cosmos.

I n the name of keeping him active, Mary incrementally handed over the household chores to Bone, at first under her hawkeyed supervision and then on his own. She sent him on daily strolls in his walking cast and each week exiled him across the street to play cards and watch TV with Charlotte, the landlady. Although Mary always sent him on these excursions alone, she didn't go back to

Cash's until he returned. Once, coming in after an especially nail-biting cribbage finale—his blue peg had squeaked across the finish line a whisker ahead of Charlotte's red one—he found Mary's face wet with tears, having, she explained, just watched a sad movie.

Another routine was Tuesday at the Food Bank. He volunteered partly to see Mary's pleased and startled reaction and partly to get at least one unselfish deed under his belt per week. Bone didn't find the chore a pleasant one, but he kept going, and gradually it got easier. Father Pepys never failed to bend his ear, but the worst part was one of the regulars, who'd lost her left leg and her husband, both to diabetes—the husband indirectly; he'd abandoned her after the amputation. She smelled bad, looked dirty even when she wasn't, and couldn't make a subject and verb agree to save her life.

Every time she came in, the woman enveloped Bone's fingers in her moist dishrag of a hand and talked *without pause* five minutes at a stretch about Jesus, how he'd come to save us, how he loved us, how he'd *suffered*—and then she would start to cry. Bone had to stay put until she was good and done, wishing he were anywhere but there. He felt ashamed of his feelings, but that didn't alter them or make him look forward to seeing her with anything but dismay.

Bone speculated to Father Pepys that the one-legged lady cried not because of Jesus but because her husband had left her, she was poor and alone, and her body was bent on piecemeal butchery.

When Father Pepys heard all this, he just gave Bone a look, like, "So what's your point?"

THE DAY BEFORE his interview at Oglethorpe, in a room as white as medical science and latex paint could make it, the orthopedist, Dr. Patel, laid the blade of the electric saw against the cast and turned it on. The blade didn't exactly cut the cast but vibrated it apart with a buzzing that reached right down to Bone's foot, crunching through the cottony crème brûlée of plaster while the bony nurse who smelled of crushed aspirin and bandage adhesive looked on. After confinement in its plaster cocoon, Bone's foot was not nearly as pink or moist as he'd imagined.

"Wiggle your toes for me," the orthopedist instructed. Bone wiggled them. "Now, stand." In spite of the momentary terror of putting his weight on his broken ankle after so long, Bone stood. "How's that feel?" It felt fine.

Mary presented him with his other shoe, which sat in a chair beside her in vacant expectation, a sock curled in its gullet. On the way home, she had him drive. His shoe felt as unfamiliar as an oven mitt.

In spite of having assigned the cooking and cleaning to Bone, on the morning of his job interview at Oglethorpe, Mary didn't let him so much as pour his own orange juice but made him the "field hand" breakfast: eggs, bacon, grits, and oven toast with crispy brown edges and buttery centers. He had a big day ahead, and she wanted him fueled up for it.

She wore a preoccupied expression, and Bone asked her why.

"Nothing," she said. "Just thinking."

Bone had sent in his vita and application without expectation, but then—surprise, surprise—Dr. Weinmeker, the humanities chair, asked to meet him for an interview. "You don't need me to drive you," Mary told Bone, and for a moment, he thought she would lean in and kiss him, but instead, she just patted his shoulder. She made him change his shirt twice and pants once before letting him go. She didn't bother letting him select a tie but chose one for him, subjecting him, before he left, to one last inspection. "You missed a belt loop. Jesus, Bone," she said, but not without affection.

Bone fixed it. "Is that better?"

She stared at him judiciously, then nodded, and for the umpteenth time, he felt an illogical transport of joy. How wonderful she was! She embraced him and this time did give him a kiss, only on the cheek, but very tenderly. She pulled away with a strange, wistful look in her eye he could not interpret.

"Wish me luck."

"Good luck," she said. Then added, "You'll do great."

That Bone managed to be late was not his fault; at the Johnson Ferry traffic light, a sedan hit the curb in a manner Bone concluded was guaranteed to pop the tire; a few rotations later, the tire itself came to the same conclusion. The starboard bumper sagged, and a plopping and grinding trailed the car as it rolled on the wheel rim. The sedan turned in to Patterson's Funeral Home, and Bone followed and, sliding down his window, asked, "Need any help?"

"God, yes, could you?" said the driver, a man with black hair oddly piled on his head like Lyle Lovett's. "I've never changed a tire. And I've got to be somewhere, like"—a moment to calculate the time—"like now."

Bone found himself stuck by the unanticipated glueyness of an offer he hadn't expected the other driver to accept. But he couldn't decently say, "I didn't really intend to help; I was being nice," so he got out of his car, reminding himself, "This is a good day," and mentally clapping his hands. He shook his head. Lord, how the fake Limongello's advice persisted.

Bone made a call but got only Weinmeker's answering machine. He opened the sedan's trunk and pulled away the ersatz carpet and particle-board covering to find the replacement tire and jack stowed as snug as Russian stacking dolls. The stranded motorist murmured approving murmurs, occasionally scratching his ankle—a skin infection, Bone surmised.

Inserting the hook end of the lug wrench into the jack's ring nose, Bone turned and turned while the device grudgingly expanded into a flattened trapezoid, thence to a square, thence to a diamond, and the rear bumper slowly hove into the air until at last the tire finally levitated, still flattened on the bottom, unable to forget its puncture. The thin sound of a speeding car grew fatter as it approached, and thin again as it went by.

This is how I feel when I'm being impatient, Bone reminded himself, and the anxiety-producing calcitonin in his bloodstream ebbed a bit, and he began to calm. After all, it wasn't as bad as all that. There were worse things than being late for Oglethorpe.

"Can I pay you anything?" the man asked.

"No, no problem," Bone demurred, giving him a smile. "Just do something nice for the next guy, I guess." As the sedan drove off, Bone examined his grimy hands. The knee of his dress pants was dirty, too, but he couldn't do anything about that. He'd have to stop in the Burger King to wash, and by now he was already a good twenty minutes overdue. His cell phone hadn't buzzed. No one had called to see what had detained him.

With the serenity that comes from the certainty that one has well and truly blown it, Bone arrived at Oglethorpe and entered the big front doors, where he consulted the building directory to find Weinmeker's office. Already framing his excuse for being so late, he ascended the wooden stairs and knocked. Oh, well, there would be other jobs.

As Bone entered, the man behind the desk rose from his chair, even his Lyle Lovett hair registering surprise to see Bone again so soon. The stranded motorist.

From time to time as they talked, Russell Weinmeker

reached down to pull up his pant cuff and scratch the skin above his argyle sock. "Can't help it," Weinmeker said without sounding in the least chagrined. "It's a skin condition. The dermatologist says there's nothing to do for it. It's not contagious." Weinmeker reminded Bone of Loundsberry, or rather what Loundsberry would have been had Loundsberry had any choice in the matter. Loundsberry apotheosized. "Anyway, now that I've given you the rundown of how we do things around here, let me show you around." From the hall outside Weinmeker's office, they descended through a dark stairwell and into the brightness of a crisp fall day. "The original campus was burned during the Civil War. Everything you see was built in 1915 by Dr. Thornwall Jacobs," Weinmeker said, explaining the medieval-looking stone edifices around them. "He was an MD who wanted it to look as he imagined Oxford College in England looks. Whenever we have to add something new, we try to keep consistent with the original design."

Leaves had changed color but only just begun to fall; crowns of trees rose like variegated red-and-orange hillsides against the horizon. At one end of the quad, yellow leaves spread like a tablecloth at the base of a maple. A carillon above the turreted clock tower chimed, filling the fall air with music. It resembled an Ivy League university in a movie where the cocky student ultimately gets the girl but first learns an enduring life lesson from Professor Witherwood, the curmudgeonly lecturer who conceals a heart of gold beneath his crusty exterior. The effect was undeniably corny but beautiful. Fulsome didn't even have a quad, unless you counted the parking lot between the English building and the main offices.

Weinmeker led Bone through the tall oaken door into the clock-tower building, where there was a library, not ostentatious but commodious, with rows of hardbound volumes ranged in muted reds, greens, and browns on the shelves of tall bookcases equipped with a rolling wooden ladder running along a rail to reach the top. Soft leather armchairs faced a pair of tall windows overlooking the campus and the early-autumn afternoon.

"Dr. Wilson," Weinmeker said, addressing the occupants of one of these chairs, "I'd like to introduce Dr. King."

Wilson, putting aside a book, extracted himself with the aid of a cane from the valley of a deep chair. He was a slight, elfin man with an absurdly precise pencil mustache. He didn't wear a tweed jacket but, like Weinmeker, had a vest and bow tie. Bone began to wonder if working here would require buying a new wardrobe.

"His dissertation is on etymology," Weinmeker said, "and his thesis won first place for Books on Grammar and Usage in the Southeast."

"As a matter of fact, I'm already familiar with it," Wilson said, smiling and holding up the book he'd been reading. To Bone's astonishment, it was *Misplaced Modifiers*.

"I was telling Dr. King about our curriculum here at Oglethorpe," Weinmeker said, reaching down to lift a pant leg and scratch his ankle.

"Yes, we're very traditional," Wilson said. "For the first two years, it's nothing but—good Lord!"

Bone's arm had shot up involuntarily.

"It's a condition," Bone explained, "or actually the side effect of my medication. Sometimes my arm goes up like that. Sorry, I know it's kind of disturbing. They can't seem to get my meds balanced."

Wilson and Weinmeker exchanged a look, but not, as Bone might have expected, one of alarm or discomfort. Rather, they seemed to communicate some silent signal of approval—even envy?—Dr. King would need no skin condition or cane to make him eccentric enough for Oglethorpe. Get him a vest and a bow tie, and he'd fit like a pen in a pen holder.

"Anyway," Wilson continued, recovering himself, "for the students' first year, it's all classics: Plato, Aristotle, Socrates. Then on to Locke, Hume, and Kant. We don't let them even touch their core classes until they have a solid foundation in the basics."

"We need someone to teach a class in good, traditional grammar starting spring semester. The other applicants—" Weinmeker trailed off and shook his head.

"Comp-Rhet," Wilson said. "They go around using words like 'Comp-Rhet.' I suppose it's okay if you like that sort of thing. But it's not for us. We're trying to impart a sense of tradition."

"Anyway," Weinmeker said, "let me show you one of our classrooms."

They crossed the quad to another building, and Weinmeker led Bone down a hallway past a bulletin board posted with notices—someone looking for a roommate, selling a ten-speed, offering free kittens, a brightly colored photo of the Mediterranean advertising a study-abroad program. A door with a frosted-glass window opened into a classroom. The gravity of the dark hardwood floor was alleviated by dust-moted light pouring though tall windows. The nose-tickling odor of chalk dust lingered in the air like the echo of a prayer. "We should probably get those smartboard things," Weinmeker said, "and in the fullness of time, we probably will. We have the budget, Lord knows. There's no fighting progress. Still, we do what we can."

Bone brushed his fingertips over the blackboard's pleasing grittiness. It had another blackboard on top that could be rolled back and forth in case someone needed to save the notes from a previous lecture. Sir Isaac Newton had been erased, but his pale ghost remained.

Back in Weinmeker's office, Bone came right out and asked his chances.

"You're definitely a strong candidate," Weinmeker affirmed. "We have a few more applicants to look at, then we'll get back to you." They smiled at one another and shook hands, and Bone left.

He was halfway down the stairs before he turned and went back up. "I'm sorry," he said, reentering Weinmeker's office. He saw himself with sudden empathy; he was worthy of having what he needed. "But that just won't do. I'm sorry, but you'll have to tell me now. I won't leave until I know I got the job. This matters. It's important."

On the way home, Bone stopped at Kroger for a bottle of chardonnay—Mary's favorite, and maybe some cheese—what else? Some fruit to go with it, for that extra je ne sais quoi. Selecting the sole pear they would divide and share, a mellow amber orb in a spongy white net, Bone rehearsed his lines as well as his dour look: "I need a drink," he'd announce as he came in—look dour, Bone, look dour—he'd let just the bottle top show over the top of the bag for corroboration, a paper bag to complete the look of wino desperation. "Well, first, I was late," Bone would say truthfully—dour, dour. The rest—how he'd rescued Weinmeker and then wowed him at the interview, about his ultimatum and the emergency Star Chamber convened to grant him the job—he'd save for when they were sharing Camembert, pear wedges, and a good laugh at how he'd fooled her; *nearly fooled her* was as close as she'd come to admitting it.

As Bone pulled onto his street, he reconsidered his tactics; dour was too obvious; she'd see right through that. Instead, he'd act *brave*: a smile, but he'd try to make it tremble a little. He'd keep the line about being late and how he wanted a drink. He'd say he didn't want to talk about it, which of course would make Mary pry it out of him. He chuckled at how well the surprise was going to work. A big bunch of birds all at once lifted from the green grass in a blizzard of black scraps.

He didn't surprise her; she surprised him. Her Honda was gone from the carport, and on the kitchen counter he found her note.

Bone,

Congratulations. I know you will get the job. I'm sorry I'm not here in person. [She had begun to add a "but" but changed her mind and crossed it out.] I couldn't leave when I thought you needed me. But you don't need me anymore because you've got everything set. The medication is working, your dissertation is finished, and soon you'll have a new job. Dr. Limongello will get your meds balanced to take care of the arm thing, but even that's not anything really serious. Good luck in your life. You're going to do great things and be very happy. The one thing I'm sorry about is I won't be there to see you hooded at your dissertation ceremony.

—M

[She had also started to add a "P" for PS but had crossed this out, too.]

For a few moments, Bone just stared at the letter.

Her strange, solemn expression. Her insistence he drive himself home from the doctor and then to Oglethorpe. Getting him to help her with the cooking and cleaning and finally making him take it over. She'd been preparing him. Seeing to it that he could get along without her.

She'd planned this all along. He shook his head at his own obtuseness. How could he not have seen this coming? He felt a mixture of gratitude and loss so poignant, it was almost unendurable. He sighed and felt his shoulders rise and fall.

So, okay, then.

CHAPTER TWENTY-SIX

Z, Z

From *zayn* ($\mathbf{I}$), "ax," the seventh letter of the Semitic alphabet. The Greeks bent the handle to create *zeta* (Z), giving it a serrated tooth in keeping with its saw-like buzz, a sound never made by any ax. The letter has not changed in appearance since. The British name for Z is *zed*, the only letter Shakespeare ever used as an insult: "Thou whoreson zed, thou unnecessary letter!" (*King Lear* II, ii).

zeugma: A pun employing the same word with two different meanings in one sentence: "The patient wasn't."

zero: One less than one, from the Arabic *zifr*, "cipher." The addition of zero to the set of whole numbers facilitated momentous mathematical achievements not possible to the inflexible numerical system of the Romans and Greeks.

zzz: A cartoon idiom for snoring, without clear onomatopoetic value but intuitively appropriate. Attributed to H. G. Wells, *Tono-Bungay*, 1909.

Time did the one thing you can count on; it passed. Bone taught at Oglethorpe, sorted out his new life alone, prepared his manuscript to send to publishers, and speculated on what had become of Flash Wye. He knew better than to ask the real Limongello the whereabouts of the fake one, but since there hadn't been anything in the news about it and no one had served him with a subpoena or asked for a deposition, he reasoned that maybe Wye hadn't been charged after all. Was it possible that—his wrist firmly and sternly slapped and a judicial finger wagged at him in no uncertain manner—Wye had been released to the outside world, supervised, of course, like a GPS-equipped coyote, "set free" by a naturalist for the purpose of monitoring? Might Wye at this very moment be working at his old job?

Bone's dreams began a few days after Mary left. These were not the suffocating dreams of attic entrapment, but they left him with the same tingling sensation of incompletion, that there was something left unattended to. He woke in the morning aware he'd had the dream but unable to recall it, and during the day he'd forget altogether. But then he'd wake the next morning from the same dream and say to himself, "Huh. I had the dream again." Only he couldn't remember what it was.

Days turned to weeks and weeks to one month, and then two, and other than the mild nuisance of a recurring but unrecallable dream, Bone fell into a not unpleasant if lonely routine, the formerly sharp divisions of Yin and Yang blending into the uniform soft gray of a dove's belly.

During a checkup with Dr. Limongello, he told the neurologist he'd been bothered by an odd recurring dream that he couldn't quite recall.

Limongello raised an eyebrow and tucked his receding chin into his neck. He was sitting on the edge of the desk, and his leg, which had been slowly swaying like a metronome, stopped midway. "Odd dreams are a potential side effect of the precursor," he said. "Or it may just be an ordinary dream." He stared at Bone as if trying to see straight through his skull until Bone shifted uneasily, repeating that he could never remember it.

The doctor's leg resumed its sway, but in a self-conscious way, and his heel thumped the desk. Limongello said, "I don't think it's anything to be concerned about, necessarily. Still, keep me posted if it continues."

"Do you think I should keep a journal?"

"What?"

"They say if you keep a journal and write in it when you first wake up, you'll remember your dreams."

The neurologist looked uncomfortable and expelled a few "well"s and soft "harrumph"s before getting out "I don't think that's a very good idea. We don't want you paying more attention to this than it deserves. Just keep me posted if anything changes. Still. Just to be safe. Let's move up your next appointment a little sooner. I'd like to see you again at the end of the week."

After his appointment, Bone went to the Food Bank, and within an hour of his arrival, who should roll in but his favorite customer? For God's sake, if she wanted to talk about Jesus, why didn't she take it up with the priest? Pepys was standing right there. But no, she headed straight for Bone and grabbed his hand.

Before she could start in on her favorite topic, Bone, hoping to forestall the inevitable waterworks, told her that he'd just seen the doctor himself and had a peculiar recurring dream that he could never remember the details of.

Her reaction was as unexpected as it was gratifying. "You gots to keep a dream journal," she said, her eyes wide, clearly impressed by the thought of a recurring but unretrievable dream. "It help you remember."

"That's exactly what I think," Bone said, marveling at the good sense of this woman who usually monopolized all the oxygen in the room talking and crying about Jesus. "That's exactly what I think." His arm went up, and it struck him how alike he and the one-legged lady were—alone with their strange afflictions; the difference was that when *he* had something to say, she listened and was interested. He began liking her a little better and vowed the next time they met, he'd take her hand before she took his.

So Bone put a pen and pad of paper on his nightstand— since finishing *Words*, he'd ceased keeping writing materials by the bed—and was rewarded that very night with the dream. As it turned out, he didn't need to write it down; waking up and seeing the pen and paper waiting at the bedside was enough to anchor the memory from floating off, and even though he still couldn't entirely recall it, he knew that if he concentrated, this would be the day that he would. He sat on the edge of the bed and mused: What was it about? What was it about?

Was Mary in it? No. He could touch the dream's delicate, fragile rim with his mental fingertips, and he sat very still as if at the slightest breath, it would scoot away from him like a dust bunny under the farthest corner of the bed.

Limongello was in it, although actually it wasn't the real Limongello but the man who'd called himself Limongello, the impostor, and Rachel the nurse was there, only sometimes instead of being Rachel, it was the lady at the Food Bank, and Father Pepys was there, and talking about the Prodigal Son and how it proved something or other, and Rachel kept telling Bone not to be a dumbass.

Bone chuckled and shook his head. What a funny dream. But what was it Limongello had been saying—something wasn't done yet—odd that Bone couldn't think of him as Flash Wye but kept calling him Limongello—somebody was feeding somebody something, but it wasn't clear who—and what had Limongello, the fake Limongello, said? It was—just on the tip of Bone's recollection—damn, what was it?

Silly how dreams are, he told himself; there's something you need to do in a dream, and when you wake up, you still feel like you really need to do it even if it's nonsense like tightening the frimjab on the lindenbob. But it didn't seem silly, and Bone clenched the edge of the mattress, his arms straight and rigid, as if he might rocket off into space if he let go or relaxed his grip just for an instant.

When he came home from his afternoon class at Oglethorpe, he set his leather satchel of papers on the kitchen counter and started water boiling for tea. He could have easily used the microwave but was comforted by the routine of watching the silver bubbles form. He changed into jeans, tennis shoes, and polo shirt, by which time the bubbles had begun to rise along the edges of the pot, and Bone read a few pages until it came to a boil, then a few pages more as the tea steeped, then a few pages more as he drank the tea, which he liked with cream and sugar.

By then it was time for his afternoon walk, and he strolled a precise circuit of streets—avoiding the street where Cash lived. Frequently, Bone ran into Mitch or another neighbor and made a point of stopping to talk. Each week, Bone watched just enough TV to come up with at least one well-rehearsed comment on the NFL or NASCAR. This was sufficient to set his neighbor off on a stream of happy chatter that required nothing from Bone but nods of simulated interest, or an occasional emphatic restatement of some point. It wasn't as bad as it sounded, and in spite of himself, Bone considered one day actually watching an entire game. Football season was over, but it was spring training for baseball, and he was already making plans to learn about that. But today, instead of sports, Bone told Mitch about his dream, of which he had retrieved the main outlines but still tantalizingly lacked key details. Mitch looked suitably intrigued and stroked his chin. He advised Bone to keep up the journal thing and see if that didn't help him remember the rest.

"Sometimes, you know," Mitch said, fumbling through a disorganized mental inventory of Freudianisms, "your dreams are trying to tell you something. It's your subconscious, you know, subliminal stuff."

Bone asked himself whose advice to trust: the professional

neurologist who was paid to treat him or random neighbors and acquaintances? The truth was, though, Bone didn't need to ask. Something in his blood had made up his mind already.

It was Wednesday, the night he traded off with Charlotte: one week she'd come to his house and he'd cook, and the next week he'd go to hers. Since it was his turn to host, he went to Kroger to pick up some snacks, and as he studied the shelf where the Spanish peanuts were, a cart turned its nose into the aisle, and behind that cart was Mary. He caught his breath at how it pleased and pained him to see her. They pretended it wasn't awkward. Her hair was shorter, and he said he liked it. She thanked him and said he looked like he was taking care of himself. He said he was and held up the jar of Spanish peanuts, explaining he normally didn't eat junk but was having someone over for dinner. Then he quickly added, without knowing why, that it was only Charlotte.

And how was Mary doing? Bone asked, and she said she was selling homemade preserves and things at Nuts 'n' Berries. A regular entrepreneur. He said that was good, and that things were going well at Oglethorpe. She asked about his condition, and he said it was fine, but the doctor thought it might be time to rebalance his meds.

They separated, each looking for the other items on their separate lists. He saw her again when he checked out but didn't speak to her this time. He tried catching her eye to give her a friendly nod, but she didn't look in his direction. Perhaps deliberately.

As he got into his car, he said to himself, "That wasn't so bad." They'd spoken, and he'd neither burst into tears nor made a fool of himself.

Later, Bone thought maybe Mary looked sad, but perhaps that's just what he wanted to see.

Months had passed since Mary had predicted it would be "about thirty days" before their divorce was finalized, but he hadn't received the official papers. Things often went slower than expected at the DeKalb County courthouse. Perhaps they'd mislaid the papers. Bone was in no hurry to get them in any case.

After supper, he and Charlotte played cribbage and watched TV. He told her about the dream he'd been having, the odd sensation of knowing it was repeating but being unable to remember exactly what it was, and Charlotte said she'd dreamed once that her niece was going to have twin boys, and that's just the way it turned out, which only went to show.

Thursday, Betty, who "just happened" to see Bone, said they were having a few people over Saturday night, nothing fancy, and could he come? There was an alarming proprietary twinkle in her eye, and Bone realized that his neighbor, with all the finesse of a kindly bear, was setting him up with a date. But after all, why not? There was no point turning into a eunuch. Bone said he'd be delighted to come, and what should he bring, bracing himself for whatever female golem Betty believed was "his type."

Once, he'd considered grammar and etymology the core of his being, the one thing he'd have pursued come estrangement from friends, unemployment, the loss of Mary—something that would justify himself to the universe and vice versa; he now realized grammar was just something he did, the way other people might grow sugar beets or do dry cleaning. Love, which he'd once thought was a period, he now realized was a semicolon. These were things he wished he'd known earlier.

Maybe Betty's golem wouldn't be as bad as he feared.

Bone didn't bring up the dream or his progress in recalling it when he saw Dr. Limongello Friday, but Limongello brought it up himself. After the customary updates, the testing of reflexes, and queries about whether Bone were having any more troubles with doors or locomotion generally, Limongello asked, trying—and failing—to sound casual, "So, have there been any more of those dreams of yours?"

"Oh, no," Bone said. And then "I don't think so," to make the lie a little milder.

"Uh-huh," the doctor said. "Sometimes strange dreams, when you wake up from them, can start to seem real. If they're vivid enough. Does that ever happen to you?"

"Oh, no, no," Bone said instantly, and maybe a little too instantly, because the doctor looked suspicious, and not for the first time, Bone suspected the neurologist might harbor a sneaking resentment, might be glad to see Bone get a little comeuppance for the fat check Rachel's lawyer-boyfriend had squeezed out of him.

"Well," the doctor said, evidently dissatisfied, "we'll keep an eye on it. Let me know if the dreams persist."

Bone left the doctor's office trembling, because the truth was that as soon as Limongello had asked about it, the missing part of the dream had flown into Bone's head all at once, and Bone had nearly blurted it out.

It was the next step of the therapy, Limongello—the fake Limongello, but Bone did not think of him that way—was saying. Bone had to take the next step. He was almost done, but he had to take the next step or his self would dislodge all over again. What was the next step? What was the next step? And that's what Limongello in his dream had come to tell him, that the next step was the part Bone had to figure out. Limongello couldn't tell him, Bone had to figure it out, but as soon as Bone figured it out, he'd know exactly what he had to do. Figuring it out was part of the therapy. And Rachel, who sometimes changed into the fat, one-legged lady, kept telling him not to be a dumbass.

As he did every Saturday morning, Bone walked a trail in a nearby park. His favorite part of the week was observing the changes of mood in that pond. Sunny mornings, it was the color of clouds and trees and sky; on overcast days, it was silver with dark ripples except in the shade, where it was dark with silver ripples. Today was foggy, and the pond was a bowl of smoke. Tonight was his dinner at Betty's.

After his walk, Bone came home and closed the door behind him.

And that's when he figured it out.

The next step of his therapy.

It was Mary.

As soon as he thought of it, he knew. It was go time. He needed to resume his therapy. Shit or get off the pot. It was now or never. He was almost there. But he could wait no longer. If he delayed one more day, it would be over. He would dislodge forever.

"God, this is crazy." Bone began pacing in circles on the kitchen floor. "Are you listening to yourself?" he asked aloud. "This is crazy. You can't be seriously thinking of doing this." But Bone's thudding heart would not let him heed his own advice.

"I'll go over there," he said, "and tell her I love her, and that I think she loves me, but that even if she doesn't love me, I love her. Although I think she does love me. And we need to try again, and keep trying, because we love each other, or at least I'm sure I love her, and if you love someone, you don't quit or give up, you keep trying, and maybe that's all love is, you just keep trying every day."

His heart was beating so hard against his rib cage, surely they could hear it down the street. "Be calm," Bone told himself. "Don't get worked up. You're talking crazy. We'll get you to the doctor. We probably just need to balance your meds."

But his heart was racing, and he could feel dopamine and oxytocin and serotonin fizzing up inside him like he was a shaken soda pop. He began to laugh. "Maybe you're crazy. But even if you're crazy—which maybe you are—what's the worst that can happen? You go over there and make a fool of yourself. Meanwhile, if you don't go—" Bone's ribs ached; how could your heart beat so hard without killing you? Bone's arm went up.

"I'm going to do it," Bone said. "I'm going over there," Bone said. He did not believe he was saying this. He did not disbelieve he was saying it, either. "I love her. She belongs with me." He merely said it. His arm went up. "She's my wife, damn it."

Bone stepped toward the door. His arm went up. He loved her, and she belonged with him. She was his wife, and he loved her, and they would keep trying. He reached for the knob.

Goddamn. Goddamn. Goddamn.

"I can't get through! Jesus!" Bone said. "I thought the medication was supposed to take care of this."

He took a breath, his jaw clenched. "It's like Limongello said," he told himself. He did not even realize he was thinking of the fake Limongello and not the real one. "You don't need the medication. You're more than just a bag of chemicals. You're already cured; your body just doesn't know it yet. Just square dance, and you can get through."

"Bow to your partner, bow to your side," Bone murmured, sweat breaking on his brow as he went through the steps. He could delay no longer. He had to get there and tell her. He loved her, and no matter what, they would keep trying. His

arm went up. "Take your partner, and swing 'er around." His
arm went up. "Do-si-do, and prah-men-ade!"

His arm went up.

His arm went up.

He strode to the door and went out.

about the author

Man Martin is a two-time Georgia Author of
the Year for his previous widely acclaimed novels,
Days of the Endless Corvette and *Paradise Dogs*. His
short stories and essays have appeared in *The Ken-
yon Review*, *The Alaska Quarterly* and elsewhere. He
also is a cartoonist whose daily comic strip Ink-
well Forest is available online and through email
feed to subscribers. Martin teaches high school
English and coaches debate in Atlanta, Georgia, where he lives with his wife Nancy.

GLENN STEWART